SIGHT SEERS

PS SINGLETON

First printed October 2022

Design by Enid Singleton

ISBN 979-8-9870541-0-9 (Paperback)

ISBN 979-8-9870541-1-6 (eBook)

Published by Enid Singleton

Email: postscriptthewriter@gmail.com

Instagram: @ps.the.writer

To my mom, who has supported me since the moment I told her I wanted to be a writer.

To my dad, who offered subplot ideas galore, only half of which ended up in the story.

To my sister, who has reserved the spot for number one fan.

And to my brother, who told me writing wasn't a real job.

Thank you

CHAPTERS

1

Shots in the Dark

Forget.

The word etched itself into the walls of my mind like a faucet dripping endlessly on stone.

Darkness engulfed the world around me, shadowless and trapping. I squeezed my eyes shut and shook my head, in a faint attempt to identify my thoughts and feelings. The seat beneath me felt like a bed. Upon finding the blankets, I gripped them close to myself, lest they let go, and submerged into the overwhelming dark.

A sound came into focus. It had been playing in the background all along. Alarms wailed, accompanied by a female computer voice. *"Please move to the nearest exit. A remmutant has been spotted on the premises. Please move to the nearest exit."*

Remmutant came as a foreign term to me, but I couldn't stay around long enough to learn the meaning.

Flinging my feet over the side of the bed, I pushed myself up to a stand as graceful as a young deer's first. I needed to get back to… I blinked. Where had I been before here? *Well, I had just … I was… I was…* My mind fell blank.

I knew nothing. Nothing but a name.

Alison Caddel.

This revelation flooded my mind and suffocated my thoughts. Several theories offered to explain my amnesia, but I hesitated to believe any of them. Shaking the distractions off, I focused on the overhead alarm. I had to get out of here. Everything else could wait.

Through the all-consuming darkness, I finally found the doorframe. I walked my hand along the wall to navigate. Suffused with paralyzing ambiguity, I treaded through the cold hall.

Crash!

All went still.

Clickclickclickclickclick…

The low, twisted purr forced my knees to buckle. Alternating hot and cold air tickled my bones. *Breathing.* The fetid odor of animal and blood reached me.

Right behind me.

My legs were sore, but I took off for a run. Earth shaking steps followed. A sharp shriek ripped through the air. My hands shot to my numb ears. In one life-threatening instant, my legs twisted and tripped, and my elbow smacked into the hard tile. Scrunching my nose in pain, I forced myself back to my feet.

A gunshot petrified me, unleashing chains of sorts to bind my feet. Shrieks bounced off the walls. I tried to keep low, not knowing what bodies around me stood on my side. How I longed for sight at this moment, one minuscule clue as to what was going on around me. *If someone can aim a gun in this dark, does that mean I'm-*

"Watch out!"

A mighty wind thrust me forward. A scratch dug across my arm as I fell. My knees hit the floor, pain jolting up my body.

Two distant shots ricocheted a few feet before me. I heard a loud shout just a few feet from me. Something shook the earth, and quiet settled in. I could feel my hands shaking before me.

Shoes battered against the floor, hesitant at first, before gathering pace and momentum. The other person caught me in a hug before I had collected all my thoughts.

At a hand's contact with my bare skin, the world lit up before my eyes. The person in my arms blocked half my vision, but the hallway stretched on beyond them. Complete with spots of light from the few that weren't broken and rubble falling off the walls, the work of whatever creature had attacked me.

Shaking breath tickled my ears. My arms wrapped around a girl who looked just as puzzled as I. Trying to decide why her shape felt so familiar, I studied her best I could with my hindered sight. When it clicked, my heart hitched. Same light brown hair, same deep blue eyes, same freckled nose. I was hugging *myself.*

I shoved myself out of the hug and ducked away. I plunged back into darkness. My numb legs staggered back, impelling me to support myself with the wall. Squeezing my eyes shut, I tried to make my vision come back. *Who are you?* The words lingered on the tip of my tongue, my mind too shaken to spit them out. And a second, further horrifying question:

If you're me, then who am I?

"Are you hurt? Let me see." The voice sounded panicked as he prodded me. My vision went in and out, exacerbating my confusion and trepidation. He managed to catch my scraped arm, holding it up. "That's a bad scratch."

With a quick yank, I distanced myself from the person. "What- What!" That summed up all my questions, I supposed. "Who are you? Where am I? What just happened?" I felt dizzy due to my hasty breathing. A reluctant footstep from him made me take a step back in unison. "I'm sorry but… I don't understand anything that's going on. I need answers, please."

"Ally…" I could hear him approaching, but I forced myself to stay and listen. He emitted a scent of cedar and sweat. "They said you probably wouldn't remember anything," he mumbled. "I'm Ashton. I was- er, I *am* your… brother." His words stumbled, hesitant and solemn, trying to ease me into the answer.

I mouthed the word over to myself. *Brother.*

Familiar on my tongue for sure, but nothing more. No memories to back it up. For that matter, I didn't have memories to back up *anything*. His voice held a twang of closeness but remained too different from my nebulous history. Could I trust him? Why would he lie to me? Could I have just made up the familiarity of the word?

"Where are we?"

Ashton cleared his throat before answering. "We're in a hospital. Seven years ago… you were in an accident. You've been in a coma until… well, now." His voice began to crack toward the end, suggesting that he wanted to reveal more. But of course, he couldn't. He didn't know a non-awkward way to explain it, and I didn't know a non-awkward way to take it.

Most of my questions could wait, but another urgent one pressed me to ask. Rubbing my arms, I let out a sigh. "Ashton, I can't see… Am I blind?" To explain why I had been able to see myself, the truth had to be more complicated than that. But for now, all I could take was a mere, straightforward "yes" or "no."

"Yeah... Here, take my hand, and we can get out of here." His hand fell into mine, cold and shaky. My world lit up again. The reflection of myself walked at my side. I tried not to think about it, to give my mind a break, albeit to no avail. My eyes wouldn't shut or look away as much as I tried. My stomach knotted.

"I wish I was better at explaining this stuff." His words broke up with a relieved huff. "I'm just really excited to see my little sis up and around again, even if you don't remember me." He pulled me along with him, hopefully out of here. My disability had forced my choice to trust. Or did it?

His voice snapped me from my disconcerting and debilitating thoughts. "Uh, can we try that hug again? I understand if you don't want to. You're clearly still discombobulated from everything."

Guilt tugged at me if I denied him a hug, and even more for not being able to remember him. I held out my arm a bit, and before I could say sure, he yanked me close. He wrapped around me tight, as if scared to ever let go.

We broke apart, but a hand still clutched mine.

"We should get out of here in case there's another remmutant around here." *There's that word again.*

"What's a 'remmutant?' Is that one of those things that attacked me?" I noted the other Ally's mouth moving in sync with mine.

"Yep. They're these creepy bird things, at least the ones in America. Other countries have some pretty scary-looking ones too. They don't usually get into the city but as always, there are some exceptions. They evacuated the hospital, but when you didn't turn up outside, I went in to look for you." He pat the gun on his hip.

"Why do they call them remmutants?"

"It's a mix of *remnant* and *mutant.* Someone coined it when they first started showing up, and now everyone just calls them that. If you ask me, a better combination of the words would've had another 'n' thrown in there, like 'remnutants' or something like that, but I digress." Ashton punctuated the statement with a short laugh. "Hang on, we're at the door, let me get it for you."

The hand released mine, and all went dark. Hinges turned, and people chattered outside. As I stepped out, I longed to see the outside world, to take it all in, but I couldn't until I figured out what was going on with my sight. A pat on the shoulders startled me. "Just a moment. I've got to go talk to some people." Ashton left me, his shoes thudding on concrete, then crunching on grass.

Rubbing my arms, I took in the crisp outside air and let out a breath. Circumstances had thrown me into this strange world. I had nothing to compare it to.

All my memories. My childhood, my family, my being.

Gone.

More than anything, I needed a little piece to cling to. *A little piece of something.*

Ashton would fill in the gaps. I had to remind myself about that to keep from falling apart in fear.

"Yeah, all I found were two, and they were relatively easy to take out, so I think we can wrap this up," my brother said in the distance. "I think you can take it from here, thanks." His footsteps came back my way, growing louder. "You ready to head home, little sis? I'm sure you're probably tired. I've already taken care of everything I had to do here."

I nodded.

"Cool. Car's this way. I hope you'll be comfortable living with me. I've got a dog. You're gonna love him."

"Can't wait."

Why did the world feel so wrong?

2

Passing Notes

When Ashton had taken me to his car, the fluffy, bear-like dog had been waiting patiently on the passenger side. Before my vision cut out for a short moment while getting in the car, I had read the German Shepard's tag as the name *Captain.*

Black and white hues decorated the landscape on the drive to Ashton's house. The fur under my palm told me my hand rested on a dog's back, but I couldn't see him. Just moments ago, I had claimed to be blind, but I now had no clue what to think. I wished to understand, to have some clue as to how my vision worked. Turning up empty on the subject, I decided to let the quiet wash over me. With how little I knew, I needed a short break from the questions.

Captain huffed, drawing my attention. I stroked his back, trying to assuage myself. With each touch, my vision glitched in and out again. I paused, my hand hovering in thought. A theory seemed to form on its own in my mind. Now would be a good time as any to test it. I let go of Captain, and everything became pitch black. Returning my hand on his back, the room returned in black and white.

It all clicked.

I could see.

Just not through my own eyes.

Ashton remained quiet throughout the drive, his eyes occasionally peeking a glance at the backseat. Due to his height, His head stretched a mere inch away from the roof of the car. An armored suit hung on his form, and he wore a backward cap on his head of curly hair. A nervous smile had been permanently glued to his face.

The city rested on a slope. At the bottom of the hill, the hospital we'd come from, shopping centers, restaurants, and the like resided cozily. Upward the slope, homes watched the town below from rows of their own neighborhoods. The dried leaves of fall drifted past the windows, all in blurred mute. Glitches across the horizon caught my attention beyond the leaves. The bright pigments of the sky were divided into panels, complete with a false sun. I squinted for a better view of the artificial vault, following the cracks in the panels up to the top of the dome shape. *What was wrong with the real sky?*

"We're here!" came Ashton's voice.

A house sat in the middle of the row, two stories

with all the windows I could see on the bottom floor. The front door waited at the end of a sidewalk path. A tall oak seasoned its leaves across the yard.

Ashton came around the side and popped open my door. Captain jumped from my lap, and my world suffocated in darkness. Yet again.

Waving my hand around, I eventually caught my brother's grip. Like a light switch, color filled my sight. Painted a welcoming green, the house smiled with its white trim. We stepped up to the unfamiliar home. A welcome mat brushed our feet. It read, *Doorbell broken, yell DING DONG really loud.* That earned a smile.

Ashton shut the door behind us. "Here, let me take a look at your arm." He walked me to the couch and sat me down.

While my brother tended to my scratch, I took in the house. As Captain rested his face in my lap, my cold knees were warmed by his fur. The couch resided to the left, and the dining area and kitchen to the right. A narrow walkway led to a set of open stairs, decked like horizontal dominoes. Atop the stairs on the second floor, three rooms hid behind closed doors.

"Her first day and she's already almost gotten herself killed," Ashton muttered. His voice seemed to be the only familiar thing I could grasp, but for all I knew, I had fabricated the vague memory. My vision once again blacked out as Ashton's hands came off me. "Let me go grab something to clean that up, and then I'll be right back." His brisk footsteps slipped away.

With the momentary quiet setting in, I grew less tense. I started by steadying my breath. My past, present, and future lay a mystery to me. A mystery imperative to unravel. But for now, breathing was my only responsibility. That would be enough.

"Okay, I'm back. This might sting a little." Carpet shuffled under Ashton's weight as he knelt in from of me. He took me by the wrist. A sharp sting bit into my arm, cold with alcohol. I winced, yanking back by reflex.

"Sorry, I warned you," Ashton said, giving a light, sympathetic laugh. "Can I keep going?"

I nodded, scrunching my nose and breathing in the pain. I felt for his hand. He took it, rubbing my wrist with his thumb. A smile crept on my face. It still hurt, but I could handle it now.

"Thank you, Ashton."

"No problem."

"No, I mean, for saving my life, taking me in, explaining stuff to me." I sighed tiredly, using my free hand to rub my cheek. That last part hadn't happened yet, but I could hope. "I guess you're my brother, so you sort of have to, but… It still means a lot to me."

He sat quietly for a while, his hand rubbing up against his nose. "T-thanks."

"I have so many questions…" I let out a heavy breath, a yawn following.

"We can answer those in the morning." He let my arm go and stood up. "We're both tired, and it's getting late. I'll show you your room. Ok, let me put it this way. I guess I can show you *to* your room. And I have some clothes for you to change into."

I liked the sleep idea. Nudging Captain off me, I got to my feet. Ashton took my hand. The world came in color. I stumbled up the stairs in my awkward perspective, but Ashton guided me the best he could.

"Careful, there's a few steps."

We came to stand in the doorway of my room, the one on the left of the hall. Sunset filled the room with fiery warmth. An empty desk rested below the window, and the closet and bed resided on opposite ends of the room. An old, oversized space-themed T-shirt and loose shorts rested at the end of the bed, folded asymmetrically. *When was the last time someone had used the room?*

"I set some of my old clothes at the end of the bed for you to use as pajamas. Kind of just what I had laying around, but it'll work." He cleared his throat, taking me toward the bed. Taking my hand in his, he set it on the pile of clothes to make sure I knew where it was. I couldn't tell him I could see yet. That would trigger a whole new conversation that would be perfectly fine waiting until morning. My bones ached with exhaustion.

"Can you change by yourself?"

I nodded after looking over the clothes and thinking it over.

"Okay, I'll leave you alone then. In between our

rooms is the bathroom, and on the other side is my room. Knock if you need help or anything." He left along with my vision.

Captain's collar jingled, and the bed shook as he jumped onto it. I grabbed the clothes before he could sit on them. "Do you mind if the dog sleeps with you? I think he likes you," came Ashton's voice.

I reached out for the dog, finding his head and ruffling his fur. "Well, I think he's neat too." I turned back to the clothes.

"Good night, Ally-gator." I heard the click of the light switch. Not that it mattered. I couldn't see anything anyways. "Love ya."

"Night, Ashton."

The smack of keys against the keyboard woke me. I kept my eyes shut, trying to fall back asleep, but was distracted by the incessant noise. Rolling over, I felt Captain's warmth in the bed. I sat up, my hand on his back. He shifted at my movement. The world came into view, the muted version, that is. The only light came from the outside moon. *What time is it?* I rubbed the sleep from the roof of my mouth with my tongue

The *tap tap tap* of the keys drew my attention again. I climbed off the bed to investigate the clatter. Captain pressed up against my leg, providing me sight. Creaking the door open, I looked over the sleeping house. The faint light of a computer filled the space.

Even though I could see through Captain's eyes, navigating the stair steps was still awkward. Nonetheless, I put one foot forward, trying to find my footing. I moved quietly, not wanting to disrupt Ashton in whatever he was doing. Captain nudged his face into my palm. We continued onward.

The typing stopped. Through the railing, I could see Ashton. His figure sat at a small desk toward the back of the dining room. A laptop monitor emitted faint blue light. Ashton glanced around, hesitating. I held my breath, hoping he couldn't hear me. He let out a yawn, then got up from his chair and walked past the staircase. He kept going, heading toward the downstairs bathroom.

With the shield of night, I quickly moved toward the computer. Curiosity tugged me to see what he had been working on. Stepping up to the desk, I loosely gripped the nape of Captain's neck for sight. An open email presented itself on the screen.

Well, it took some digging and time, but I finally got the reports on M1. Unfortunately, it seems like they've kept tight-knit on anything concerning the HDE. Anything new on your end? Communication is still safe, right?

-Marksman

The reply email said:

Thanks. I've got A2 and C1's, so only 3 left to get. And, to answer your question, yes, I believe we're still in the clear. But things might get a little rough with Ally here. I don't know how much I can keep from her, or for how long. For now, communication via email will be few and far between, just to avoid suspicion. I can't tell her until we find a way to save her. All of them. Pass the message to Mother. I will look over these reports, then see if there's anything we can do about them. We can discuss this at the office.

-Scientist

Context clues proved futile in understanding the emails. A file hung at the bottom of the email, labeled M1. I hovered the mouse over the file and was contemplating clicking it. If Ashton was *Scientist*, what was he hiding from me? More pertinently, what was he saving me from?

I didn't like being left in the dark.

With a deep breath, I went for it and clicked.

A dark, dungy lab viewed from a static security camera lit up the screen. Captain tugged at my shirt, but I ignored him. Two figures lay on operation tables in the middle of the room. The scene stood still. A few doctors were discussing something in the back, too mumbled for me to decipher anything. The fuzzy computer light hurt to look at for too long after still being half awake. Narrowing my eyes (or rather Captain's), I waited for something to happen.

A loud snap erupted from the video. I flinched, hoping Ashton wouldn't hear. I didn't know how he would react if he saw me watching the video he specifically did not want me to watch. The room in the video went dark. It took a moment, but eventually, everything lit up again.

"What was that?"

"Some sort of power outage, I think."

The figure on the right table let out a loud scream. The doctors rushed to him. Their shadows flickered strangely, making wild shapes and forming almost another figure. The boy on the other table started to convulse. I was flooded by a sudden urge to run back to my room before I got caught, and a chill ran up my back.

The scene continued. *"Quick, go get Dr. Cleo!"* a doctor said in a strained tone.

A bark startled me. I glanced down at Captain. Ashton definitely heard that. I moved quickly to the escape button. The video disappeared with a click, returning the screen to the way I had found it.

I raced on my tiptoes. Captain didn't follow, stranding me in the dark sea. Grabbing the railing, I swung myself up the stairs. I could only hope my footfalls kept quiet and my steps were correct. I made it to the top of the stairs when I heard Ashton's voice.

"Hey, Captain," he said in an immature yet hushed voice. I put a hand over my mouth to keep my breathing quiet. "Who's a good boy…?"

No one spoke for a while. I heard Ashton's shuffling. *Does he know?*

I instructed my thoughts to shut up as if Ashton might hear my internal panicking. If I went back to bed now, I could fall asleep, wake up in the morning, and call it all a dream.

Only, it wasn't a dream. Ashton was hiding something from me. Something bigger than the things I had wanted answers to before.

Until I knew what he was hiding, I couldn't trust Ashton.

I had been here one day, and already, the cracks began to show.

3

Research

Pacing my room, the video from the email replayed itself repeatedly on the wall of my mind. I could hear Ashton talking over the phone downstairs. The new morning wasn't quite the welcome respite I was hoping it would be. It brought new challenges. New insecurities. New questions. Not only about my life before my amnesia, but the truth behind his emails. My stomach cartwheeled, anxiety building up in my chest. Why had I crept downstairs last night? Why had I watched that *cursed* video?

Ashton would be expecting me for breakfast soon. *Should I tell him I saw the video? He would be expecting me to ask questions... No, I can't. He wanted those emails hidden. I'll ask him the questions he wants me to ask until I get more information. I can't trust him until then.*

Everyone has their secrets. Most, however, don't involve videos of unconscious children and dark labs.

I stepped down the stairs through the looming dark. Forcing on a smile, my unsteady foot found the solid ground of the bottom story floor. Putting the video out of my head, I focused on the smell of breakfast floating in from the kitchen. For now, I would ask Ashton a few questions and clear up as much as I could.

"Morning, Ally! Here, let me help you." The creak of a chair followed my brother's hand on my arm, providing me sight. He helped me into a seat at the table and left to another part of the room. When he came back, a plate clattered on the table before me. "Made ya eggs. I think I burnt them a little, but whatever, it's fine." After ruffling my hair, I assumed he went back to his own seat.

"Thanks…" The conflicting feelings in my gut made me reluctant. My vision lit up in the grays, Captain laying down at my feet under the table. The lower view made my vision wonky, but I didn't know how to fix it. I figured it would be easier to eat in the dark rather than at an inconvenient angle. Lifting my feet up, I returned to my sightless view.

"So, Ashton, about…" I bit my lip, trying to figure out ways to phrase my concern. "Everything. There's just so much missing, and I'm so lost…" I rested my elbows as supports on the table. "It's overwhelming."

Ashton's utensil clattered against his plate. "Well, that's what I'm here for. To make it more 'whelming.'" A light smile spread across my lips. Truth be told, it wasn't easy to remain suspicious of him when he made everything sound nicer. Probably the angle he was playing.

"Ashton…What was my life like before the accident? I mean, did I have any friends? Hobbies? Dreams?" Cracks broke through my voice.

Ashton stayed quiet. "Well… Yeah. There were a good amount of people who loved and cared about you, but… they're all gone now. Either grown up or moved away or..." His sigh fell heavy. "Who knew so much stuff could change in seven years?"

I nodded along, but all his responses were vague at best. These weren't answers but shields, blocking me from what I should know. Ashton continued to hide more than I thought.

I managed to get some eggs into my mouth. They certainly smelled burnt, as I had been warned, but the taste was fine. As the taste filled my throat, I realized how hungry I had been. *When was the last time I ate?* After I had swallowed, I let my legs drop back down. My feet brushed against Captain, allowing me to see again. I stared up at Ashton.

Ashton took on a quizzical smirk. "Hey, that's interesting…"

"What?"

"Your eyes just changed colors. They've actually done that a few times since you got home." He squinted, trying to decipher something.

"What do you mean? How?"

"Well, your eyes are usually a cool grayish blue, like how you'd expect a blind person's eyes to look, of course, but then they sometimes change to a dark blue. Neat." I raised my feet a bit to test an idea. "Hey, they just changed back to the gray."

Huh. My eye color changed along with my sight. In the words of Ashton, *neat*.

I opened my mouth to ask another question, but a beep interrupted me. "Oops, I'm running late for work." Shuffling followed, and Ashton scrambled to get ready. "That's what I get for wanting a slow morning, I guess. You can hold your own here, right?"

There goes my opportunity to get some answers. "Yeah…"

"Take Captain with you if you feel like going somewhere."

"The…dog?" *Ashton trusted a dog to keep an eye on me?* I knew I wasn't really blind, but *he* didn't.

"What? He's trained," he responded, suggesting that it was a perfectly reasonable explanation. A jingle of keys followed the front door opening.

"You trust me to just wander around town?"

"Yeah, you're fifteen. See you later, Ally-gator. Love you." He blew me a kiss before shutting the door.

My thoughts lingered after him. More than emails, Ashton was hiding as much as he possibly could about my history. I knew one thing for certain.

I could not trust him.

Getting my vision back via Captain, I stared after

my brother. "I guess I'm being babysat by a dog," I said, trying to avoid ranting about the lack of my freedom. I got up from my seat, and Captain followed my lead. I pat him on the head. I could use some vitamin D after being in a coma for so long. Navigating the stairs only slightly better than before, I made my way to my room. I dressed for the day and started on my way.

Capris that rose just below my knees dressed my legs, allowing me to brush up against Captain. I needed to get to know the neighborhood. I explored the possibility of running away, and to do that, I'd need some sense of direction.

The windy fall air blended with the cold filter of black and white all over the world. Yards rested between each house, with sidewalk outlining the properties. The street rolled out to meet the main road. Glancing back and forth, I ruminated on which direction to take. The city leaned on a slope, funneling down to the left. Everything circled together at the bottom. I assumed the upward road led out of the city and to a more open country. I didn't want to be too far from Ashton's house, since I didn't have anything to contact him with if I got lost, so my feet started downward.

Captain's leash rested in my hand as we walked into town. Some time had passed before we came up on the city library. As good a place as any to gather information. Towering brick pillars like a castle welcomed me in. After entering, I scanned over the books, hoping that they would answer *any* of my questions. Waiting for Ashton to give me answers was clearly taking too long.

Thankfully, they allowed dogs inside, I wandered around the interior. Rows of shelves lined the area. People scrolled through them slowly. A few kids cried and laughed as they ran around the library, their mother chasing to reprimand them. Finding the nonfiction section, I found the Dewey decimal for history. *Research time.*

Scrunching my nose, I ran my hand over the smooth book bindings. The air was imbued with the aroma of old books, redolent with wisdom and experience. Part of me liked the scent. One book title caught my eye. *Remmutants, Dragons, and Other Things: An Incomplete History, by Blake Landerson.*

Slipping it out of its designated spot, I took it over to a table a few feet away. The hardcover book thudded as I dropped it. I pulled out a chair, which proved harder than necessary by a combination of my view stuck in the third person, carpet flooring, and the weight of the chair (There also might've been a piece of gum under it too, which grossed me out). But I managed and finally took my seat.

Glancing back and forth, I checked for anyone around. With the coast clear, I picked up Captain's top half and set him on my lap. "Here, read this for me." His weight on my chest made it hard to breathe, whereas his claws dug into my knees, much to my chagrin. I winced, trying to focus on reading the book.

With my hands, I moved around the dog to turn through the pages. I skimmed over the table of contents. *What is a remmutant, What is a Dragon, and where did they come from, The Readjustment...* The list went on numbering the chapters. The book was way too thick to read in one sitting, and I didn't know how to get a library card here. I would have to pick and choose chapters. Ashton and experience had already told me about the remmutants. What about Dragons?

Thumbing through the pages of the book, I found the chapter on Dragons.

Humans born with special abilities in today's world go by the term Dragon. These abilities are typically genetic and can range from something as unnoticeable as being able to blink fast to as powerful as flight or fire manipulation.

I began to contemplate the passage. My ability to see through others' eyes came to mind. Was I a Dragon? I kept reading.

Most powers are hereditary, meaning if one had the ability, or most known as a talent, to produce fire, their children would likely be able to produce fire as well. Some talents can mutate through several generations, but in most cases, they stay in the same realm of ability. One could theoretically trace their heritage based on who had what talents, however, two unrelated families could carry similar powers. Though hereditary, not all talents will carry over to another generation.

Talents have, for the most part, remained a mystery. These notes are mere observations, though more research on Dragons continues to grow every day. CAIN, a branch of government founded a decade after Dragons started showing, has put most of their resources toward the study of these beings. They also manage most research toward remmutants (see chapter 1).

I frowned at how little information I had. Several ideas crossed my mind. If talents passed through generations, it was possible that Ashton could be in possession of a power he wasn't telling me about. Was that what he was trying to hide from me? The thought calmed my nerves about him a bit. Of course, none of that explained the video.

Leaning back in my seat, I let my head drop and sighed. Part of me wished I had never seen that video. It only served to make me more anxious and confused. But I *needed* to see it. I couldn't stand to be left in the dark. I took a deep breath. *Alright, Ally, it's not the end of the world. You'll adjust. Eventually.* I longed for my memories, for the puzzle pieces to fill in. A chunk of me was missing, and the longer it went without it, the more lost I became.

Captain jumped down from my lap, growing uncomfortable. Any view I had left with the dog. "Come on, Captain, I still need you." I groaned. How was I supposed to solve this mystery if I had to rely on someone else to even see?

I reached down until I found Captain's head. I

stroked his fur, lost in my thoughts. I needed a plan.

The clattering of books caught my attention. Using Captain, I looked behind us to find a pregnant woman who had dropped a few miscellaneous books. She frowned at the mess she'd made, pushing her dark hair out of her face. It flowed down her back in shiny waves. She squatted down to pick up the books. Her legs spread, stretching her light colored dress, she tried to pick up the books. Her fingertips just barely grazed the cover of one.

"Do you need help?" I asked.

"Nah, I've almost got it…" She narrowed her eyes at the books, her tongue stuck out determined. Bending back, she tried to get them from behind herself, only to result in more struggles. Chuckling, she straightened, giving up. "Yes, I do need help."

I got up from my seat, and, through the dark, collected her books from where I remembered them to be. I bounced up, holding out the books to her. "Here you go, ma'am."

"Didn't realize I was getting 'ma'am' old. Wow." The woman took the books from me. "Thank you," she said, her voice naturally lined with laughter. I started to go back toward my table, but she stopped me. "Hey, you kind of look familiar. Have we met? Sorry if I'm terrible with faces, but I'm certain I've seen you before."

I turned back to the woman. "I don't think so…" *I've been in a coma for the last few years, so who knows?*

"Hang on, I think I know where I've seen you

before…" The woman hummed as she thought. "You look just like this girl that was in the paper a few years back. Of course, she was younger than you, but you look like an older version of her. She was my neighbor, too. Guess I was mistaken. Sorry, I don't know you." She let out an awkward laugh.

"In the paper? For what?" It could've been me. My heart jumped at the thought. I wished more than ever to have some piece of my past.

"Oh, it was a little girl, she went missing. I don't think they ever found her, unfortunately. Her name was…"

My vision filled in grays, Captain suddenly sitting against my leg. He must've gotten up from under the table. The woman's mouth hung open as she thought, but her eyes froze to Captain's (which were technically mine at the moment). I watched her curiously.

"Her name was what?"

The woman seemed to snap out of her trance. "Uh, I don't remember. Well, nice talking with you, but I've got to go. Again, thanks for the help." Something was amiss. She walked past me, somewhat abruptly. I watched after her.

"What was that about?" I mumbled to myself. Captain rubbed his head into my palm, pulling me away from the strange woman. I turned back to the book I had been reading. I shrugged off the lingering unnerving feeling and tried not to think about the missing girl. My thoughts wandered as to whether she could be me, but I pushed them out. *Just focus on solving one thing at a time.*

Rather than sitting Captain on my lap again, I found a lounge area with beanbags. Reclining on one, Captain cuddled up next to me. I ran my hand on his back, feeling the stiff texture of his fur.

Flipping through the book, I found the chapter about remmutants.

Dragons and remmutants came to being in the same event. Nearly 200 years ago, a disease broke out across the globe, called the Wyvern-X. Historians have yet to pinpoint the start of the disease, but with every person infected, they were granted special abilities. Wyvern-X had a different effect on animals. They grew disfigured and more violent, mutated remnants of their previous being, (hence the term "remmutants"). In certain parts of the world, some remmutants were stronger than others. Most remmutant variants came to be extinct, picked off by the stronger species. This is why every country has a specific version of remmutants.

With remmutants and Dragons making appearances across the globe, people were struggling to adjust. Each country managed its remmutants on its own, coming up with innovative ways to ward off the monsters. The United States of America, as it was called back then, became the United Colonies of America, as the native bird-like creatures destroyed most of the usable land. They rebuilt into colonies, constructing higher walls and domes to keep the eagle remmutants out. In turn, they sacrificed natural sunlight, but the domes are capable of recreating the health benefits almost perfectly. Not every country changed so drastically, as Canada simply cleared out more trees where people were living to make their giant moose easier to spot, and China built up stronger defenses against the vicious pandas and reptiles. A catalog for different breeds of remmutants can be found in appendix 1.

The book tempted me to check the catalog, just to see what exactly had attacked me, but I refrained. Of course, I had to focus. The next chapter title hung at the top of the page: "The Readjustment."

While some Dragons used their newfound abilities for good, others used them to manipulate others, gain wealth, bully people, and more. The world leaders felt a need for something to be done about these overpowered people. Some even questioned whether they should still have all the rights of a normal human being. The world was divided in half: those with powers, and those without. A band of Dragons made the first move, launching an attack in Europe. War broke out.

As the war continued, the fighting spread to surrounding countries, and the Dragons became more and more ambitious.

For the first two years of war, the Dragons had the upper hand. Some Dragons kidnapped humans as trophies, using them as slaves. Meanwhile, some cities took joy in hanging their Dragon captives. Both sides had blood on their hands.

After four hard years of fighting with the supernatural, we finally came to an agreement. They formed a treaty. As long as Dragons refrained from breaking the law with their abilities and using their abilities in public, they would be permitted the rights of normal humans. Although these laws are more lenient when it comes to children who do not yet know what they are capable of, efforts have been made to keep a close watch on Dragons since. For the most part, Dragons have slowly gone into hiding, most refusing to use their powers at all and blending in with the rest of humanity.

The United Colonies to date are the only country with a specific military division to deal with the Dragons and remmutants. CAIN, otherwise known as the Citizens and Abilities Investigatory Network, primarily deals with remmutant control, but if a Dragon gets out of hand, they'll be there too. They were founded in the aftermath of the Readjustment.

The chapter continued, but I had to stop due to Captain getting up. I sat up, mulling everything over. Particularly whether to tell Ashton about my newfound ability to see through others' eyes. I didn't see how my talent could be used for evil, but the thought of any special ability being used wrongly made me uncomfortable about mine. So I decided to just hold on to my secret for a while.

Captain's huffing snapped me out of my thoughts. "What's up, boy?" I hoisted myself up from the bean bag, stumbling through the dark to find my dog. As if noticing my struggle, he soon came to my side.

Following him, the dog led me out of the building. He seemingly wanted to go back home. Puzzled, I allowed him to lead. He glanced back several times, and I thought I almost saw a figure watching us, though I couldn't quite make them out. My gut tightened, and I stopped questioning the dog.

Once Captain stopped looking back, I thought we had lost whoever had been watching. As we turned into our neighborhood, his tail began to wag, trading fear for joy.

"What's got you so happy?"

When we got back to Ashton's house, his car sat parked on the driveway. I stepped inside. Ashton sat on the table, eating a slice of pizza. The sight of me made him smile. "Hey, you're back! I'm on my lunch break right now, and I had some leftover pizza, so." He gestured at the slice in his hand.

"Does Captain know when your lunch break is?" I asked.

Ashton nodded, taking another bite and getting off the table. Coming over, he knelt in front of the dog and scratched behind the ear with his free hand. "That's because he's a smart boy, huh, Captain?" Ashton made baby noises at the dog, somewhat unsettling from my view. "You're a good boy. Good boys get pizza." After giving Captain a bit of pizza, Ashton went on to take a bite. I shuddered, sticking out my tongue.

Ashton laughed at me. "Aw, does Ally want some

too?"

I made quick to shake my head. "Nope."

With one last pat, Ashton stood up and walked back to the dining area. He dug through the fridge, pulling out a jug of milk. "So, where'd you go?"

"Just the library, it's only a few miles away."

"Pft, of course, the first place you explore is the library." Ashton laughed to himself, pouring a tall glass of milk. I stared at him confused. He looked up, catching my expression. "Right, amnesia…" A sad smile spread across his lips. "When you were little, you loved reading and blabbing on and on about whatever book you were reading. If I remember correctly, historical fiction was your favorite." The more he talked, the brighter his face grew. "But it used to drive you crazy that the only way you could read was if- "He stopped himself, eyeing me weird. "-Uh, Braille. If the book was in Braille. You'd get upset and your face would turn red whenever you wanted to read a book that wasn't in Braille." His awkwardness fell off after he rubbed his nose. "It was really cute and funny."

I squinted at him, questioning his hiccup. "Okay…"

He sighed. "I wish I could give you all your memories. Fix everything you lost. Then at least it'd be somewhat easier to help you adjust. And there are so many things I want to tell you, but I can't. I don't know how."

"Ashton." I stepped toward him, standing across

the breakfast bar. I could no longer see as Captain had gone to lay on the couch. "It's okay." The gesture proved more for me than him, but he seemed to appreciate it.

"Thanks for being such a good sport." Ashton ruffled my hair. "My break will be over soon, so I've got to head out. Love you, Ally-gator."

"Bye, Ashton." I waved to where I thought he would be. The door shut behind him.

Again, I stood alone in the dark.

4

Testing Theories

"Good morning, beautiful sister-o-mine!" Ashton burst into my bedroom, singing on too high of a note for this early in the morning.

Sitting up in my bed, I rubbed my eyes. "What?"

Captain barked off-beat to my brother's song. The bed shifted as Ashton sat down. He set his hand on my bare knee. I watched my face, contorted at the tiredness of just waking up and the chaos that had just let himself into my room. "No time for sleeping, girly! It's October 7th, and you know what that means!"

"No, what does that mean? What time is it? Why are you in my room?" My face rested against my palm, tangled hair loosely falling over me.

His expression fell; I could tell in the way his eyes dropped and his gaze turned. "Oh. Well, let me remind you. 16 years ago, on this day, a certain little girl whose name starts with an 'A' was born."

He stopped talking, and I realized he was waiting for an answer.

"Was it me?"

"It was you! Happy Birthday, Ally-gator!" He shoved something in my hand, a considerably wide chocolate chip cookie, complete with a single, unlit candle stabbed messily into the middle.

"My birthday?" I eyed the desert. "Thanks." I had lost a lot, but I hadn't stopped to consider each and every little thing missing in my past. That stood too tall of a task. But now, the mention of having something as common as a birthday made my eyes sting. Just a little.

"Dessert for breakfast. I like my birthday."

Ashton's cheeks peaked in a smile. "I've got work today, but after that, what would you like to do? Anything today, as it's your day."

"I don't know… Maybe we could just hang out or something. I don't really know much about anything to do." I took a bite of the cookie to keep myself from thinking about all the years I had lost. It melted against the roof of my mouth, disappearing just like every aspect of my life before now. I hardly knew anything about Ashton, any parents I had, or even myself. I was just a girl trying to copy the person Alison Caddel had once been.

Stretching his arms behind his head and cutting off my sight, Ashton let out a wistful sigh. "Just a few days ago, you were just nine, a short little thing. And then I blink and you're sixteen, all big like an actual person." His tongue clicked. Following in a smaller voice, he said, "We sure have missed a lot." Those nervous and painful thoughts had reached Ashton too. In an attempt to shake them off, he poked me in the knee. "If you don't stop growing, you'll be in trouble. Quit it."

A small laugh escaped me.

"I'm serious, Ally. You're my baby sister forever, right?" He yanked me into a suffocating hug, tickling me as we lay on the bed.

He took my uncontrollable laughter at his teasing as a yes.

"Good."

We took a moment, enjoying the calm as I ate the cookie I had somehow managed to save from Ashton's roughhousing.

I cleaned out the last of the cookie from my teeth when Ashton grabbed me by the legs and yanked me up over his shoulders - all in one swift movement. I let out a squeal, Captain barking at the cacophony.

"Ashton! What are you doing! Put me down!" Feeling my shirt falling up, I pulled it back over my stomach. My long hair only landed at his ankles, which is when I noted how tall he stood.

"Where do you want to go for actual birthday breakfast?" He passed the doorway of my room and walked around the house, hauling me upside down. His sweaty palms on my ankles allowed me a view different from the lightheaded one my body felt.

"Put me down!" He trotted down the stairs now, my head repeatedly knocking against his back.

"Fine." Ashton decided to drop my skull on the couch. I lay there upside down, my face bright with giggles. The cushions bounced as he took a spot next to me. "You're too much fun, ya dork."

I often wondered where Ashton worked, or if it was somehow related to those weird emails. Today, I shut the door on those thoughts, though. I wouldn't spend my birthday worrying about the suspicious things Ashton did. No, I had something else in mind for the afternoon.

Using Captain for sight, I dug around the kitchen junk drawer for a sticky note and pencil. Sitting on the floor so Captain could see, I made a list of everything I knew about my sight.

1. *I can see through others' eyes.*
2. *My eyes change color, depending on whether I can see.*

Tapping the pencil to my chin, I scanned the small list. Glancing at Captain's paws, a thought came to me. *Could I control him, or had I only gained his vision?* I focused, trying to move Captain rather than my own body. Captain's head acted as I wanted, his paws at my command as well. After a few more tests, I let the dog have control again. I added it to the list.

3. *I can control the viewer's movements.*

I still needed to test the limits of my abilities.

Taking my hand off the dog, the world returned to black. What next? Did my powers work through clothes? Pulling Captain up next to me, his body leaned against my shirt. After double checking that my skin had no contact with him whatsoever, I found my view still blacked out.

4. *Skin contact only.*

I set down the pencil and gave Captain a scratch behind the ears for being a cooperative test subject. "You're such a good boy, huh?" I said, talking in the childish voice I had heard Ashton use before.

Ding dong!

The doorbell made my skin jump. I turned Captain's head to the door. *Would Ashton use the doorbell?* I got to my feet, and Captain moved to press against the leg. He'd gotten used to being my eyes.

Three men stood at the door, dressed in matching black and white suits. The only thing difference between their uniforms was the tie colors, which I only made out by shade using Captain's color-blind vision, and name tags.

"Can I help you?" My hand remained on the door, which opened only halfway.

"Good day, young lady." The man at the front looked somewhat surprised to see someone home. "We're here with CAIN for a monthly house check. May we come in?"

I hesitated, my heart quickening from a mix of suspicion and surprise. "CAIN?" According to the book I had read, they only showed up for remmutants or *Dragons*. "Can I ask why?"

"All employee homes are inspected randomly once a month, to ensure everything is in order."

Employee? Does Ashton work for CAIN? "Okay…" Still unsure, I stepped out of the way.

I eyed them as they entered one by one. The last one to enter was an Asian man with thick, dark hair, who gave me a welcoming smile as he came. His tag read *K. Kiyano*. I gave him a short wave, unsure if the smile made me feel better or worse.

Captain seemed strangely calm. I sat my hand on his head, more comforting myself than anything else. The CAIN men checked every feasible space, and even some less feasible spots, taking care not to mess anything up. Under the fridge, the paper-thin crack of the door jam, *on* the coffee table. They came up with nothing so far, making me wonder if they were looking for anything specific in the first place.

"I'll do a quick sweep upstairs, and then we'll be done," I heard Kiyano say to the lead man.

My gaze darted upstairs at the mention of it. If Ashton kept something private, he would probably keep it in his room. An idea crossed my mind. These people would be the perfect excuse to go into my brother's room, and if I did find out anything that explained that video, it'd be a great birthday present. *I know I said no investigating Ashton today, but...*

Kiyano strode up the dark wood steps. After a

moment, I followed. The other men seemed to ignore me, either too focused on their search or not caring. The man dug through my room first. He just shuffled through my clothes, searching for any secret compartments in the drawers. There weren't many hiding places as I had only moved in recently. Once he was sure he'd found nothing of suspicion, he walked out, nodding to me as he did so.

Next, the man moved onto Ashton's room. The air conditioning blasted cold air into the space, not to mention that cedar-sweat scent that followed Ashton everywhere returned. Clothes struggled in strewn, crumpled piles across the floor. A bowl and a cup stacked on the nightstand told me Ashton ate in here often. A desk leaned against the wall, neat in comparison to the rest of the room. Except for a journal and scattered sticky notes with random scrawlings and phone numbers, the tabletop proved tidy.

Looking over the sticky notes, Kiyano found nothing worth lingering on. He moved to the bed. He slid it away from its prior spot easily. I noticed a faint indented streak in the carpet, almost as if the bed moved over often. Under the bed, I spotted the outline of a small hatch, probably a good hiding spot for secrets. I could tell by the man's eyes he had seen it.

He slid the bed back into place and left the room.

Startled, I made to follow Mr. Kiyano. I knew he saw it, yet he just moved on, uncharacteristic to the rest of the search party. I decided to keep mum, though. *Investigate later.*

"Sir, there's nothing here. Everything's in order."

The lead man nodded. He spun his finger as if to say *wrap it up*. The third man joined the other two, and together they stood in the front room. I came to meet them once I made my way down the steps.

"Thank you for your cooperation. We are done here." The lead man pulled a pair of sunglasses out of his pocket, flicked his wrist to open them, and set them on the bridge of his nose. His hand came out to mine. I pulled my leg from Captain and shook his hand.

I smirked, wondering if I could make him do anything in this small moment we were touching. I decided to have some fun and tried moving his hand. Didn't budge. I frowned. Our hands split.

The men turned and exited the house. Waving, I closed the door behind them. Once the quiet washed over the house, I let out a sigh of relief, having gotten rid of those intruders.

I thought over the possible reasons I couldn't control the man. Species became the only difference I could think of between man and dog. With another limit to my powers found, I added it to my list.

"What's up, Ally-gator?" Ashton poured a bowl of soup, watching me from the kitchen. I leaned back at the table, Captain at my bare toes.

I was wondering if it would be appropriate to tell him about the CAIN men. He could probably read it on my face. But every time I opened my mouth, my lips ran dry.

Probably bored of the quiet, Ashton said, "Did you know sunscreen works by absorbing ultraviolet rays before they get to your skin?"

I should tell him. Ashton went on talking, going more in-depth about sunscreen and its history. *Just go for it.* "Earlier some people came by. They said they were with a group called CAIN, for some mandatory search thing." The ladle clattered against the pot of soup as he dropped it. I straightened, curious. "You wouldn't know anything about that, would you?"

"Oh, dang, was that today?" His voice hitched. Thankfully, he didn't sound too upset about the interruption to his sunscreen story. "I mean, I guess that's why it's random, so I don't expect it, but- What happened?" His voice lingered with a tinge of uncertainty, but he did a pretty good job of camouflaging it

"Uh, I don't think they found anything, just walked around and then left. But it's not like you're hiding anything." I punctuated the sentence with a hard laugh. *Oh, the irony. You most* definitely *are hiding something.* "Are you?" I flashed him a smirk. He would think it was a joke, but it wasn't.

"Nope, nothing." He rubbed his nose. Taking two steamy bowls in his hands, he headed to the couch. "Come on, we'll have a movie night."

I rose from my seat, only momentarily blind as

Captain caught up. Just as quickly, the dog ran off to go beg his master for food, only to get reprimanded. "Uh, aren't you going to tell me *why* those people came here?" My hand found the back of the couch, and I sat down.

"Oh. Right." Ashton landed next to me, setting the hot bowl on my lap without warning. I made quick to pick it up. "You know what a Dragon is, right?"

I nodded.

"Good, so you remember some stuff. I work for this place called CAIN. They keep an eye on Dragons and stuff. But they've got this whole loyalty thing, so they need to make sure that their employees aren't holding out information or something."

"You work for CAIN?" I hesitated in asking my next question. "Have you ever encountered a Dragon? Someone with real-life superpowers?"

He ran his hands through my hair, his eyes watching me. I stared at my own face. "No." His hand slid across the bridge of his nose. "If I did, I wouldn't know. Most powers aren't visual unless it's in the eyes or something."

"The eyes?"

"Yeah, depending on the power, some peoples' eyes are really cool. They'll be a weird color or something. Kind of like yours."

"Huh." *Little do you know?*

"But no, I don't really deal with Dragons so much as remmutants." *So that must be why he showed up at the hospital during the attack.* Ashton readjusted himself on the couch. I settled in under his arm, taking a spoonful of cheesy bean soup. His hand pressed against my arm, letting me see. "Anyhow, back to a movie. You've got two genres to choose from. Contemporary romance or western."

"Why only two?"

"Well, back in the day, they had fairytales and superhero comics, but then Dragons started showing up, and stuff that encouraged the use of special powers was unofficially banned." In a shrug, Ashton hunched up to slurp his spoon. "Some stories still stuck around, but most of them faded away over the years. I've got of a friend who's got a book of fairytales she managed to find."

"You have friends?"

Ashton burst into a snort. "Yes, for your information, I do have friends. Two best friends, Kade and May. I should invite them over." He smiled at the thought of them. "You'd like May. She's real sweet. And Kade might seem intimidating at first, but he's loyal until the very end once you get past that." His expression turned bittersweet, his gaze fixed on the soup. "They just haven't been over in a while, since I've got to take care of you, and I thought it would take a minute to adjust."

That reminded me of another question I had. I had no clue who my parents were. Whatever accident I had been in stole that from me. I doubted I would like the reason as to why I hadn't heard mention of them, but I wanted confirmation. "About that… It's not that I don't enjoy living with you, but you're an adult. Wouldn't it be better if I stayed with our parents?"

"Oh, well…" Ashton's hesitant breathing interrupted the answer. "They're gone… They died in the accident."

Even though I had already guessed that to be the case, it didn't make it easier. Instead of feeling sad about their demise, I felt worse I couldn't even remember them. My whole world had been stolen from me. At least I had Ashton. "What - What were they like?" My words came out cracked, a break in the silence.

Rubbing his hands together, Ashton began to string the words in his mind. "Your dad… Hank Caddel. He was a brilliant man. He was a scientist at CAIN, and he loved you more than anything. Some nights, he'd come home late and tired. He kept multiple journals of different observations but rarely allowed anyone to read them. I mean, he let me read a few lines out of one, but that was it. When he was writing, that was his serious time." A bitter-sweetness hung in the air. "He was a good man."

"And mom?"

"Her name was Lauren, and she was a quiet and reserved woman. She wanted you to be the best you could and loved it when you guys would find something new to be interested in. And her eyes…" As Ashton turned, his body faced me more. He seemed to perk up as he reminisced about our parents. "They always seemed … sad? Or maybe that's not the right word. Mixed with myriad emotions, like pride and contentment, but also worry. Something else behind that?" He shook himself from the topic of her eyes. "And, she really liked Shakespeare, particularly the insults. Whenever she had the chance, she'd use them. She might've been a nurturing mother, but she was also subtly snarky. She would tell you plainly if you did something she thought was idiotic. She truly was a great woman. Actually, you look just like her." Ashton sighed, holding me closer.

My eyes watered and warm butterflies filled my stomach. I shook the feeling off. "They sound amazing."

"Oh, they were. I still miss them, but I've had seven years to deal with it, so it doesn't hurt as much to think about them. But you-"

"Don't remember them." I shut my eyes, focusing on sweet nothing.

"Ally…" Ashton pulled me into a hug. His warm body sent a comforting sensation through me, and I wasn't keen to resist it either. He stroked my hair as he held me.

I don't remember if I started crying or not.

5

Quantum Entanglement

Since waking up in the hospital, the world had seemed like a strangulating trap. The suffocation percolated every aspect of my life. It forced me to stay in the house, stuck in my marred knowledge of my past, present, and future. And so I seemed destined to be until the day I died or discovered how every piece of my history fell into place.

I wished I could demand my brother answer the millions of questions fighting for attention in my mind. But I drew a blank every time I thought I had gathered the courage. Behind that innocent smirk of his, in truth, he held the key to my cage. He simply dangled it above me, only allowing me to get as close as he wanted me to. Perhaps a ludicrous thought, but without any clue as to what exactly happened to me, the ridiculous posed itself plausible.

After grabbing a snack from the fridge, (pudding, I think, but I couldn't see), I flopped down on the couch.

"Captain!" I called, throwing an arm over my face dramatically. The pitter-patter of his paws came along. I pat him on the head, popped open the chocolate pudding, and ate it without a spoon.

Snap!

The sharp noise interrupted my train of thought. I straightened and listened closer.

Snap! Squeak!

Captain huffed at the source of the sound. I shushed him, trying to focus.

Snap! Snap!

The crackles accompanied an animalistic squeak. Closing the gap between Captain and me, I used him for sight. He continued huffing, his focus fixated on underneath the couch.

Now that I could see as Captain saw, I nearly yelped. A small rat skittered from under the couch and escaped between my feet. A childish scream ensued instinctively. Captain went after it, stranding me in the dark and almost knocking me over, barking at the rodent.

I shuddered, shaking out my hands. "Captain?" I stalked through the dark, chasing after sounds.

After finding his fur, sight returned. The rat backed against the wall, cornered under the computer desk. Its weighted body moved up and down with shaking breath. Topped with a red lens, a cylindrical camera emerged from its scuffed black fur. Brown goggles hung strapped across its face, and a metal skeletal spine ran along its backside, reaching the tail's tip.

"What in the world…"

A wire poked out from under the camera. As the rat's face came closer to it, the rodent met another shock, resulting in the *snap!* The rat squeaked in response. I frowned, the smallest portion of me pitying the creature. The rat looked half mechanical, unlike the biological mutants, Ashton had described to me. I crossed out the idea it could be a remmutant.

Sucking up my nerves, I held my hand out to the rat.

It looked at my fingers very reluctantly. I didn't exactly trust it either. As the rat scampered up on my palm, I let go of Captain, only needing to see through one pair of eyes.

With the rat in hand, I realized I couldn't see back behind the rat while using my powers. I frowned and moved to touch Captain again. Shutting one eye, I found myself only looking from Captain's view.

I perked up at the new development.

5. *When touching two things, my eyes each take one perspective.*

"Hey, that's neat." I wondered if I'd be doing this for the rest of my life: talking to animals while waiting for Ashton to get home.

Taking my pinky, I tucked the wire back under the camera. I noticed an imprint in the metal plating. *BL-*

32. The rat tilted its head at me, scanning me over. I watched it, wondering what it could be thinking.

In my carelessness, the uncovered tip touched me, resulting in a light shock. I quickly whipped my hand back. In the process, I smacked Captain in the nose. That set him off with a loud bark. The rat leaped away among the chaos. I yanked Captain's collar to keep him from going after the rodent. After bonking my head on the bottom of the table, I found my way to the sink.

Captain came to my side, done chasing the rat. I rolled my eyes at him. "Thanks, boy. Now I'll never figure out who was spying on us." *Or why.*

"Ally…"
Soft pink lips flashed.
"Ally… Can you hear me?"
Warm cheeks. Bouncy blond curls. I couldn't make out her face.

"Ah, dang, this was a bad idea." The world around me glitched. Blurry images flew past my vision. Voices. Mumbles. A gate. "For all I know, it's not even you."

"Just wait right here." A different voice from the first one. A grown man.

A scream pierced the air. Crying. "Abort! Abort!"

These voices came foggier than the girl's defined tone.

The girl's voice returned. "There's something else here. Someone..."

Fire. So much fire. Glowing. Bright yellow.

"Lee!" Another alien voice.

"Oh shoot." Trampling footsteps followed the girl's voice.

The world shifted to black. Eyes, peering through. The knocking. Remmutants.

"I'll be back. Please, just hang on till then." Everything went still, all except an eerie ringing. "Please."

"Lee!"

Ashton's laughter filled the space. Disappearing as soon as it came.

"Well... You're in good hands. I'll see you again... I promise."

Quiet. A void. The water rippled in the center. Drip. Drop. Drip.

Drop.

"You're in good hands."

I gasped and woke up from my nap on the couch. Groaning, I rubbed my face with my palm. *Weird dream.*

Even weirder was how I could see right now.

I stopped, the thought connecting. My whole body was fixed visible from a distance. I double-checked to make sure I wasn't touching anything that could give me sight. Someone else's view took over mine *without* making contact.

A yellow sticky note stuck to my forehead. In Ashton's scribbly handwriting, it read, *Sweet dreams, dork! See you after work!* How long was I asleep?

Shoving the note in my pocket, I focused. *I must find who I was seeing through. From under… the coffee table.* Captain? The low angle exhibited the scene in color, canceling out the option. I glanced down toward my watcher's feet. Toothy toes and chubby legs moved toward dark fur and metal plating.

My eyes widened. The rat from earlier. My mind was swarmed with several different thoughts. *1, gross, 2, how, and 3, why!* Peeking around the coffee table leg, I searched for Captain. He lay curled up on his bed, by the stairs. Probably for the best, lest he scares away the rodent. I needed to find out how I could see through the rat's eyes.

Before I could, the rat took control again. It darted across the floor and squeezed under the closet door beneath the stairs. I moved to get up off the couch but decided against it. After all, a strange cyborg rat would certainly have interesting places to go. He could take the lead for a while.

A misplaced sense of freedom fell over me.

Climbing up a broom handle, the rat made his way up into the roof vents. He had a route already planned out, but there had to be someone who had programmed it into him. *Who could it be?*

After the rat reached the end of the vents, he

climbed downward, landing in the kitchen walls. He scampered out from a hole and made his way into the outside light. The grass padded his soft steps. He reached the end of the concrete sidewalk, before pausing. His head turned back at the house, nose twitching in thoughts. His will stood strong.

Some more nudging from me, and the rat moved. Going as fast as his tiny rat body would take him, he finally reached the end of the street. Attempting to cross the road, he took a step forward.

Dark red letters rolled across my view. It only served to worsen my confusion until I remembered the rat's goggles. *Glitch detected. Return to Cleo's lab.* The rat retracted his arm, moving back onto the sidewalk. He raced uphill, crossing the road to the right.

Cleo. That name was mentioned in the video I had seen on Ashton's computer had mentioned someone. Who were they?

Finding this rat had not been a coincidence. I clicked my tongue, thinking.

"What's up, Ally-gator!"

I flinched, startled at the sound of Ashton's voice. The world went dark, disconnecting from the rat. "No," I yelped under my breath.

"Ally?" I felt his hand on my shoulders.

"Ashton, you're back. Hey." I gave a smile, trying to sound enthusiastic.

"Okay, weirdo." He ruffled my hair and moved on.

I pulled myself up from the couch. "Hey, Ashton?" I needed to ask him at least one of my questions. I genuinely considered, but couldn't bring myself to trust him entirely. If I asked, I didn't think he would tell me the truth. About any of it.

"Yeah?"

"Maybe… tonight we could just hang out? We could play a board game or something." An honest diversion. He said he was my brother, but I knew so little about him. Maybe some quality time would rid me of trust issues. Then I could hopefully have the guts to ask him anything I wanted.

"Yeah, I'd like that." Warmness lingered in his voice. Maybe he felt the same way.

6

The Journal

The house stood still in the absence of Ashton. My hand led the way through the darkness of his den, moving from doorway to bedframe. With what I could muster, I shoved the bed from the wall. Plopping on my knees, I brushed through the carpet, searching for the indented secret hatch.

A bark broke my chain of thoughts. My hands went tense. I let go of my breath after no one spoke. Captain barked again, rubbing up against me. My fingers found the hatch latch. He huffed, tugging on my shirt with his teeth.

"What is your problem?" Captain not wanting me to find whatever Ashton had hidden in here proved the answer I needed lay beneath the trapped door. I shoved the dog away, keeping contact with sight. He whined, but I persisted.

I hooked my finger in the latch and yanked it up. After some tugging, it gave loose. The hinges scratched at the carpet, revealing a hidden space. A small book tied closed with a string of ribbon rested inside. Taking it with my free hand, I examined it over. Imprinted in the bottom right corner were two letters. *B.L.*

I hoisted myself up with the bed, and I managed to shove it back against the wall. Captain snarled at me.

Captain nipping at my sleeves, I made my way to my room. I pat a spot for the dog on the bed. "Come on, Captain." Giving up, he joined me on the bed. Pouting, he placed his head on my lap. I stroked back his fur, setting the book in front of him. "Now, there's a good boy." He huffed, staring up at me.

Opening the cover, the first page held a title laid out in pen. *The Scientific Findings of Blake Landerson.*

My finger dragged through the book until I found the first written page, a report with a pencil-shaded rat in the bottom corner. Turned out, the time-stained page dated back nine years.

Today begins the start of a new project: the BL experiment, named after me. We're designing a new form of spy, one that will go beyond the human ones we have recruited now, not to make our agents obsolete, but to work as an addition to our current assets. Imagine rats being able to investigate places discretely and report back information. The concept seems ridiculous. I thought it was ridiculous when I first considered it. Once suggesting it to our CAIN supervisor, Vix, I have been placed as head of the experiment. I still have no clue how we will achieve this, but I have a few ideas. This is only day one, but soon, I'm hoping we'll reach our goal. I will report more as things advance. Signing off,

B.L.

I scrunched my nose at the report. "Who are you, Mr. Landerson?"

Click, turn, creak.

I straightened, startled by the front door. "Oh, shoot." My fingers drummed along the leather cover as my mind raced for a place to hide the book.

"Ally! Are you home?" Ashton called from downstairs.

"Yeah, in my room!" I moved to slide the journal in the pillowcase in the back to prevent Ashton from noticing it. Something in plastic wrapping crumpled under my movement. After a curious pause, I held the object for Captain to see. A dark-colored, see-through wrapping encased a fortune cookie.

"What-"

Ashton swung my bedroom door open. "Want lunch?"

I shoved the fortune cookie into my lap, out of view. My mind retraced the simple question Ashton had just asked. "Uh, sure." I tried hard to ensure I didn't sound too strained. Ironic as can be. All this mystery stuff was making me lose my mind. Some food would do me good.

Ashton sat me down at a fast-food place. They didn't allow dogs inside, so we ate out in the chilled air.

I found it cute that my brother cared so much for his dog.

My soft side for my brother conflicted with my suspicions of him. Just because someone liked their dog didn't mean they were innocent. Ashton clearly wasn't.

Ashton set a sandwich in front of me. "There's your lunch." He took my hand, moving it to the food. I smiled, wondering how long it would be before he found out I could see. Would I ever trust him enough to tell him? Maybe after I figured out what skeletons hid in his closet?

"Hey, did you know stomachs can't hold much after 5 liters of food? If you eat more, your stomach will pop."

A red flag went off in my head. I gulped down my food and gaped at him.

He chuckled at my embarrassed expression. "Sorry. I dislike silence, so I fill the quiet with random facts. They make good ice breakers." He lifted his sandwich. "Besides, your brain stops you before you reach that point, so you'll gag before your insides burst."

"Why would you need ice breakers? I'm your sister." I took another bite of food so I wouldn't have to talk much. I tried to shake off Ashton's "fun" fact, but it didn't help his case.

"Not really. You're the same, but... different. I

feel like we barely know each other." My brother crinkled his food wrapper as he spoke, avoiding eye contact.

I frowned, realizing the truth in his words. "Well, then, let's get to know each other. I'm Ally Caddel." I stuck out my hand, more as a joke than anything else. He shook it.

"Nice to meet you, Ally, I'm Ashton Caddel." I could see through his eyes momentarily. His hand came up and scraped across his nose. "What's your day look like, Ally?"

"Well, I play with the dog and…" I scrunched my nose, trying to think. *Tell him about your powers.* Convinced that this would be a bad idea, I gave up. "I sit around bored all day. That's it."

"Oh man, sorry about that. We should do something fun sometime soon."

Part of me fondly thought over the idea of just spending a day with my brother, but I reminded myself of the emails and the journal. *I cannot trust him until I know the truth.* "So, how about you? What's your day look like?"

"Well, I go to work-"

"At CAIN." I hoped the interjection might spring up some wanted information.

"Yeah, at CAIN. I come home for lunch, or sometimes I go out. And then, I go back to work. And then after that, I finally go home and stay home. I go to bed, and I do it all over again. But I do have the day off on Sundays." Taking a bite, he continued with a mouth full of food. "And once a month, my friends and I do game night, but we kind of paused that a few months ago."

"What do you do at CAIN?"

"Hmm, I can't tell you." Ashton smiled at me wistfully. A hint of sadness hid behind his eyes. I couldn't see him as far as he knew, but that didn't stop him from concealing his true feelings behind a mask.

"Why not?" I crumpled up my wrapper into a ball, making a small trash pile.

"Can't tell you."

Ashton grew harder to trust every day. He let me into his bubble just enough for me to like him, and that was exactly what made him so unlikeable.

He must've read the discontentment on my face because he rolled his eyes. "Just because I don't tell you something doesn't mean it is some dark, profound mystery."

Sort of feels like it. "Is there anything you can tell me?" Over and over again, Ashton abandoned me in the dark.

Ashton shook his head.

Realizing this conversation wasn't going anywhere, I found myself eager to leave. "I can get your trash," I said. Before he could answer, I reached across our table and collected his wrapper. Captain looked up from his nap. He arose, yawned, and followed me to a nearby trash can.

"Thanks, the trash is just over…" Ashton watched me toss the trash. "There."

My breath hiccupped at my mistake. Ashton wouldn't expect me to know where the trash bin would be. As he got up, I heard his chair squeak. When I turned to see him, I saw his expression change from a confused to a light smile. Did he already know?

He ruffled my hair. "Come on, Ally. I've got to get back to work, so I'll drop you off back at the house. It was fun having lunch and spending time with you."

Ashton's smile proved contagious. "Yeah, thanks."

When he dropped me off, I stood on the porch. I waited to see him off. He kissed me on the forehead and then, left.

I stared after him, Captain at my side. *Wonder what he* actually *does every day.* A scheme formed in my mind.

As I stepped back into my room, I remembered the fortune cookie I had found on my bed.

I called for Captain and grabbed the cookie from the sheets. With my sight reactivated, I sat down on the carpet and started to unwrap it. He sniffed at the cookie, watching it as a toddler waiting for permission from their mom to have a piece of candy. After removing the inner note, I gave the dog the cookie. The paper stretched between my hands. The black text stood out in bold.

You've been watching me.

Ashton's gaze moved to the stove clock as he took a sip of his coffee. The sweet scent rose with the steam.

I leaned against the kitchen island, where he stood on the other side. One more swig and he slid the mug over to me. "I've got to get to work. Here, want some?"

It heated my cold fingertips, sending chills through me. I lifted the mug to my lips, and the drink sent a warm sensation down to my bones. The drink tickled my throat, and I could actually taste it once the burning left. I clicked my tongue and scrunched my face. "This is extremely sweet. Are we sure there's any coffee in this?"

"A little." Ashton grabbed his cap from the counter and plopped it on backward. He jaunted to the door.

"Hey, Ashton? I was thinking…" I considered my wording. "Could you give me a ride into town? I've been cooped up here for days and kind of wanted to explore."

"Okay. Let me just grab Captain's leash." He turned back and went to the closet under the stairs. Upon his return, he clasped the leash on, up close from my perspective. Patting his dog on the head, Ashton stood up to his full height. "Alright, come on, gang."

I watched the scenery blend together out the car window. The dog sat on my lap, passing along gray vision. The town formed the shape of a raindrop, pouring out into a mix of small businesses and government-funded facilities. The sky panels shifted from early sunrise to mid-morning light. A far-reaching obsidian wall stretched along the other side of town. I stared over it as the car rolled down the hill.

"What's out there? Past the fake sky?"

Ashton glanced in my direction. "Oh, that's where the remmutants live. They kind of took most of the country when they started showing up. The ones here in the Colonies are especially annoying, because they can all fly. They're like big, freaky eagles. That's why we have the dome."

"And the wall?"

"That's a barrier as another line of defense, in case a remmutant does get in. Sometimes they do get past the wall, though, like when you first woke up from your coma, and we have to hunt them down. They station a bunch of CAIN agents at the border. They don't let me down there anymore though, seeing as last time didn't go so well." Ashton gestured to the scar on his cheek.

"So… This small town is all that's left of America?" I sat up in my seat, readjusting the dog on my lap.

"Oh no, that would be sad." He punctuated the statement with a laugh. "No, America split into three colonies on the land that was still usable. More cities exist in this colony; they're just spread farther. We're in the Second Colony, up north by Canada. And then, southwest of here, there's the Third Colony. Up toward the tip of the United Colonies, at the East end is First Colony. That's where the capital, New Old York is."

"How do you get between them with the domes and remmutants in the way?"

"Underground tunnels. They're really long and really dark. Yes, there are lights down there, but not much. Rich people take trains between them, but I usually go by car. There are underground hotels and pitstops too."

"Which city are we living in?"

"Tintview. I've been living here for five years now."

The car pulled up to an empty shopping center. Ashton parked in front of a wide, unlabeled building. A small sticker slapped on the glass door tagged it as a CAIN rented space. Along with a motorcycle, two other cars, one short and compact, the other a jeep, took up the parking lot. *Wonder what Ashton's work friends are like...*

"Well, you're free to explore for the day. Oh! And..." Ashton reached over into my already cramped space and dug through the glove box. I pressed my body against the back of the chair, hugging Captain tightly, to give Ashton as much space as possible. He retrieved a phone, a shiny black screen, and a dark colored case. "Here's an old phone of mine I figured you could use. I probably should've given this to you when you first moved in, with me so busy with work and such. But better late than never. I already put my number in it."

"Thanks. I'll let you know if I get into trouble."

"See you after work, Ally." Popping open the door, he left. With one last wave at me, he went inside.

Biting my lip, I fixed my mindset back on my plan. CAIN held the key to discovering what Ashton was hiding. I figured this wasn't the main base as the headquarters for an elite branch of government would probably have a bigger budget than an old shopping outlet.

Patting Captain on the back, I said, "Come on, boy, let's go spy on Ashton." Reaching past the dog, I popped open the latch and let us out of the car.

I turned into the small gap between buildings. A dumpster beneath a thin window on the side sat building up rust. I hoisted myself on top of the dumpster. My vision left.

A low growl rumbled like thunder from Captain. I rolled my eyes. "And Ashton expects me to trust him, even though his dog barks at me whenever I get too close to one of his secrets." I crossed my legs, sitting on the plastic dumpster lid. He barked at me when I pat a spot for him next to me. Hoping no one inside would hear, I shushed him.

The dog finally jumped up, but only keep me out of trouble. Nonetheless, I set my hands on his shoulders and forced him quiet. I rested his front paws against the wall, so I could peer through the window. *What are you up to, Ashton?*

Inside, four desks were arranged in two neat

rows, each complete with a computer and miscellaneous desk decorations. Other than Ashton, I recognized two other faces: the pregnant woman from the library and the Kiyano man from the inspection.

Ashton did some sort of handshake with Kiyano. Another man, hidden behind a computer, typed at his desk. His blond hair laid back, glistening with smooth gel, accompanying his put-together suit.

Ashton found himself a seat at his desk. The dark-haired Kiyano man continued to stand, while the woman rested in a wheeled chair. They laughed and talked, except for the blond man. I frowned, unable to make out any words.

Taking a breath, I focused, hoping for some way to hear them.

"…Come on, May, why won't you listen to me?" Ashton. It sounded so clear, but… I stopped. *Could I access* all *of Captain's senses?*

"Oh hush, you're so dramatic." May, the woman, shook her head, smiling.

"Not this again," Kiyano said.

"Come on, Kade, back me up here. I just worry about you. Shouldn't you be on maternity leave already?" Ashton frowned.

"You've been saying that since the moment I suspected I was pregnant, Ash. The baby's due in three months, I think I'll be fine." May rested her hands on her stomach, leaning back in her seat.

"Can you get to work already?" Uninterested in

their conversation, the blond man glared at them.

"Casey's right. Back to it, guys. We're not getting paid to mess around." Kade spun his finger, moved to his desk, and placed it next to Ashton's. Kade logged onto the computer, clicking the mouse a few times. He stared at the computer before glancing sideways at Ashton. "Messing around sure is a lot more fun than this, though. Remember when we were on the front lines?"

"Now it's just the exciting life of moving documents from one file to another. Dangerous stuff." Ashton smirked.

May snickered.

Spying on them was turning out to be an exercise in futility. Just small talk. The idea of just leaving crossed my mind.

"Speaking of dangerous," May started, her hazelnut eyes glued to her computer screen. "I met a certain little girl the other day, Ashton. Your *baby sister?*"

Or maybe I could stay a little longer.

"Wait, really?" That seemed to catch Ashton's attention. "You didn't tell her anything, did you?" *Tell me what?*

"Oh, nothing. But I did almost spill the entire can of beans. I first didn't realize it was her, but then I saw Captain, and that certainly shut me up. Everything is still a-okay." A guilty smile crossed her face. She fidgeted with a ring in her right hand.

"Dude! You thought she was a random stranger,

so you were just gonna tell her everything?"

"You guys are the worst agents ever," Kade said with a chuckle.

"This is why I should've been the one in charge of that mess." Casey frowned. "You've been leading on the experiment for a couple of weeks now. When will you make the move?"

"I'm sure Ashton has a plan," Kade said, shooting Casey a look.

Ashton let out a breath, rolling his eyes. "She's not an experiment. She's a person." The part of me that suspected they were talking about me blushed at the idea he'd defend me like that. But that would also mean that I was the "she" he was leading on. What did that mean? My distrust for him only deepened.

"I thought you were assigned a different project, anyways." Kade glanced back at Casey. "What was it called again? Something pretentious, I bet." May's eyes moved to Casey, waiting for his reaction.

"Station 42. Any details further than that are classified."

"Who has what case doesn't matter. Let's just finish our work." Done with the conversation, Ashton turned his attention to the monitor.

May frowned and Kade turned stiff.

"You guys are just jealous because you only ever get Abel cases," Casey muttered, his dry voice only making it quieter.

I was certain that more lay beneath the surface of

Ashton's annoyance. Whoever this Casey guy was could easily press Ashton's buttons.

An eternity passed before anyone spoke again.

"Hey, Ashton, you're tall. It's kind of stuffy in here. Can you open the side window to let some air in?" May smiled at him.

My heart jumped. Pulling Captain down, I ducked out of view. I heard footsteps approaching the window. My sneakers squeaked sharply as I slipped down. *Captain, you better not bark at me!* Gripping the strap of his collar, my backhand pressed against his fur. I forced him to keep his mouth shut. The creaking of the window behind me followed. My breath shaking, I crouched down in the dirt.

New theories dug their way into my mind. More were in store about the things that had put me in the hospital, I just knew it.

If Ashton wouldn't make his move, I'd make mine.

7

Phone Call

Ashton burst into the house clumsily with bags of groceries draped on his arms. He sang out of key as he set the bags on the kitchen table. I watched him from the stairs, Captain sitting at my feet.

I knew "lovable dork" merely acted as his cover-up. I just hadn't deciphered for what yet.

Reaching across the table, he began sorting the groceries into their spots. "How has your day been, Ally-gator?" *The fun nickname is part of his façade. What's he playing at?*

"The same as every day," I mumbled, my hand pressed against my cheek.

"We're gonna take a trip together or something one of these days." He slid the milk onto a shelf in the fridge. "You know what's amazing? The fact that two gasses make a liquid. You take Hydrogen and Oxygen, smoosh them together, and then it is water."

"And?"

"I just think that's crazy. That's it! Science is so cool." Ashton took off his hat and slapped it down on the kitchen island. "Since we don't have a vacation now, how about we go to the ice cream place downtown tonight, huh?"

Before I could answer, his phone began ringing with an even stranger song than the one he had been singing. He held a finger up. "Just a moment, Ally…" Pinning the phone to his ear with his shoulder, he greeted, "Go for Ashton." While I waited patiently, he paced the kitchen, putting away the last few groceries. Scratching the back of Captain's ears, I tuned in on the conversation.

"Caleb, this is Vix. We've been looking over your work. With the HDE resurfacing and how smoothly it's going, Titus thinks you're due for promotion."

Ashton's face lit up. "Really?"

"Yes, though he does have a few notes. For one, you have yet to bring in the girl…"

Ashton's eyes moved toward me. The moment he caught me staring, his gaze darted elsewhere. "Well, these things take time. But, I-"

"I don't need your excuses, Caleb. Come up to Envision City today. We'll pay for a hotel and anything else you might need. We'll talk in the morning. I hope things go well." The phone beeped as the other line hung up.

A mix of emotions showed up on Ashton's face. A moment passed before half his mouth curved upward in a smile.

"Who's Caleb?" I asked, spite layered in my tone. I grew fed up with all the secrets.

His skin jumped, my voice surprising him. "What?"

"You left it on speaker." A cheap lie, but he would probably believe it.

"Oh, silly George," Ashton mumbled to himself. "Caleb is my middle name. Sometimes I go by that." He shoved the phone back into his pocket.

"Anything else you would like to explain about that call?"

He continued collecting the grocery bag and kept on ignoring me. He wouldn't be able to hear me over the shuffling.

Intentional? I wouldn't be surprised.

Ashton hesitated, clicking his tongue. "Hey, how'd you like that vacation tonight instead of ice cream? I've got a free night at a hotel." He smirked, spinning on his heels. "As you heard, I've got a job thing in the morning. But it'll just be us the rest of the day." He stuffed the loose plastic bags in a drawer on the island. "What'd ya say?"

If Ashton would take me near a bigger branch of CAIN, well then, "Okay! Sounds fun!"

8

Envision

Envision City. Anthony Vix thought the name described the Second Colony's capital perfectly, and by proxy, himself. Greatness lined his blood, waiting like a lion patient for his pride. It stood at the finish line, beckoning him onward, to push through to the inevitable moment when he would rise with grandeur and craft his legacy as a royal seal on mankind's timeline. The only man who stood in the way of Vix's envisioned greatness was his boss, Mr. Titus.

Taking in the new morning, Vix threw his bedroom curtains open. Sun filled up every dark corner of the space. His gaze swept over the city, breathing with life and potential. He glanced back at his bed, the comforter disheveled in the night's sleep. However, his wife Cherry was missing from her spot and could be heard from the bathroom. Her voice drifted through the air in a honey-like melody. Mouth curved in a smile at her song, he crossed over the room to the closet. Selecting a white dress shirt, he knotted up each button one at a time.

As he finished dressing, Vix stepped into the shared bathroom. "Good morning, my love," he greeted.

Dressed in a scarlet bathrobe, she stood fluffing up her deep red locks. "Morning," she said, too fixated with her reflection to glance back. Picking out a cluster of silvery strands, she puckered her lips in a frown.

Vix reached past her for the hair gel. His knuckles brushed against a pair of red hair dye boxes. Taking one, he examined it closer. "What's this for?"

"I'm touching up my grays." Taking it from him, Cherry looked it over. "Let's see, what do I need…"

Vix rubbed his wife's arms, smiling at her through the mirror. "But, darling, you look so gorgeous with them. Who wouldn't want hair like fine metal?"

Cherry chuckled at this comparison. "Anthony, silver is not the best; it is only second best. Besides, I'm not ready to look like an old lady just yet. People only watch the news for the pretty women, you see." Turning, she planted a kiss on his cheek. The reporter began opening her dye box. "Today I'm doing a special on some sort of endangered species that the remmutants keep eating. Exciting stuff," she added sarcastically.

After the two had married, Cherry Vix had taken up a job as a reporter for the news station downtown. Although Vix watched every one of her broadcasts, she never covered anything exciting. Any time something interesting sprang up, typically attacks from Abel, she couldn't cover it because Vix would persuade her not to. They didn't want to alarm people. As far as the average citizen knew, there wasn't a group of terrorists running around the city causing trouble.

Vix went back to gelling his hair. "How does a fancy dinner out tonight sound?"

Pulling her bathrobe tighter around herself, Cherry smirked. "What's the occasion?"

"Well, my project is back and kicking again."

Cherry gasped, turning her whole body to face him. "Really? At this point, I was beginning to think it was over."

"Nope. It might've spent seven years dead in the water, but tomorrow, I should be able to move on to the next step."

Throwing her arms around his neck, Cherry smiled. "Anthony, that's great!"

Wrapping his hands around her back, they swayed together in a small dance. "Soon, I'll be able to give you everything you've ever wanted." With his palms, he could feel past stretch marks on her stomach. *Almost everything.*

Cherry had gotten pregnant years ago. Vix was more than happy at the news. Unfortunately, he had been called back from work with a phone call from her telling him it had been a miscarriage. Ever since they hadn't been able to have a kid.

"That will be wonderful." Smiling, her bangs fell over half her face. She didn't bother to push them back. Standing on her tiptoes, she gave him a quick kiss again.

Letting go, Vix turned to the bathroom door. "I'm off to work, but tonight we'll have dinner at wherever you'd like."

"I'll see you then."

Giving a small wave to the guards out in front of the CAIN building, Vix made his way to his car in the side lot. He slid into the driver's seat, humming happily to himself. *It may have been a slow day at work, but meeting Cherry for a dinner is surely a nice way to end a tiresome day.*

Pulling out his phone, Vix moved to press call on his wife's phone. It began to buzz before he found her contact, a new name on the caller ID.

Mr. Titus.

Vix frowned.

Phone pressed to his ear, Vix rested his hand on the steering wheel. Traffic inched along as slow as his dreams for the future but moved nonetheless. The highways in Envision stretched over the tallest towers in the city, laced in an intricate spider web of suspended roads. The sky panels mixed in a blend of blues, starless due to the city lights, but Vix liked to imagine those lights as stars instead.

Mr. Titus had called to complain about the

progress of Vix's project, making the drive to the restaurant even longer.

Vix's finger tapped along the wheel. "I think he'd just rather play the waiting game. Caleb is young, and this is the first time he's had to do something like this. But I think he can pull through."

"Don't be naïve, Vix."

Shoulders hunched, Vix tried to keep from frowning. He bumped his car forward, eager for the ride or the phone call to end. "I'm giving him the benefit of the doubt." He just had to hold through until this rough patch washed over. Once his project was over, Vix would impress Titus, get a promotion, and move to the First Colony as Cherry had always wanted. *Just keep your head up.*

A jolting *thud* smacked against the car. Vix's attention shot up, finding a man rolled onto the hood. The man jumped to his feet, locked eyes with Vix, and then took off. Gunshots could be heard from some direction, accompanied by screams.

"Hang on, Mr. Titus. I'll have to call you back. I believe we've got Abel trouble." Without waiting for his boss' response, Vix hung up and threw the door open.

As his shoes hit the highway pavement, Vix's hand went to the gun on his hip. He scanned over the chaos. Weaving between the cars, he searched for any civilians who could be in the crossfire. Ducking past a gunshot overhead, he picked out a blue van. After helping the family, he moved to the next several cars.

"You've got to get out of here!"

"Get off the highway as quick as you can!"

"Go!"

Vix was slammed into the concrete by another body. The kid who knocked into him jumped to his feet, aiming his gun at Vix warily. Vix did the same, finally unclipping his weapon. Though the kid wore a mask to guard the bottom half of his face, Vix recognized him as the same redhead kid he had seen in multiple Abel attacks. It made him wonder how sick Abel must be to hire a bunch of kids.

They stood locked in a glare. Hesitant steps crossed the pavement. In the blink of an eye, the kid kicked the gun from Vix's hand. He flinched back, his hands forming fists. Rather than fight, the boy took off in the direction of the person who had knocked into the car. Vix stared after him, only loosening slightly.

"Mr. Vix!" Glancing back, Vix found two CAIN agents running to meet him. Their chests lifted with heavy breaths. "Are you alright?"

Letting go of his tension, Vix dusted off his suit. "Yes," he said with a sigh. He knelt, collecting the gun again. The smell of asphalt and car fumes mixed with the cold worsened his mood. "Report?"

"Abel launched an attack at Dr. Cleo's old lab by the border."

"How many?"

"Just three couriers, a small extraction team. Our agents are figuring out who now."

Vix's gaze swept over the messy street. Shattered windows, busted bumpers from a few drivers who didn't stop their vehicles in time, and bullet-punctured tires took up the halted highway. Vix's own car was now adorned with a dented hood. "This is going to be a hard one to cover up."

Vix turned back to the CAIN agents. With the wave of his hand, he said, "You two can go. I'll see what I can do here."

With a nod, the agents left.

He moved toward his car, wincing at the dent. Shaking himself, he took a deep breath, trying to reset his evening. *Just keep your head up.*

Just keep your head up.

9

Sneak Out, Rinse, Repeat

We reached the hotel, and Ashton checked in under CAIN. Sliding the key card through the door lock, he pushed it open into our room.

Ashton chucked our two bags on the bed, Captain tagging along behind us. "Here we are. I'm going to take a shower and head off to bed since I've got an early start in the morning. But after work stuff, we'll go find something in the city to do."

"Can't wait," I said. If Ashton could put on a mask, so could I.

After a steamy shower, Ashton settled into bed, just as he had said. Not much time had passed before his snores fell on my ears.

Go time. I crept out of bed, stepping around the dog. Ashton shifted in the sheets, setting me on edge. Taking a deep breath, I grabbed my brother's jacket from where I remembered it to be. My hand fished for the door handle in the ever-watching darkness.

One step out, then the other. The door creaked behind me. I waited.

In the pitch black, I hoped I would be able to find what I was looking for. I snuck through the hall. I thought it better to use the stairs than the elevator since I could find my way with the rails. *Time for answers, Ashton.*

My fingers brushed along the phone in my pocket, and something else… Fortune cookie wrapper. A small gasp escaped me. Whoever was leaving behind these cookies not only knew where I lived but knew where I was going. Only one person crossed my mind who fit that knowledge. My fingers tightened around the fortune cookie as if I might lose it by letting go.

I felt the cold of the lobby and heard the hush of the sliding doors. My sneakers squeaked sharply on the marble floor.

Crisp October air washed over me as I exited the building.

Slipping the phone out of my pocket, I held it up to my face. My thumb pressed the button. "Directions to CAIN."

"Finding directions to CAIN… Turn left on 3rd street."

Without anything to guide me, I wouldn't get very far. The cracks showed themselves in my plan. Part of me considered going back for Captain, but it would be too risky. Not to mention he would bark at me for going behind Ashton's back.

Squeezing my eyes shut, I rubbed a hand over my face. Only bad ideas rattled around my head, this one no different. I would get myself kidnapped or something. I let out a sigh and turned to go back inside. I opened my eyes.

And I could see.

I froze. Not my eyes. It was… The rat. What was he doing here? I watched myself from the bushes, seeing my backside. I turned around, confusion in my expression.

Focusing, I forced him toward me, and he came to crouch at my feet. Kneeling, I picked him up and faced him forward. "Why do you keep following me?"

The rat only groomed himself in response. I looked down the city and spotted it with blue and yellow lights. Turning my attention back to the hotel, I bit my lip.

Now or never, Ally.

Setting the rat on my shoulder, my gaze moved to the directions on the phone. *Now.*

The eerie quiet of the night was starting to get to me. The cold nipped at my nose. I rubbed my hands together, hoping to muster some sort of warmth. Walking alone at night in a wide, unfamiliar city looked less and less wise. Dogs barking, cars scraping against the pavement, and sirens howling from somewhere made the hairs on my neck stand up. With the mysterious rat tucked warmly in my hood, I pressed on.

I took the fortune cookie in my fingers. Raising it for the rat to see, I discovered the wrapper's pigment to be red tinted. I cracked it open for the new note.

I've been watching you too.

My gaze narrowed. *Is Ashton the one leaving these?*

The small parchment lingered between my fingertips. *If Ashton wanted me to trust him, why was he leaving these ominous notes?* Not wanting to think about it anymore, I shoved the paper slip deep into my pocket.

Was I making the right choice? How did I expect this to end? I needed the truth. Not whatever nonsense Ashton was trying to feed me. Beneath that smiling mask lurked something dangerous and cunning. I would demand my answers, one way or another.

After the long walk, I found myself near a tall building. In glossy letters, the sign on the building read *CAIN.* Two men stood at the entrance, and the closer I got, I learned they were armed. My heart sped up, but I kept my expression calm. *Of course, a government facility would have high security. Why didn't I think of that?* My on-the-spot plan broke apart with every step I took.

This was a *very* bad idea.

I kept moving past the building, so as not to arouse suspicion. Once I stood out of sight, I stopped. I leaned on the side of the next building over. My mind searched for some way around the security. Everything I wanted to know waited in those doors.

The rat rubbed his face against mine, giving me the chills. Raising my hand, I pushed him back a little. An idea sprang into my head.

Setting the rat on the floor, I focused my powers. Maneuvering him, I made my way around the back of the CAIN building. I blended in with the shadows, avoiding sight.

Behind the building, I discovered a lone door, guarded by one man. One man would certainly be easier to fight than two, but I had no skill when it came to combat. My gaze moved to the man's utility belt, several smoke bombs clipped to it.

I counted down in my head, working up the courage to make my move. I darted across the ground as the rat, determined not to be seen. Placing scraggly paws onto the notched wall, I climbed upwards. The late night had taken its toll on the man, causing him to lean against the wall in a complacent style. Stretching out, I carefully grabbed a smoke bomb from his belt. A smirk crossed my face. The rat's miniature paws let go.

Smoke erupted from the bomb, and the man let out a gasp before bending over and coughing. His hand moved to his gun, ready for any unseen attackers in the smoke. I found it surprisingly easy to see through the smog, as the rat's goggles provided protection.

My window of opportunity shrunk. Watching myself in the third person, I clumsily came to the door. I pulled my jacket over my mouth, holding my breath.

After getting a grasp on the door handle, I yanked as hard as I could. It smacked forward, hitting the guard in the back of his head and knocking him unconscious. He fell forward, and the smoke cloud cleared.

My steps hesitated. *Should I stay and help him? Is he okay? Did I just kill someone?*

The rat took control, staring at me in disbelief before starting to run off without me. I shook my imagination away. *He'll be fine.* I lifted my leg over the man, stepping into the building and corralling back the rat. The door thudded behind me.

My eyes scanned over the area, my breath heavy. I stood in a dimly lit hall, a single door sitting at the end of the corridor. I set my hand against the wall closest to me and started on my way.

My mind wandered to the rat as I walked. "If I'm going to keep you around, I can't just keep calling you 'the rat,'" I said in a hushed tone, in case more people waited inside. "You're labeled *BL*, so maybe… Bolt?" The rat didn't seem to care either way, so Bolt it was.

Opening the door, I found a flight of stairs tumbling downward. I grabbed the railing, curiosity digging into my skin. Checking around, I started my descent. My footsteps added to the echo of noises. Chills ran up my spine with each step down into the unknown.

I reached the last step. I found myself at the beginning of another long corridor, just as poorly lit as the first. I recoiled, seeing a few people at the other end of the hall. They hadn't noticed me yet. I darted for the nearest room. Yanking shut the door, I stranded myself in the dark. The lights turned on at my movement.

I held up my hands defensively, ready for anyone who might be inside. But after closer inspection, I found the room vacant. Exhaling, I let my guard down.

Four walls boxed in the tight space. A map hung to the back wall, a few locations pinned. A pair of tables met adjacently at the corner. The room's light spilled from a single dangling lamp. It squawked like a crow as it swung back and forth. My footsteps clipped against the ground as I moved toward the tables. Miscellaneous objects in bags labeled *evidence* spread out in disorganized piles across the tabletops.

My hands hovered over the tables as I walked past them. I scanned over the objects, trying to decide what could be important. A screwdriver zipped in a clear bag held a note labeled *Found in the aftermath of the Hidden Dragon Experiment, next to P2.* "What is all this stuff?"

"Don't move!"

I stiffened at the sharp tone. Turning on my heels, I raised my hands. Sensing danger, Bolt moved to the neck of my shirt, only making it harder for me to see. Three men stood in the doorway, weapons aimed. For the first time, I noticed a camera wedged up in the corner near the entrance.

Dang it.

My mind panicked. The guards approached me, one moving behind me. "Come along quietly, or we will resort to force." The stern order sent shivers down my spine. I moved in step with the lead guard. Every thought that surfaced told me to fight back, take a risk, and run for it. The odds stood insanely against me, though. *I should've stayed at the hotel like a good little girl.*

"We'll take her to Vix. He can decide what to do with her."

The leader wrapped his hand around my wrist, and instinct kicked in. My free hand launched forward in a fist, but he easily ducked without any fighting skills. Tightening his grip on my arm, he twisted it back and kicked my knees in. My body hit the cold, hard ground.

Flinching, I scrunched my nose, the pain mostly in my arm. The second man came at me, hitting the side of my head with the butt of his gun. I gave up, unconscious.

This whole thing had been a *very, very* bad idea.

10

An Improvised Job Interview

Ringing throbbed in my ears.

Darkness shrouded my sight. I groaned, slowly coming to. Something scratched against my face, a potato sack. The cold metal seat pinched at my back and sored into my bones. My heart thudded in the back of my head, making it hard to think. Rope rubbed against my wrists, my shoulders knotted back behind the chair.

Ashton has no clue where I am. He can't save me now.

The dark was void and uncertain.

"In just a few minutes, he should be here. Maybe we should start…" The hushed voice snapped me out of my thoughts. I wasn't alone. There went any scrap of hope for escape I had.

Someone from behind removed the bag, but it didn't change a thing. I still could only see the suffocating darkness and nothing else.

"Good morning, young lady," the voice said. "Do you break into places often?" The man chuckled. "Relax, you're perfectly safe here. No one is going to hurt you." His uniformed footsteps approached me. I pulled back, scrunching my nose like a scared rabbit. "You'll be a great help in the fight against Abel."

Doors creaked on hinges, smacking hard against the wall in urgency. I stiffened, inhaling sharply.

"Ah, good. You're here."

"Mr. Vix…" Ashton's voice. I didn't know if that made me relieved or worried. Either way, trouble hung over me like a blade waiting to drop.

"She came here by herself, in the dead of night. Guess she got bored waiting for you." The first voice let out a laugh, though light bitterness lingered beneath it. "Relax, it's a joke."

"How?" Aston hesitated. "Sir, I said I would take care of it. I was waiting until-"

"Watch what you say, Caddel, she's listening."

The room settled in suspicious quiet.

"Ally?" A warm hand appeared on my arm, and my vision lit up through familiar eyes. *Ashton.* "What are you doing here?"

"This is for the best, I suppose," the first man cut in. Ashton glanced back at him. The man stood fitted in a nice suit, oil black hair gelled neatly. A bright crimson tie dangled from his neck, the only colored thing on his attire. His eyebrows arched in a way as if he were always smiling, always proud of some achievement. His lips spread to a long smile, and his shoes clipped as he walked across the room. "Now, Caddel, about that promotion."

"Now?"

"Yes. In fact, we can discuss the other thing now that she's here. A new recruitment." His gaze went past Ashton, landing on me.

Ashton rose to his feet, shaking his head. His touch left, leaving me both literally and figuratively in the dark. "Sir, surely it's too early for that, not to mention-"

"In my opinion, you've waited too long. You can give her the tour and welcome her in. I have a few things to attend to, but you can meet me at my office in, let's say… half an hour. Sounds good?"

The door opened. "Alright."

"Good." It swung shut.

Ashton and I breathed in unison.

"Mind explaining *what* exactly you are doing here?" Ashton moved to untie me, his voice bitter. The trenchant criticism in his tone was piercing, to say the least.

Once I was free, I leaned over, rubbing my wrists. "Well, uh, I was curious…?" It came out more of a question than I had intended.

"You broke into a well-guarded government facility, blind, might I add, because you were curious? Smart. Ever heard the one about the cat? Curiosity killed it." Ashton helped me to my feet, his hand in mine.

"In case it wasn't obvious, I'm not actually blind."

"I know."

I turned up at him, gaping.

"And yes, you were very obvious about it. You're my little sister, of course, I knew you were a Dragon. Just 'cause you don't remember telling me years ago doesn't me you never did. But I just figured you'd tell me when you trusted me." Ashton directed me to the door of the room. "Unlike *you,* snooping through my stuff, trying to get one up on me. You're not as sneaky as you think. And I'm not an idiot."

Well, now I feel like one. "Will you tell me what you've been hiding?"

"Yes, now that you've broken my trust, I'll tell you all my secrets." Sarcasm peeked behind his dry voice.

"Alright, I shouldn't have snuck off. I get it." I shot him a glare.

"Whatever. I guess I *have* to give you the CAIN tour now, otherwise, I'll probably be fired." Ashton didn't sound too thrilled about it. He took my hand, leading me toward the door. "Don't tell anyone else about the Dragon thing, by the way. That's a secret for you and me."

"How come?"

"Do you have to question *everything*? Just trust me." Annoyance lingered at the surface of his words. He gripped my hand a little tighter, in a way that said, *shut up, and maybe I'll forget I'm mad at you.*

I shrunk a bit, turning my head from him. *Why won't he just tell me things? Then I wouldn't have to get kidnapped to figure anything out!*

We entered a busy lobby, CAIN agents going to and from different rooms, like ants on a mission. A front desk shaped like a horseshoe sat with two people working it. Light poured in from the windows, clueing me into the morning. Two staircases on either side and a twin set of elevators to my left lead to the second floor. The doors stood straight ahead of me.

"This is CAIN's front," Ashton said, gesturing to everything. "This is where you'll be."

"Where I'll be?"

"Yup. Vix, the guy in charge wants to make you an agent." Ashton ran a hand through his hair, extra fluff with the morning air and lack of a hat. I noticed he wasn't dressed in uniform like the other CAIN agents. Had he just woken up to come to pick me up? That probably added to the mix of things going wrong with his morning.

"Why does he want me?"

Ashton rubbed his nose tiredly. "You broke in here, didn't you? He must think you're tough enough to handle it."

"How did you get hired? Did you commit a felony too?"

"Nah, I just went old school and filled out

paperwork." That made him lighten up a bit.

Ashton took me upstairs to the second layer of the building. Doors lined the hall, decorated with labels of everyone's last names. "Up here we've got the offices and filing stuff. There's also bathrooms and bedrooms, complete with showers and lockers for those late nights when you're only running on caffeine and willpower, and you haven't cleaned yourself in a week." He gave a crooked smile, slowly warming up to the tour. "Just like high school."

"Has that ever happened to you?"

"Oh yeah. A lot of times, actually. But not anytime recently." Finding the only door missing the plaque label, Ashton pushed it open. "And here's my office, for when I'm working up here. But usually, I'm down where we live, in Tintview." He flopped down on the wheeled chair, spinning it back and forth. "So, yeah, that's pretty much everything. The top floor is just Vix's office and an infirmary."

I frowned. He hadn't explained the area I had been anticipating most. "What's in the basement?"

He rolled his head back and let out a sigh. "You'll want to go down there if I tell you, and you'll want to go down there if I don't tell you, so I might as well tell you." He slipped his hands into his pockets, robbing me of sight. "That's where they keep the secret projects and stuff. But you are not allowed down there. Heck, I'm not allowed down there, unless someone with more authority goes with me."

"Got it."

"Ally, I'm serious. Don't. If I get another call about you snooping where you're not supposed to, I am disowning you."

Dang it, he read my mind. I let out a huff. "Fine."

He put out his hand to me, taking mine. "Hey, I love you, Ally-gator. If I tell you to do something, or keep something from you, it's because I have your best interests in mind. I'm not always going to get it right, but… We've got to learn to trust each other."

"Right. Trust."

But I still didn't.

I had unraveled what Ashton was hiding from me. Just CAIN, I guess. No, something more lingered. *Is it about time that I started trusting Ashton? Maybe not.* This onion of a mystery still had more layers to peel.

Ashton's squeaking sneakers followed the ruffling of my hair. "Now come on. Let's go see what Mr. Vix wants."

I trailed along in my mind, noting the rights and lefts to Vix's office. Toward the end, Ashton took hold of my hand, allowing me sight. Did Vix really invite me to work for a covert branch of government simply because I had broken in here?

The man's office proved quite a sight. Glass replaced the outer wall, allowing a clear view of the streets below and the frosty sky. As we made our way to the desk at the end, crimson carpet brushed the bottom of our shoes. The man stood straight and strict, scruff beard and hair set in sage and wise with time. A shiny, silver plating decked on his suit read *A. Vix.* His hands were anything save small. Holding a phone to his ear, he held up a finger, signaling us to wait. Ashton would not let go of my hand, and despite being able to see, he had clammy palms, so I tugged away.

"Yes, Mr. Titus, you can count on me. Goodbye." Vix cleared his throat after hanging up. "Thank you for waiting," he started. His tone made me straighten. Dressed in clothes thrown on in the middle of the night and hair scrambled by the wind was *not* how to come to a job interview. "So, Ashton. About your sister. How would she like to work for CAIN?"

"Well-"

"Can I ask why?" I had not meant to cut Ashton off, but my mind jumped ahead of me.

A bellowing chuckle came from him. "If you must know, I was watching your little break-in from the beginning through security cameras. You've got potential. And being Ashton's sister, you're trustworthy. It's hard to get agents for CAIN. Soldiers rather fight man than the supernatural. Perhaps you'd like to fight with us?"

If it meant getting more answers to my past, of course, I did. I opened my mouth, but Ashton got back at me for cutting him off.

"Don't you think she's a little young?"

"If *you* train her, I'm sure she'll be kept safe. Children have a unique perspective on the world, Ashton.

Don't you think we could use more of that sense of wonder and potential?" Vix's body heat implied he leaned into the desk. I didn't know what sense of wonder he was talking about, I wouldn't exactly call myself an optimist, but I wasn't about to help Ashton's case to not let me in.

"This isn't exactly a safe line of work. I'm just trying to look out for her. What if she ends up dying?"

"No one's going to die. You would make sure of it," Vix said, confidence in his voice.

"I don't want-"

"Ashton. This isn't about you."

Ashton stopped talking.

"Alison, was it? What do you think?"

I couldn't see Ashton's expression right now, but it was apparent that he was silently frustrated. "I would like to become a CAIN agent." *If it's alright with Ashton,* I considered adding, but honestly, I didn't care what Ashton said. Trust goes both ways, and clearly, Ashton did not trust me.

"Excellent. You see, Alison, most people don't know it, but we are at war."

I sat at attention. "War? What do you mean?"

Vix cleared his throat. "There's a group of disorganized individuals trying to put an end to CAIN. They are fighting against progression and any attempt we make to fix the damage done to the world. People are still shaken up over the arrival of Dragons, and as CAIN, it is our job to mend the gap between those with powers and those without," Vix said.

Ashton started up, "Well-"

Vix interrupted once again. "If you could step out for a moment while I discuss something with your brother, my dear?"

Nodding, I rose from the cushioned chair. Ashton wordlessly helped me to the door. His hand on my arm provided me with some idea of direction.

"Just wait for a minute," Ashton said as he nudged me out of the office. "Love ya, Ally-gator." He left me in the dark sea, the door clicking behind him.

With a huff, I leaned against the wall. I considered listening in on the conversation, but they spoke at too low of a volume, and I could only pick up their faint mumbles. *Where's Captain when you need him?*

The thought of the dog reminded me of Bolt. I must've forgotten about him after the mess in the basement. Focusing, I searched for him. When I opened my eyes, I was somewhere else. Uncertain darkness took up the space, but I could make out vague shapes. Bars walled in front of me. Bolt paced in a cage. As my vision readjusted to the dim light. I spotted several more cages. More rats, complete with mechanical alterations and cameras. *That's how Vix was watching me.* I shuddered at the thought. If Bolt belonged to CAIN, why the need to spy on Ashton and me? I had found him in our house. It hadn't been a coincidence.

Doors swung open. Broken from my train of

thought, I flinched and lost sight. Ashton let out a heavy breath, but I couldn't tell what emotions lay behind it. "Well, Ally, guess who's got a job at CAIN?"

I beamed. "Really?"

"Sort of. More like an apprenticeship. I'm going to train you." His tone seemed to have perked up. He took my hand. I stared at my own smile.

Vix exited the office behind my brother. "You'll be extending your stay here in the city for a time. Ally, you can sleep in one of the rooms here while Caleb remains at the hotel. How does that sound?"

"Great! Thank you!" *Hello, answers.* Sure, my last plan to dig into CAIN's background didn't work that well, but giving up now would be pathetic.

"Then we start tomorrow." Vix flashed us a grin, his lips spread wide. "And, might I add, your eyes are an incredible color, miss Caddel." Hands comfortably shoved in his pockets, he walked off, heavy footfalls marking his descent down the hall.

Ashton looked back at me. "Well, I did say we should spend more time together. Welcome to CAIN, Ally."

11

Combat 101

"Here! Catch!"

Something fabric slapped against my face, tumbling to the ground before my feet.

"Oh, right, forgot about the blind thing." Ashton took my hand, allowing me to see the black coat he'd just thrown at me. Picking it up, he held it out to me. "This is your CAIN-issued jacket. Do you like it?"

I unrolled it with one hand, raising it to see the full suit. A name tag reading, *A. Caddel* decorated the pitch-colored fabric. "It's very black." I set the jacket on the bed. The room I'd been assigned was framed neat, with a bed, desk, and bathroom.

"Harder to see at night. Supposedly harder for the remmutants to find you." Ashton rubbed the back of his neck. "I don't think it makes much a difference though. The eagles have expert eyes."

"What are they like?" I flopped down on the bed, losing vision. "Are they dangerous?"

"They're terrifying. You can't look at them in the eyes. They trap you in a trance."

I rubbed my arms, frowning. "Has that ever happened to you? What's that like?"

"It… doesn't feel great. It shows you all your greatest failures. That's part of why I prefer to work with Dragons. But at least it's not African remmutants." Ashton's voice perked up.

I fidgeted with my hair, done up in a ponytail with a red tie. "What are those?"

"Giraffes. With long necks. I mean *real* long necks. Anyways, let's get to training." Ashton gave me a pat on the back before taking my hand. "Come on."

Ashton showed me to the training room. A pair of windowed doors swung open to a wide space. The air conditioning echoed loud enough that conversations could barely be heard. Red mats padded the equipment, and a confined shooting range resided in the back of the room. Various weapons and equipment decked the right side wall. A button protected with a plastic casing and a key lock waited near the door.

"Welcome to the training hall. Do you smell it? The sweat?" Hands on his hips, Ashton took in a deep breath. He kept his elbow against my arm. "This is where dreams are crushed. Enjoy yours while you still have them." He smirked. I had wondered if he was still bitter about me joining CAIN. Well, now I knew.

"Very supportive of you, Ashton," I said dryly. I readjusted my red tank top, a black pair of sweatpants accompanying it as my training clothes. If I was going to take on Abel and Dragons, I would have to push myself to train as hard as possible

Ashton took off his CAIN jacket, readying for physical work. I couldn't help but notice his tag missing.

"Where's your name tag?"

"I'm getting a new one so that ours won't match. The new one's going to say 'C. Caddel.' For Caleb." Scratching his nose, he stepped ahead of me.

He tapped the button lid next to where we stood. "This is the emergency shut-off button. If there's ever a problem with things, this button will turn off all the electric-powered weapons and even some Dragon powers." Turning me toward the wall of weapons, he set one hand on my shoulder and positioned himself behind me. He pointed out the various weapons, noting that most of them just electrocute people.

"There might be a few grappling hooks in here. I don't know. I'm going to show you how to use the electric bo staff. I think it'd be the best weapon for you. Even though I'm not great at it, I usually use a gun. On the other hand, my best friend, Kade, is quite the marksman. Speaking of marksmen ..." he said, motioning to the gun range. Two other agents were shooting at the distant targets. Thick, soundproof glass separated the range from the rest of the training room. "Behold. Guns."

"Cool."

"And, finally, we have where we'll be training today." Ashton dragged me along behind him to the horizontal bar in the middle of the room. Red padding covered the stands of the bar as well as the floor below, to dull the pain if someone were to fall off of it. He ran a hand through his hair, proudly. "After skimming two books and watching a video, I now know how to train someone. This is going to be a piece of cake."

"That doesn't convince me." I turned to him. "How did *you* learn to fight?"

"Uh, the unorthodox way." Ashton rubbed the back of his neck, smiling nervously. "My friend's uncle used to spar with me. If he hit me, I learned to block it the next time, but that's not how I want to teach you." He pointed to the mat before letting me go.

I did as directed. A wary sensation came over me, stemming from being unable to see what he was doing. "What fighting style did you say this was called?"

"Jujitsu. Now, shut up and get yourself ready!"

"Ready for what?" A hard shove overcame me. I tumbled to my side, a startled yelp escaping me. I held my arms up in defense, laying on my back. "What was that!"

"We're learning how to fall down. You did it wrong."

"I did it wrong? Is there some special way to

fall!" I sat up, wishing I knew where he stood so I could glare at him.

"You've got to put your arm out or something."

My arm stung. "I think I scraped my elbow." Pushing myself up, I added, "What's the point of this anyways."

Ashton molded my body in the proper formation, sporadically letting me see. Once he was ready, he stepped back. "You must know how to fall down in a way that you can get back up. If you're unprepared, you could get knocked down and lose any opportunity to get to your feet. Wait, I think there's a life lesson in there somewhere." His hand clasped with mine, and he yanked me up. "I'll warn you this time so that you can be better prepared. I'm going to push you."

"You're going soft on her, Caleb," someone called from across the room.

"Mr. Vix, sir." Ashton's hand still clutched to mine. Vix approached us, hands in his pockets. "I was trying to ease her into it."

"Please, she'll never get anywhere with that attitude." Vix scoffed and set his hand on my shoulder. "Listen to me, kid. Remmutants and criminals aren't going to tell you before they push you. You've got to jump right in without a second thought."

"What exactly does CAIN deal with? I get the remmutant part, but how do you deal with Dragons?"

"Well, they take care of *any* Dragons that get out of a hand." Ashton shrugged. "Just a glorified police force for people with superpowers."

"I believe we do much more than that," Vix said, laughter engraved in his voice. "We also find new ways to help and use those powers for the greater good. Playing with the limits of those abilities, dedicating years of research to learning more about them, all so we can invent a new and better future." His chin rose proudly.

"You really do have a way with words, don't you?" Ashton chuckled. "I guess CAIN's a lot more than I made it look like. Our division just does the fighting stuff."

"For now," Vix added. "But give it enough time, and you could be a great agent working with lab or forensics." He pat my shoulder before slipping his hand back into his pocket. "I'll let you get back to it then. I just wanted to check in with you two. We'll talk later, Caddels." He turned to leave, waving behind him.

Ashton's gaze lingered on our boss, leaving me to wonder what he was thinking. He clapped his hands together. "So! Back to me shoving you over."

"I've got a surprise for you," Ashton sang.

"A surprise?"

"As your basic training is almost over, we can now go back home to Tintview soon. So I've set something up to celebrate the occasion." My bed bounced as my brother joined me.

I frowned. "What do you mean back to Tintview?

I thought I was going to stay and become a full-time agent?"

Ashton blew through his lips, in an attempt to avoid the confrontation. "Well, this CAIN stuff was a fun adventure and all, but I don't think it's the best thing for you…"

I pulled away from Ashton. "What?"

"Ally, listen, I only want to protect you-"

"Ashton." My hands clenched on my knees. After teaching me how to defend myself, he still didn't trust me to do that. I wanted to prove to him that I could handle myself, almost more than I wanted to uncover the secrets of my past. *What is he so afraid of?*

Ashton's voice picked up into frustrated franticness. "Please, just." A sharp snap whipped through the air. He stopped, flinching with a gasp. I stiffened, wondering what had happened. All I could hear was his breathing.

"Ashton?"

"It's a blackout," Ashton cleared.

The radio on his belt went off. "*I think a remmutant took out the power box. If someone could go down there and take care of it… Security footage shows it's only one.*"

Ashton unclipped the radio. "Silly George, they only ever come in pairs. I'll take care of it. Caleb out." He gave me a pat on the knee. "Fine, you want adventure? Come on. We'll take care of this, then go to the surprise I've got planned for you."

I rolled my eyes, rising to my feet. "But you were just talking about how dangerous this stuff is. Make up your mind."

"Can't hear you. I'm waiting for you in the hall." He whistled to himself, waiting for me.

Deciding not to argue against myself, I dug around for my jacket. "Who the heck is George, anyways?" I mumbled.

We walked outside into the cold night. The clicking I had heard at the hospital returned, echoing off the alleyway walls.

Ashton handed me a long electric staff, powered at either end. "Here. You can use this, that way you won't have to aim if we split up."

A figure crawled along the end of the alley. Ragged feathers glinted like gold and draped along its back in a cloak, its bloodstained beak as a decorative mask. Growling in its twisted form, the bird paced back and forth. It locked eyes with Ashton, consciousness thrown away in the mesmerizing pool that overtook its iris. The world blended into a blur as its gaze grew bigger and all the more inviting.

Ashton's hand clenched in mine.

My own eyes blinked. The monster had Ashton in its trap, but not me. Unsuccessful, I tugged from my brother's grip. I remembered what he had said about the remmutant's trap. Staring into its eyes could hold you in a replay of all your worst failures. Blood thudded in the back of my head as the eagle drew closer.

"Ashton…" His hand held tighter, and I wondered what he truly saw behind the hypnotic gaze.

The air whipped above us, a screech accompanying it.

"Ashton!" I ducked, yanking us both face first into the asphalt. Ashton's hand let go of me as the second beast's attempted grab failed. It tumbled into its partner, resulting in an earsplitting argument between the remmutants.

Ashton's breath came heavier. "Ally, I- I'm so sorry- I'm usually more careful-"

"Later!" Taking hold of my weapon, I stumbled to my legs. A screech pierced through my eardrums, a powerful gust of wind knocking me into a defensive position.

"I knew there was a second one. There's always a second one." Ashton stood next to me. "Be careful."

The eagles let out an awful tune, and commotion broke out.

Staff in front of myself, I jabbed it forward. I wished for some sense of direction, but the darkness stranded me on my own. If this was what it took to prove myself, so be it. The remmutant screeched as I made contact with its right side. Pressing the button on the staff, venomous sparks bit at the creature. A hard thrust from a weighty wing nearly knocked the tool from my grip. I promptly caught the other end, only to be knocked back by a hard impact on my chest.

I smacked against the concrete and cried out, my

eyes widening from reflux. The eagle's massive beak jabbed at me, stopped only by the pole between us. I desperately chased my next move. The bar caught in its serrated teeth. My fists clenched tighter over the weapon, my lifeline. Wet saliva hit my cheeks. With the beast so close, its twisted, offbeat heart rang in my skull.

I pushed off my back, thrusting my legs upward into the remmutant's neck. It lumbered back, allowing me space to breathe. With a right hook, I worked my way to my feet.

A few grunts and gunfire from Ashton came from behind me.

A mound of feathers slugged my cheek, nearly knocking me out. I stumbled back, shaking myself. I warily stepped forward, keeping my focus on my breaths. The dagger-like beak dug into my shoulder, causing me to cry out. I knocked upwards with my elbow and gave it another hard punch.

"Ally! You alright?"

I staggered back, holding myself. "Yeah," I groaned. "I think so."

His back supported mine. "Don't worry, we've got this."

Nodding, I raised the power on the bar. With a diagonal swing, it thudded at contact. The bird let out a gurgled scream. A *snap-crackle* rang through the alley. The eagle tumbled back. Heavy flaps and harsh wind followed. I waited. The only sound after came from Ashton.

"Nice work, Ally-gator!" Even before I could react, Ashton swept me up in a tight squeeze. "You fought that thing like a champ, and double points because you couldn't even see it!" When we broke apart, he took my hands.

I stared at myself, before letting out a curt laugh. Wild hair, dirty face, blood from my shoulder all over my uniform, and a shaken expression summed it up.

"Are those things going to come back? Should we go after them?" I asked, still pumped with adrenalin from the fight.

"They can send a small team to hunt them down, but I think you've had enough adventure for one day." Ashton ruffled my already-messed hair.

"I thought the walls kept them out." We stepped out of the alleyway.

"Sort of… You get a few that get by without anyone noticing, they start having kids, and before you know, there's a whole secret civilization of murder birds running around…" Ashton waved it off. "But CAIN does a pretty good job at keeping the population low." He rubbed dirt from my face. "Did you know in some places, remmutants are a rare delicacy? Even more expensive if it's a non-native breed." Wrapping his arm around me, he walked me back to the front of the building.

"Come on, let's get you a shower before we go."

As Ashton led me up the stairs of the hotel he had been staying at, he held my hand, swinging it back and forth. Empowered by the fight with the remmutants, I smiled a little.

"It's not the greatest surprise in the world, but I think it's… nice." Ashton rubbed the back of his neck, eyes drifting around the dingy hall.

I allowed my thoughts to drift away. Something new lined itself with my view of Ashton. His comforting hands kept me safe, his steady laughter brought me confidence. *Don't worry, we've got this* - these words reverberated in my mind. His voice shined so certain, so reassuring. I actually wanted to trust him. But the lies I had yet to uncover prevented me from doing so. He left himself open just enough for me to trust him.

Was that trustworthy at all?

Ashton knocked on his room door, before he swiped the key card over the lock, twisted the knob, and opened it.

"Surprise!" Two grins met me at the door, May and Kade, the two agents I had seen while spying on Ashton. Captain sat next to Kade, wagging his tail at the sight of me.

Ashton squeezed my arms, his vision squinted with a smile. "Ally, meet my two best friends in the whole wide world- Well, other than you, of course. This is Kade and May."

May smiled warmly, moving to shake my hand. "I've met you before, at the library, remember? But glad to meet you officially. Hi!"

Kade gave a wave, his monotone face forming a small smile. "And I raided your house. How's it going, Ally."

Still shaking my hand, May's vision blended with Ashton's, making me somewhat dizzy. I decided I would lead the two on that I was blind, just to keep the Dragon thing a secret.

"We've got pizza to celebrate your training!"

Ashton let me go, which helped with my sight. May dragged me over to the small coffee table on the other side of the room. Steam arose from two pizza boxes waiting on the tabletop, one pepperoni, and one pineapple and ham.

"Thanks," I said, unable to think of anything else to say.

Ashton took a spot on the bed, the sheets billowing. "Not only is Ally here a fighting master now, but she also fought one of those eagles before coming here." He smirked proudly, which made my chest rise just a little too.

"A remmutant?" Kade leaned against the wall, arms folded. "Pretty cool, kid. Did you get any scratches?"

May began to investigate me, looking for any scrapes.

"Uh, yeah, it got me in the shoulder. Ashton helped patch it up, but he says it'll probably leave a scar."

"Aw, baby girl," May said, concerned. "Ashton, she could've gotten really hurt."

Ashton coughed. "Well, she *did*, but she's fine now. I was watching her the whole time." He shuffled from the bed, passed between me and May, and took a slice of pizza. Mouth full of food, he added, "Can't be any worse from the scars Kade and I have gotten from them."

"Is that how you got the scar on your cheek?" I asked.

"Sort of…" Ashton's snicker accompanied May's. I listed my head curiously.

Kade sighed. "How many times do I have to say I'm sorry?" He didn't sound as amused as the other two.

"What happened?" I hoisted myself up, feeling my way to the bed. I kicked my legs back and forth and felt the soft fabric beneath me. Ashton joined me on the bed, pulling me close. With his fingers on my arm, I could see.

"It was some years back." Ashton waved his hand dramatically, readying his tale. Kade shook his head, though hidden beneath his reluctance, he smirked. "We were outside the dome, investigating some suspicious activity. I don't remember what it was, maybe a squirrel or something." He rubbed his nose, taking a moment to get his story in order.

"You told Vix it was a squirrel, which I still find funny." Kade nodded, loosening up to the story. "But we didn't figure out what it was." Kade cast his glance at

May. She idly rubbed her ring, enjoying the story. I didn't know how a squirrel warranted suspicious activity, but Ashton went on.

"The squirrel doesn't matter. While we were out there, we came across a remmutant, kind of just chilling in a tree. I was whistling some song-"

"We Didn't Start the Fire," Kade said.

"The eagle woke up and began to circle us. We could've totally escaped it, except, turns out, these things never work alone. Do remember that, Ally. It'll save you a lot of trouble. We just thought we had to get away from one, so once we thought we were far away enough, we were less careful." Ashton talked with his hands a lot. "We accidentally woke up two more with our running. Now we were surrounded, nowhere safe to look without getting trapped in a trance, so what do we do?" He looked at me as if expecting an answer, but he continued before he gave me a chance. "I tried getting past one, but it traps me with the trance thing, so now Kade has to figure out how to escape and how to get me out too. Kade, would you like to tell her your ingenious plan?"

Kade looked unamused. "Why am I friends with you?"

Waving off the comment, Ashton continued. "He pulls out his gun and tries to shoot them off. We managed to escape the remmutants while they got distracted fighting each other. When we're walking, I feel something wet on my face, and it starts stinging. Kade pulls out his flashlight, and surprise, he shot me in the face." Ashton shot a glare at his friend. "Kade went to medical school, so he sort of knew what to do, but I was freaking out. He must've apologized a thousand times." He laughed, Kade starting to smirk a bit and May snickering to herself.

I smiled, scooting closer to my brother. "I thought you said he was good with guns?"

Ashton shrugged. "Eh, that was when we were young and didn't know what we were doing."

"You still don't know what you're doing." Kade shook his head, holding back a laugh.

As the night went on, the adults exchanged stories of their missions at CAIN. The conversation, for once, felt real. Not some hidden meaning behind the smiles or avoidance of questions.

By the time the pizza party ended, only two and a half slices (half being eaten by Captain) remained scattered in one of the boxes. Everyone began to wind down, sweet laughter replaced with tired yawns. Ashton sat asleep on the ground, snoring as he leaned against the side of the chair Kade was sleeping in. May sat on the bed, smiling at them and rocking her head back and forth. Her arm pressed against mine while I sat next to her.

"Ashton really cares about you, you know," May said softly, breaking the quiet of the hour. I turned to her. "He often tells us he worries that he's not doing enough for you, but I think he's doing just fine. You've got a good brother." She ended with a smiling, contagious yawn.

Folding my hands in my lap, I gave her words a thought. Was I being too hard on him? I tried not to stay on it too long. "How did you guys all meet?"

She tilted her head, thoughtfully. Rubbing her stomach, she leaned back on her free hand. "Kade and Ashton met in high school, and my uncle was friends and neighbors with Ashton's family." She paused a moment. "I guess your family, too."

"And how did you guys join CAIN?"

"Nothing fancy. We just walked in and tried for the job. We thought it'd be more fun together, to make sure we have each other's backs." May let out a sleepy groan, shutting her eyes momentarily. "I don't know what time it is, but it's probably too late. The guys have the right idea." She gestured to the boys by the chair.

"Are you going to sleep here?" I asked.

"Well, I would hate to take Ashton's bed, especially when he's on the floor but... yeah, probably. I've also got a long drive in the morning."

Starting to feel uncomfortable trying to make contact, I lay back on the bed, submersing myself in darkness. "Where to?"

"I don't live in the Second Colony, so I like to stay in Tintview for a short amount of time and go back home between work. I can't stay too long because..." May chuckled. "Well, I've got a kid at home and one in the oven. The joys of being a mother, I guess." She brayed through her lips in a carefree way. "You're fun to chat with, Ally."

"Thanks," I said, unable to think of anything else to say in response. I shut my eyes, unable to keep them open.

It felt nice to be included in Ashton's strange world.

12

The Basement Theory

Dressed and ready for training, I anticipated Ashton's arrival. I jumped at the knocking on my bedroom door, but upon opening it, I could sense a different someone, a firmer figure.

"Hello, miss Caddel."

I recognized the voice belonging to Vix. "Hello, sir." I stepped aside as he invited himself in.

"What's wrong?" Vix probably noticed the awkwardness with which I stood around him.

"Just expecting someone else, I guess."

"Ashton. Well, he won't be coming today. He's out on a mission. That's what I came here to tell you. I thought I'd take the opportunity to talk to you."

"About what, sir?" I asked.

The bed creaked under Vix's weight. "No need to be so formal, Alison. Just call me Vix. I wanted to discuss your future here at CAIN. You are a very special girl, and I want to help you harness that potential."

Does he know I'm a Dragon? I nodded, wondering where this was going.

"I think you should be doing more than just waiting around for the occasional remmutant attack. In fact, I want to help you fulfill your great purpose. How would you like a mission?"

I grinned, my mind wandering to possible futures. "I would like it very much, sir- Vix. Do you think I could handle one by myself?"

Vix gave a hearty laugh. "Of course. With you as my protégé, I can build you into the best that you can be. You've shown you can manage yourself. Ashton's training may be good and dandy, but I certainly have more to offer." He shifted some, rising from the bed. "I'll tell you what. In about two weeks, some of my supervisors are coming down here for a gala. You and Ashton can come, and we'll discuss your promotions there. And if you make a good impression, who knows where you might go!"

Smiling, my chest rose at the thought. Vix playfully nudged me in the shoulder, making my wound sting. I hadn't realized how close he was to me.

"When I was around your age, I had a good head on my shoulders and a dream for the future. With my scrap of ideas, I worked my way up. And now, I run a whole branch of agents, soldiers fighting for a greater cause than themselves. Plus, I was the youngest agent to take on my position ever. I mean, I was, until a few months ago some other agent became the supervisor of her branch, but it was a nice brag while it lasted." Vix took my arm, letting me see. "Here, walk with me, and I'll get you started on the mission."

Vix's palm was cracked and calloused, worn with age. I hadn't used anyone's eyes much except Ashton's, so seeing a slightly different perspective intrigued me. Oddly enough, Vix's vision held a faint, rose-colored tint. As I walked in step with him, I caught myself standing straighter, trying to make a good impression.

"Has Ashton shared any additional information on Abel yet?" Vix glanced at me.

"Not really. What else is there to know?"

"That's who we're fighting against. In CAIN's more recent years, we've grown enemies. Abel is a terrorist group bent on destroying our research. They remain quiet to the public but carry out their nefarious activities surreptitiously. We don't want to raise an uproar, but we often fight them more than rogue Dragons. Lately, their attacks have been more frequent, but we still don't know what their plan is. Someday, I hope we can get rid of them for good." Vix's grip tightened around my hand in pride, and his lips split into a grin. "That's what you'll be helping me with." He turned us down the stairs, pausing to wave at the agent running the front desk.

"These Abel guys, how tough are they?" My shoulder ached as I remember how hard my last fight had been.

Vix gave me a pat on the back in an attempt to reduce the element of formality between us. "No stronger than remmutants, I assure you. They're just people scrapped together of those who want to see us fail, without any experience or training. They were founded by an old detective named Abel. I'm sure Ashton meant to warn you about them but just forgot with that easily excitable brain of his."

Or Ashton just didn't want me to know. "Where are we going?"

"The filing room. You're quite an astute investigator, Alison. Perhaps you can put your calculating mind to use in there and figure out where Abel will strike us next." Turning down a door, Vix led me to a library.

Filing cabinets and bookshelves lined the walls and came out in rows in the middle of the room. Two tables sat in the front, decorated with desk lamps. A pair of bright blinking lights from the top corners allowed me to identify a duo of security cameras. The walls closed in tight, painted a faded brown, adding to the dim air of the room. A poster hung by one table, displaying the word *WOW!* over a kitten's head. I had no clue what I was supposed to be wowing at.

"Here we are. I could read the files to you, or I think we have audio versions of some. Whatever you'd like." Vix let go of my hand, stranding me in the void.

I walked around, getting a feel for the space. My

hand found a place at one of the desks. I thought over Vix's offer. Deciding it might be more efficient to work alone, I said, "I'll listen to the audios. I'll let you know if I find anything." I knew that I wouldn't be able to see with Vix's eyes, but I wanted to try another idea.

"Alright. I'll show you to them, then be on my way. I'll pick you up some lunch later." Vix led me to a box placed above one cabinet filled with a mix of mediums, from cassettes to DVDs. With one more pat on my good shoulder, he left.

The air stilled. Taking a breath, I shut my eyes and focused. *Where are you, Bolt?* My eyes fluttered. When I opened them, the dark cage enclosed me. I put my will into the rodent, maneuvering around the lock. Scrawny fingernails tugged at the latch, sliding up, over, and out. The cage opened. I now had to find my way to the file room.

I hoped to keep the rat closer from now on. I still needed to find out how I could see through him in the first place.

As I squeezed under the door, I found myself getting secondhand claustrophobia. I carried its bottom-heavy body in leaps across the halls. If an agent found him running out, he may have put him back in the room, so I stuck close to the wall, hoping Bolt's dark fur would blend in with the shadows. After a few wrong turns, I managed to find the lobby.

If my memory's correct, the library should be...
Going through a doorway, I found my tall

likeness from to the rat's point of view waiting by a desk. I scooped him into my hand. Rubbing my finger across his head, I scrunched my face in confusion. "I don't know what you are, but I'm going to figure it out. Best you stay with me. They've got enough rat spies, anyways." I set him on my shoulder, striding over to the cabinets.

I didn't know what I was looking for, but if CAIN knew anything about a secret Ashton was hiding from me, it'd be here. Deciphering Abel's plans would have to wait.

As I dug through the cabinets, trying to find somewhere to start, I noticed they were split into groups. I rolled one cabinet drawer open, finding a list of all the agents in this branch. I scrolled through, searching the A's. Realizing they would more likely be listed by the last name, I found the C's, only a few drawers down.

I squatted down, reading through as quickly as I could. Thankfully, *Caddel* wouldn't have much competition as first in the C's. The B's ended, thus started the C's.

And… Nothing.

From *Byron* straight to *Calihan.* I frowned. Where did Ashton's file go? The more I thought about it, neither Caddel files resided in the cabinet.

A red-wrapped fortune cookie waited where the files should've been.

I opened it and cracked the cookie in two for the piece of paper.

You're so much like your father.

I lingered on this note longer than the others. Ashton knew every step of mine. He knew what I wanted so desperately to know. Was I that predictable?

I fell back into a sit, frowning. *Ashton didn't remove the files, did he?* Ashton was leaving these notes for me, but I was sure if I brought it up, he would deny it. What did the note even mean? I knew nothing of my father because my brother wouldn't tell me anything."

"You're so much like your father.' Dang it, Ashton. Why can't you just give me a straight answer for once?"

I knew so little of my past, and now that my father was mentioned, it held more questions than answers. Ashton, CAIN, Blake Landerson, and now my father all played a role in this mystery I called life.

I hoisted myself up, making sure to keep Bolt on balance. His tiny hands dug into my shoulder. I moved away from the agent cabinet, searching for where Vix had shown me the Abel one. I shuffled through the basket of digital files. *I guess it's time for me to do my job.*

I dug through a few drawers as well, so that everything was laid out in front of me. A thick folder found my attention. It read *Skylor* on the cheap piece of tan, ugly painter's tape slapped on the top. Just behind it, another full folder marked *Skylor II.*

"What's so important about this Skylor stuff that it gets two whole files worth?" Taking them together, I moved to one of the tables.

I smacked them down on the desk top. Dust rose up from the movement, causing me to cough and Bolt to sneeze. I started with the first file. Newspaper clippings, photographs, and plastic bags containing various items tumbled out. I held up the pictures by the corners, careful not to get thumbprints on the actual image. All of them were blurred attempts at catching sight of a man. A brown trench coat, red shirt, and a tie that changed depending on the picture dressed the man. He often had some way of blocking his face, either with his coat, a hat, or some object close to him. Hoping to find more information, I flipped the first one over. Scribbled in pen, it read *Detective Skylor,* along with a month and year.

I set the photographs aside. The newspaper pieces slid out of the folder, begging me to read them. A paperclip loosely held the snippets together. I slipped the first clipping into my hand. *THREE CHILDREN REPORTED MISSING ALONG WITH PARENTS* went the headline. Was that what Abel had done? Kidnap children? How could someone be so cruel as to make a whole family disappear?

To my surprise, I found another folder within the folder. Scrawled along the top with permanent maker, the label read *Hidden Dragon Experiment.* Six pages held a portrait in each corner, the rest of the paper taken up by notes on the person portrayed in the image. The first detailed a young redheaded boy, no older than the age of ten. A gap split his teeth, an unsure smile on his face.

Shaking from my control, Bolt crawled down my arm, giving me a closer view. Basic information revealed itself along the top side.

Name: Aaron???

Experiment: A1

Sex: M

Talent: Electricity manipulation

Origin:???

Labeled *Cleo's notes,* below the initial facts, resided the science behind how the child's talent worked. Setting it off to the side, I started on the next page. A younger version of me, not even bothering to look at the camera, sat in the top portrait. I froze. My hair sat shorter, my eyes clear blue like how they showed when I couldn't see. I gaped, trying to process.

Name: Alison Caddel

Experiment: A2

Sex: F

Talent: Accessing others' senses

Origin: Daughter of Hank and Lauren Caddel

I examined the paper to its limits, ignoring the rest of the reports in my hand. I allowed them to fall, only caring for the one. "What is this?" I hadn't meant to voice the question aloud. *Why did Abel have this? What experiment! Does Ashton know?* I paused to think, my heart rate thundering in the back of my head. Searching for any clue I could, I read over the bottom part.

Cleo's notes: In transfer to the basement, A2 refused to be away from her brother. Perhaps it may have something to do with her talent. When we asked Lauren what A2's powers were, she refused to give us any information, but the girl herself didn't seem to care that much and told us. Very similar situation to E3, except not even E3 would tell us her abilities.

The rest continued with more science vocabulary. I scrunched my nose at the cryptic notes. I was desperate to find something from my past to hold onto.

Nothing here was helping me. All these files lay out in the open for any CAIN agent to look over and investigate, but the information was way too cryptic. If I were to find my answers, I needed to go somewhere I wasn't allowed to be.

The basement... My eyes widened as a light bulb went off in my head. The one place Ashton told me not to go. *Forget Ashton.* I rose from my chair, reaching down to take Bolt. I hesitated, remembering the camera on his back. Peeling a piece of tape from a folder, I pressed it onto the lens with my thumb. *Problem solved.*

I passed down the stairs, though the hall, and to the basement, ready to run if need be. My body went stiff with the lurching feeling that someone could be watching. I tried to ignore it, but a sense of pervasive uncertainty remained in the back of my head. Bolt tucked in close to my neck.

My steps echoed throughout the hall. Some doors had blackened windows, and I tried peering through a few of them. I squeezed Bolt under any of the doors he would fit, as the locks remained steadfast. After no sign or mention of the "Hidden Dragon Experiment," only one door remained. I reached the end of the hall.

I lowered Bolt under the tight space. "Come on, buddy, just unlock it for me," I whispered.

The blinding dark waited before me. Bolt's ears picked up on a faint beeping, coming from below. I took a hesitant trod forward. Squinting, I managed to pick up on distant lights, hovering in blue.

Bolt climbed up the door. Using his scrawny claws, I inserted them into the door lock. *Click.* I turned it downward, setting my whole weight along the L-shaped handle. The door popped open.

With Bolt back on my shoulder, I kept my hand along the wall as I made my way down.

My foot created a phantom step, nearly causing me to trip. Taking in the room, I stopped. The room was dug out like a cave, no proper ground, roof, or walls. Six canisters in rows of three led to a panel. These cylindrical canisters stretched tall enough to fit a person and closed with glass doors. The panel proved the source of the beeping and soft, blue light. The light glinted off something overlooking the space, an observation room, separated by glass.

The glass door to the cylinder on my right lay open. Overhead, a small screen darkened with a lack of power. Someone had taped a sheet of notepaper over it, labeling it as *A1*.

The left side canister's door had been shattered, a spider web of cracks spiraling from the point of impact.

Leftover shards crunched beneath my feet. Trying to avoid getting any glass in my shoes, I made myself lighter. *P2* marked the canister label in blocky digits.

The second set seemed better off than the first pair. Next to *A1,* the digital screen above the canister door read *M1.* A collection of dust building up on the glass was the only thing wrong with it.

My gaze shifting to the cylinder across, I found myself strangely drawn to it. There was a glitch in the number assigned, but I managed to make it out. *C1.* Before I realized what I was doing, my fingertips pressed against the door. I stared into my reflection, to decipher what this strange sensation over me was. As I took in the old air of the container, I was inundated by a mix of bottled-up emotions. *Uncertainty, anger, pain, and… something else.*

I had been here before.

I tried to make sense of it, still staring into my own questioning eyes reflecting off the glass. *Something… Something was stolen from me here. But what?*

I pulled away from the door, my nerves sinking in. I wanted to get out of here as quickly as I could. But not before solving the mystery of *why.* I forced myself to move on to the last two containers, *A1* and *E3.* Unfortunately, they only deepened the sensation.

E3's essence pressed more words into my mind. *Innocence, family, and lies.* The last word threw me off.

My fingertips landed on the final cylinder. *A2.*

It's me. I was here. Why? I drew closer, setting my forehead against the glass pane. I longed to remember. The beeping of the panel played along with my thoughts. Who were the people that filled the other containers? What was the experiment for? Every time I got a clue, it threw up more questions than answers.

The basement door opened, and I snapped to attention.

"Hello? Alison? Are you down here?" *Vix.* What had I stumbled into? Vix came around the corner. My gut tightened, my hand grounding me as I leaned against the A2 container. "There you are, Miss Caddel. I've brought you lunch, but you were missing when I arrived at the library. With the files you'd left on the table, I figured you came down here."

I hesitated, my mind turning up empty in the search for an escape plan. *He knows...*

Vix let out a small laugh. "Relax dear, I know all about your powers. The secret's safe with me." He finished with a wink.

Taking a deep breath, I readjusted myself. "Where is 'here?'"

Vix let out a hearty laugh, coming closer. "I guess it does look intimidating. This is my magnum opus. I've spent almost my whole career on this project. It was going to revolutionize the world." Hope and pride glinted in his eyes as he ran his hand over the dusty glass of *M1*.

"What did it do?" I came to stand next to him. Back turned to the *C1* container, and I tried to avoid analyzing how it made me feel. I could hear Vix out. *Stop jumping to conclusions.*

"It was an attempt to replicate Dragon abilities and use them for the greater good. Just imagine, doctors able to save lives at the snap of a finger. Fire fighters able to put out fire in a heartbeat. And so much more!" Vix's smile lit up. "We were creating the cure for death. The science wasn't perfect, but we tried."

"What happened?" Bolt looked between Vix and me. Several questions ran through my head. I straightened, trying not to show worry on my face.

Vix shoved his hands in his pockets. "Abel. He ruined everything. He sent two spies here. Little did I know, but they had infiltrated CAIN a long time before the experiment. We managed to stop one of the spies, but the other one escaped, and she blew up our experiment before we could catch her."

"And?"

"And that's all." He set his hand on my wounded shoulder, making me flinch. "Not everything is some crazy conspiracy. What has that Ashton been teaching you?" Ending with a light chuckle, he shook me by the shoulder. "Now come on, let's go eat our lunch." His hand moved on my back, pushing me along with him.

I forced myself not to be so defensive. Maybe Vix was right. Maybe I was getting worked up over nothing. Ashton had said I needed to trust, so might as well try.

13

Halloween and a Handful of Did-You-Know's

Music hummed over the drug store. Ashton's hand kept in mine, swinging back and forth as he scanned over the aisles. Reaching a row toward the back, he tugged me along. The candy aisle.

"What kind of candy do you like?" Ashton gestured to the row, grinning.

"I still don't get this holiday." I frowned upward at him. "You said 'Halloween' is where we go from door to door and demand people give us candy. The very concept carries several problems with it. One, that's hardly socially acceptable-"

"Not any less acceptable than spying on your big brother," Ashton cut in, letting out a smirk and glancing at me. *He's never going to let that go, is he?*

"And two, why are we buying candy if we're just

going to get it for free from a bunch of strangers?"

"Oh, Ally. You can never have too much candy."

"That's not true. Also, accepting candy from random people can't be safe. You said adults let their kids just roam the streets for this holiday? And another thing-"

Ashton interrupted with a laugh. "It's just a tradition, ya silly George! Goodness, I didn't think explaining Halloween would have to be one of my brotherly duties when I picked you up from the hospital." Clicking his tongue with debate, he grabbed a bag of individually wrapped chocolates. "Here. Chocolate makes everyone happy." He shoved the bag into my chest, and I took it with my free hand. He grabbed a small bag of sour gummy worms for himself. "Just wait until you hear about the costumes."

"What costumes?"

"I'm not wearing this the whole night."

"What are you talking about? You're adorable!"

"You made this up. People don't wear costumes on Halloween."

"Yes, they do. You know, when everyone's wearing a costume, the only one who stands out is the one who *doesn't* wear a costume. Come on, it's not *that* embarrassing." Ashton hid behind a snicker.

I stood awkwardly in the middle of my room, one eyebrow raised at Ashton. "Really?" I had half a mind to let go of Ashton's hand so I wouldn't have to look at what he'd tricked me into. A soft gray onesie hung to my body, white for the furry underbelly, and a thin pink tail on my backside. He had used a permanent marker to draw dark whiskers on my cheeks, smudging with my freckles and my embarrassed red hue.

Smiling sadistically, Ashton slipped a mouse-ear headband into my hair. "Adorable."

"Ha ha." I pat down the costume, unamused. "You better be wearing one of these too."

"Naturally."

Ashton walked me out of the room and into the hall. To avoid the eyes of other agents, I wanted to get out of the CAIN building as quickly as possible. "Can't have matching costumes with only one person. And you better believe I'd never miss out on an opportunity to humiliate myself." With his elbow, he nudged me as we went down the stairs, nearly causing me to trip.

"What's yours? A cat?"

Ashton let out a thinking breath. "Oh, a cat probably would've been more obvious for the predator-prey theme. Why didn't I think of that?" he mumbled. "No, I'm in an eagle onesie. Not as terrifying as the remmutants, but I still think it looks neat."

As we walked out of the building, Ashton gave a corny grin to the guards at the front. He led me to his car and opened the door for me, before leaving to the driver's side. Captain greeted us from the backseat.

Climbing in, I decided to make the most of this

weird holiday and get over the costume. I could humor my brother this once. *It might be nice to let myself have a mental break from the mystery I have been tracking down.*

"Got a neighborhood in mind?" I wouldn't be surprised if Ashton had a whole battle strategy for getting the most sweets.

"Sort of…" The engine began to run, and the plastic bag on the passenger side rustled. Ashton dug through the candy we bought. "But it's not in Envision." Wow. If Ashton was willing to drive out of town for the optimal row of houses, he had invested more into this holiday than I thought. Something heavy landed in my lap, which made me flinch. "Here. It's the candy we bought, in case we don't get much."

I frowned, picking up the bag. "Candy means this much to you? I knew you were immature, but…" I cut off with a chuckle, but no warm laugh returned.

Silence ensued after we began our drive. I reclined back in my seat, wondering why Ashton was acting so quiet.

Ashton read the awkwardness on my face. "Hey, uh, you're aware of that rumor about drugs and razorblades in kids' candy on Halloween?"

I gaped, wondering where on earth Ashton got these icebreakers from. "No… up until this morning, I didn't know what Halloween was. Amnesia, remember?"

"Oh, right. Well, these rumors started from two incidents. In one instance, the drugs weren't even in the candy. The candy was just a cover to protect this one guy-"

"Ashton. Where are we going?"

"That is a surprise. But you'll like it, I promise." Ashton's hand reached over and ruffled my hair.

After breaking the silence, Ashton didn't seem to know how to stop talking. He went on and on about whatever nonsense popped into his head. All to avoid what *really* stayed on his mind.

The car took a round turn before slowing to a park. "Well, we're here."

"Where exactly is here?"

The driver's door popped open. "A little town by the name of Serendipity Shores. Nice name, huh?" Ashton took a brief moment to come around and help me from my side. My hand slipped into his. I gasped as my vision filled in. The row of houses circled at the end and rounded out onto the main street.

Half of them had been burnt to the ground.

"This is our old home."

Ashton pulled me up out of the car, and Captain followed behind. Ashton stood behind me, my hand occupying one of his while the other rested on my forearm. His breath waited by my ear as I took it all in.

Like the perfect cul-de-sacs of Tintveiw, all the houses lined up symmetrically, except for the houses to the right. Half the houses showed signs of being rebuilt. The other ones told that a fire had been the cause of reconstruction. Ashy wood settled in pieces on the floors.

The fire had stretched though most of the homes, but it had been put out before spreading to the opposite street. The humble home directly at the end stood just as sad as the untouched houses. Ashton's gaze lingered on it longer than the others.

"Was that where we lived?"

Ashton's gaze darted away from the house, realizing he was staring. "N-no. It was… a family friend's."

"Then where was-"

My brother's arm stretched straight forward, landing on one of the burnt-down homes.

"What are we doing here?"

Ashton leaned into my ear. "I might not be able to tell you anything about what happened, but that doesn't mean I can't show you," he whispered.

The wind chilled down my spine. Captain stood close to my side, awaiting my command. I rested my hand on the dog's head and swapped visions. I turned to read Ashton's face. He wore an almost nonexistent smile, nodding me to go on.

"As far as *they* know, we're just out trick-or-treating."

Is Ashton… trusting me? And even more unsettling, he is admitting that something had happened. So then… What stopped him from telling me?

I opened my mouth to ask more, but a bark from Captain reminded me to take advantage of this time. Hesitating, I gave Ashton a thanking smile before leaving to investigate the block.

I carefully crossed over the outline of my past home, ash kicking up beneath my feet. I glanced down the row of houses. The sound of water clashing against land reached my ears. I tread across the backyard, only to realize that the neighborhood looked over a cliffside. Below the steep drop, the earth sloped into a thin beach before stretching out into a river. Through Captain's colorblind view, the dark sea blended with the shades of the night sky.

I glanced back to where Ashton once stood, finding it vacant. The end house's door swung back and forth with the wind. This trip was as much for Ashton as it was for me.

I turned back to my own investigation. *There has to be more here.* Everything that had once stood had been turned to ash. The cause of the fire stood a mystery in itself.

Something clicked in my head. With my sneaker, I scraped away the ash beneath me. I knew it would stain my costume, but I couldn't care less. Tracing the floor plan, I dug for any sort of secret entrance. If I had learned anything from CAIN, people hid their secrets in basements.

Whereas the rest of the earth had been paved over with concrete, one spot where the master bedroom would've been was covered with mere wooden planks. I knelt down and tried to lift them up. They weighed down my arms, so I threw the planks belly-up with a huff. They clattered away.

I wiped my grimy hands off my knees before taking the scruff on Captain's neck. Beneath the plank, a dark hole led downward on dusty, uneven concrete steps. Captain walked down with me, and as we grew farther from the surface, the world faded into trapping darkness. My foot stopped after attempting a phantom step.

Squinting, I tried to make out the space before me, albeit to no avail. Running my hand over the nearest wall, I found a crude switch with no cover over the wires. The ugly yellow light flickered on, humming with a buzz. Somehow, the air hung colder down here than the windy outside. I tucked my hand into the cozy onesie sleeve.

Tacky fold-up tables lined the back walls of the cramped basement. Several journals lay scatted across them, and only one was open. I crossed over to them, looking the book over. Dark and light ink went back and forth: two different handwritings. I determined the true pigments were red and blue. My hand rested on the journal as if scared it would disappear.

My eyes scanned over the walls in front of me. Posters hung, decorated with the biology of remmutants. The sketches of their bones and muscles made them more unsettling than decorated with feathers. The poster in the corner held a different sketch. The bird depicted wasn't an eagle, but a crow. The crow's feathers dripped off its wings like molasses, and notes on the poster read *Cannot fly* and *"Myth."* I listed my head, noting the quotations on the latter word. Whoever had designed the graph did not think the inky crow was a myth.

Moving on, I looked back to the tables. Miniature metal skeletons lined up on stands, each with slight variations. With a piece of painter's tape, someone had marked the date for each prototype. The skeletons grew shell-like before changing into something more harmonic of the two designs. The last skeleton-like armor created came with wires. Squinting at it, I got a sense of familiarity from it. Whether from some piece of my memories returning or just something I had seen, I didn't know.

"What would armor that small even be put on?" My breath pooled in a cold cloud.

Barring the notes and inventions, miscellaneous dirty dishes waited on the tables. A stuffed toy cat leaned against the wall, its dead button eyes watching me. My gaze swept up to the ceiling as I imagined the home that had once stood above me.

This wasn't just a conspiracy I had to unravel. These walls held a whole history, *my* history. The life of a family I had nothing of. Just my brother and a few scraps of evidence that my family did indeed exist once.

My thoughts shifted to the journal. As I flipped through, the red and blue inks went back and forth, until the red overtook the other color for the better part of the second page. I turned it over, finding all the writings ended there. Frowning, I turned back to the beginnings of the writings, oddly placed in the middle of the journal.

The blue started the notes in rougher handwriting. *Hank, this is Skylor. I don't really know how to start this, nor do I even know if writing in this book will change anything, but Blake told me to take a chance on you. I'm sure if this message finds you, you'll have a lot of questions, but you always have a lot of questions. I told Blake this was a waste of time. Please don't prove me right.*

The red's handwriting flowed in a smoother cursive. *Skylor? Wait, by Blake do you mean- This is incredible. I never thought that anything like this could be possible! How far in the future or past are you?*

Something seemed odd about the way the notes flowed like dialogue, as opposed to letters. As if they had been written and read in real-time, from two different places between two different people.

The blue picked up. *That's beside the point. Look, you know I would never agree to anything as crazy as time travel if I didn't think it was important. This is a warning, not a friendly conversation. You have to stop using your talent. I can't tell you why, you've got to just trust me.*

The red ignored blue's warning. *What are you talking about? My talent is part of who I am. I can only keep the life I have because of it. Even you are using it for a greater purpose. I'm careful with it. I'm currently building a log of its limits and rules if you must know. I assume you're from the future if this is a warning. Well, tell future me I said hi.*

Blue ended the page with, *I hate being right. This was a waste of time.*

I thumbed through the pages prior, discovering the conversation seemingly went on forever. The pages of the journal before the conversation held scientific writings in the blue pen. One flip to the cover gave me a loose explanation. *Notes on the Interval, by Hank Caddel.*

Too much hung on this one book for me to understand. My father's name, mention of "Skylor" again, time travel, and this "Interval" thing. Was this what Ashton had been hoping to show me by bringing me here?

With utmost caution, I started up the steps, slipping the journal into the onesie.

I walked up to the door of the end house, finding the lock had been broken into. The house had been untouched by everything but dust, a once happy home frozen in time. Shuffling from upstairs drew my attention. Ashton came to stand at the top of the stairs, an old shoe box in his hands. He flinched when he saw me.

"Ally. Hey." He stepped down to meet me. His face grew nervous. "Find anything?"

"No…" Was I still trying to lie to Ashton even after he had shown me this place? Some cards remained best kept close to my chest. My gaze moved to the shoe box. "What's in the box?"

"Oh, uh…" Ashton glanced down and pat it, as if to make sure it wouldn't leave his hands. "Candy."

"Sure."

"No, really." My brother lifted the lid for me to see. A handful of candy littered the top, though I knew something was hidden beneath it. "And some old pictures."

"Can I see?"

Ashton slid the lid back over the box, frowning. "That's something I'm not quite ready to share yet…" His sentence drifted off into quiet.

We both are keeping our distance, so the game goes. "Why is there a box of candy in this abandoned house?"

"Oh, you don't want to eat any of it. It is *years* old." Ashton bit his lip, thinking over how to explain it. "The family friends that lived here, they had a kid named Dylan. He's a little older than you. He hid his secret stash of candy in the picture box under his bed. He didn't know that I knew exactly where it was. And now, five years later, I stole it from him." He smirked. "Poor kid has no idea."

I let out a small laugh. "These family friends still around? Maybe I could meet them." Even if it didn't give me some large piece of the puzzle, it would at least be nice to talk to someone I had known back before the accident.

"I would reintroduce you, but Dylan's sister and I aren't exactly on good terms." Ashton frowned, but a small chuckle escaped him. "Do you want to go trick-or-treating for real now?"

My thoughts went to the book that was awkwardly shoved at my stomach. I nodded, deciding the journal could wait. "Yeah. That would be nice."

14

Distractions

I got to work the moment I woke up.

With Bolt as my sight, I dug through the library cabinet labeled *Abel*. Finding a recording device in one drawer, I moved to one of the closer tables. The rat sniffed at it, investigating the build of the device. I had to know about the role Abel played in the experiment I had found in the basement. Why had he been so determined to put a stop to something so revolutionary? Not only had he stopped the experiment, but he had gone out of his way to plant deep cover spies. If I found out his motives, I could probably decipher this piece of the puzzle.

Finding the switch on the listening device, I watched as the wheels churned and whirred, a little green light flicking on. Several labeled cassette tapes sat next to me. Simple, one-word titles marked on white painter's tape labeled them. I figured any order would do as they didn't have dates or time stamps.

Selecting one marked *Split*, I inserted it into the player. Hunched over, I listened carefully.

A dial tone began.

"Hank? Hank, pick up, or I promise I'm divorcing you." The woman's voice came raspy and desperate.

The phone clicked as someone answered.

"Hello? Lauren? What's up?"

"Hank! Thank goodness you're okay."

"Why wouldn't I be?"

This wasn't just any other conversation. It was a phone call between my parents. Why would CAIN have a recorded call between my parents?

"Listen, Hank, you need to come home right now. Your project- It's not what you think. You're not safe! The kids aren't safe. I've been down in the basement, and I found your journal."

My mind wandered to the journal I'd found in Serendipity Shores. Whatever my mother had found in there hadn't been good. I scrunched my nose in a frown.

"Oh, don't listen to that nonsense. You and I both know Abel's crazy-"

"But-"

"Everything is under control."

"You're hopeless. I'm coming over."

One of them hung up, and the recording ended. I sat, confused, and in the dark. My parents meant more to CAIN's mystery than I thought. Granted, Ashton did have the courtesy of telling me a little about them, but it wasn't enough. Far from it. Whatever he told me, it was *never* enough.

Popping out the tape, I inserted the next one. *Emergency,* as it read. I pulled my legs up on the chair and blew through my lips.

"Come on. I just want some answers. Please," I said. Bolt crawled up my knee and came to snuggle against my neck. I gave him a small scratch on the head. The tape clicked as it set into place.

"Hey, kid. Just wanted to let you know we'll be coming home later than expected."

Another voice came muffled from the background. *"Did he pick up?"*

The first voice returned, quieter. *"No, but I'm leaving him a message."*

"Why wouldn't he pick up-"

"Uh, anyways..." The first voice directed back to the phone. *"No need to worry, but be careful. Lock the door and don't answer anyone. If anyone comes, you guys can hide in the basement. Some very bad people might be dropping by the house later, so I need you to keep alert. Call your family and let them know too. In fact, you might be better off with the Skylors. Just... stay safe."*

A slam ended his talk, followed by some loud shouting. *"Dr. Landerson, put your hands up!"*

"Call me back-"

The recording ended.

"Blake Landerson…" I thought it over to myself. I recalled his journal about his testing with the rats. I added his name to my list of things to find out more about later. The mystery of my past had too many loose pieces, I questioned whether I would ever solve this. Maybe I had missed something. I reset the tape and waited as it started back up.

"Hey, Ally-gator. How's it going?"

My brother's voice nearly made me jump from my seat. He stood at the doorway of the library, Kade standing just behind him.

The duo came to meet me. Ashton watched the tape player curiously. "What is that?"

"Oh, uh…" I straightened in my seat, frustrated at allowing myself to get caught. "Just some old tapes I found. I thought I might find something Abel related on them." *Not a total lie.*

Ashton popped the tape from the player when it was only halfway through the audio. "Huh." He looked it over, frowning. He set it on the table and turned back to me. "Anyways, I just wanted to let you know that I'm gonna be on a mission, so Kade's taking care of your training today."

Kade gave a curt wave. "'Sup."

"Alright then." I frowned, a little disappointed I wouldn't be spending the day with Ashton. As much as I didn't like him, he was still my brother, familiar and safe. *But hanging out with someone else might mean new information.*

After cleaning up things in the library, Ashton headed off for his mission and left me alone with Kade.

"Come on, kid." Kade led me out the front door.

Not wanting to divulge the secret that I was a Dragon, I sent Bolt off and stranded myself in the dark. I followed after Kade as best as I could. We crossed to the outside, in the opposite direction of the training hall. "I thought we were training."

"I told May we'd meet her at the mall, and we're already running a little late."

I listed my head, trailing the sound of his footsteps. "Are we training at the mall?"

"Nope." Kade helped me into the passenger side of his jeep before he left for the driver's side. "Today was supposed to be my day off, and I intend on keeping it that way."

I sat awkwardly through the drive. I didn't know Kade that well, and he had already derailed my plans entirely. I fidgeted with my hands in the dark.

"And I thought I was quiet," Kade said after we had been driving a while.

"I just wasn't expecting to go anywhere."

I could feel Kade staring at me instead of the road. "Wait, do you actually like working at CAIN?"

"You don't?"

Kade laughed. It sounded weird. "Oh no, I hate it there. Look, I know you think all the detective work is fun, but it gets tiresome beyond a point."

I listed my head. "If you don't like it, why do you

work there?"

Kade sighed, thinking the question over. "Ashton. I only applied to work at CAIN because Ashton was going to get himself killed if he didn't have anyone to keep an eye on him."

I scrunched my nose. "How come? I think he handles remmutants pretty well."

"Oh, I'm sure Ashton is more than capable of taking on a thousand of those birds and making it out perfectly fine. But he doesn't know how to keep his nose out of places he doesn't belong. That's how he got the job in the first place."

I frowned, not liking how much that reflected me. My hunt for the truth wouldn't get me killed, would it?

May waved us over from a pretzel stand in the mall food court. When we came to meet her, she took my hand. My sight lit up for a moment as she shoved a fluffy pretzel stick into my grip.

"Here. You have to try this! It's amazing!" May's cheeks perked up.

Taking the pretzel, I tore off a piece and slipped it into my mouth. Once I had swallowed, I smiled. "Pretty good."

"Right?" May sounded like she had stuffed her mouth full of the salty bread. "So, which stores should we check out first?"

"What is it that we're doing here?" I asked.

"Nothing much. Just hanging out." I heard Kade shove his hands into his pockets.

"Plus," May sang. "I just got my paycheck. Let's see how fast we can waste it."

"May, no."

I followed along after them as they perused the shops. There was no point in shopping mindlessly. I needed to find Abel. I needed to find my past. I couldn't waste my time like this, but I'd be stuck here until Ashton got back from his mission. My worries seeped into the back of my mind. Even if I tagged along on that, I would feel more productive than now.

"You good?" May nudged me with her elbow, pausing from flipping through the dresses on the rack. Kade had opted to wait at the electronics store across the way, stating that clothes shopping was boring and telling May to enjoy herself. "What are you thinking about, girly?"

"Well." I fiddled with one of the sleeves on the clothes in front of me. "We're CAIN agents. Don't you think we would be better off trying to find Abel or hunting remmutants? Who knows whether either could attack next? We should be doing something productive, like training. Not wasting time at the mall."

May chuckled. "It's okay to take a break every once in a while. Don't you think you should have a life outside of secret agencies and dark conspiracies?"

"Why? What's the point in that?"

The shifting of hangers against the bar stopped.

"Silly George. Ashton should let us watch you more."
May clicked her tongue when examining another dress.
"What do you *really* know about Alison Caddel?"

I listed my head. "What do you mean?"

"What does she like to do for fun? What is
something she can't stand? What is something she would
absolutely lose her mind over if she got it for her
birthday?"

I paused May's browsing as background noise.
My mind blanked, and my mouth ran dry. Shaking
myself, I started again. "None of that hardly matters,
May." I punctuated it with a mild, short laugh.

"Nonsense. Matters just as much as the edgy
backstory you're so determined to find, if not more."
May hummed over to herself. "What do you think of this
one?" She held up the dress to me. "Oh right, you can't
see. Well, you're more of a red, anyways."

"Well, what about you?" I marched after her steps
as she moved to another rack. "If you think 'personal
interests' are so important, what are yours?" I huffed,
crossing my arms. "If you ask me, they're just
distractions."

Sighing, May set her hand on my shoulder. "Ally,
Ally, Ally, do you know how ridiculous you sound?" She
laughed a little. "What nonsense has Vix been feeding
you? And to answer your question, I like to watch anime
and read books with my son for fun. I can't stand loud
noises or people who insult art, and I am petrified by fire.
I lose my mind if I get flowers for my birthday,

especially freesias. Now you go."

I could almost see May's smug look searing into my skull. "I…" I scrunched my nose and huffed. "I don't know, okay?"

May snapped her fingers. "And that's your problem. You're too focused on who Ally *was*. Not who she is now."

"What are you? My therapist?"

May gasped. "Is that sass I hear? You better watch it or else I'ma tell Ashton." She nudged me playfully.

Before we walked to the electronics store, May bought a few things. We found Kade playing on one of the demonstration consoles. May held my hand, her other occupied with her bags.

"Kade just likes to come over here for the free games," May whispered to me. "He likes to play racing games, but on one occasion, he brought Ashton with him, and they both got kicked out. They get a little too competitive." She smirked.

I smiled at the thought, my mood lightening. "How come?"

"It's the one thing Kade can't beat Ashton at."

Kade looked at the sound of his name. He came to meet us, smiling. "What are you telling her about me?"

"Just that you're a sore loser," May said with a chuckle.

Kade rolled his eyes, slipping his hands into his

pockets. "So, where to now?"

May looked at me. "Ally, want to pick?"

I opened my mouth as Kade's phone buzzed. He pulled it up to his face, checking his text. "Ashton says he's done with his mission."

"We could head back now, then," I proposed. I wanted to return to my investigation anyways.

Kade knocked against Ashton's office door. Opening it without awaiting a response, we found Ashton at his desk, playing the *Emergency* tape from earlier on the listening device. He paused it, turning to greet us.

"Hey, you guys are back. Have fun, Ally-gator?"

I nodded. But the fact of the matter was that I had spent the whole time wishing I could be back in the CAIN library.

"How did the mission go?" Kade said, his voice on monotone.

"Good… and bad." Ashton sighed, hunching his shoulders.

Kade raised an eyebrow. "Bad how?"

"Uh…" Ashton's eyes wandered to me. "Ally, could you step out for just one second?"

I figured. I did as told, leaving Ashton's office. When my hand let go of Kade's, deceitful darkness came over me. The door shut behind me. I sidestepped so they wouldn't see my silhouette under the door. I listened.

Kade spoke first. "Ashton, you could let her in on

something."

Ashton's voice followed. "I know, I know, but I can't."

"Why not?"

"I just… haven't found the right time yet. That's not the point. Look, I dug up some stuff on C1."

"C1?"

"Uh, Clay. This CAIN stuff is getting to me. Anyways, that secret project Casey's been working on? That's where they're keeping him. But there's something else."

Kade waited. "What?"

"I don't quite know yet. It's called Station 42. They're launching it in, I don't know… A week? Maybe two?" Ashton sounded stressed.

Kade sighed. "That's not a lot of time. And we still don't even know what it is…"

"Plus, it'll probably be a lot harder to find him once this project launches. Kade." Both men went silent. Ashton broke the air. "I *really* don't know what I'm doing."

I leaned in closer, finding their voices growing quieter.

"Well, I could've told you that."

"Alison."

Vix's voice startled me. I straightened, moving farther from the door. "Mr. Vix. Evening." I forced a smile, trying to seem inconspicuous.

"How was your day, my dear?" I could feel his

figure come closer.

I hunched my shoulders. "Fine, I guess. I spent the day with Kade and May since Ashton was busy on his mission."

"His mission?" Laughter hung in Vix's tone. "Caleb didn't have a mission today."

"He… didn't?"

"I might be wrong, but I thought he wasn't scheduled for anything today. I'll have to check when I get back to my office." Vix gave me a pat on the shoulder. "Good night, Alison." He passed me and continued down the hall.

"Night," I called absentmindedly.

Once he was done talking to Kade, Ashton opened my room door. I sat on my bed, hands folded in my lap.

"Hey, Ally. Just wanted to stop by and say goodnight before I head back to the hotel." Ashton paused, reading my expression. "Is… something wrong?"

"Yeah." I didn't bother to look in his direction. "You lied to me."

"About?"

"About so many things that you can't even pinpoint a specific instance. But, at the moment, you lied about having a mission." I stood to face him. "Why?"

Ashton grew defensive, his voice higher in pitch.

"No, no, I didn't. I did have a mission today. It just wasn't from CAIN."

I rolled my eyes, my face getting hot. "But that's not the only thing you lied about. You lie about *everything!*"

"Ally, just- You don't understand-"

"No, I don't because you won't tell me a thing." I clenched my fists.

"Now, hang on." I could feel Ashton's tall figure towering over me. "I tell you what you need to know. I know what's best for you."

"No, you don't!" Frustration stung my sinuses, but I was too determined not to cry. "You don't know anything about me. *I* don't know anything about me! All you've ever done was leave me a confused mess!"

"Ally, stop." Ashton's stern voice sent a shiver through me. "You don't know anything you're talking about. You have no idea what I go through just trying to keep you alive! The world's a lot more dangerous than you think it is, and if you don't stop digging, you're going to get yourself killed!"

I flexed my fingers. "Well, then, tell me! Help me be prepared. I've fought remmutants, and I've been training to fight Abel. What more do I need!"

"Ally, you're crazy." Ashton turned to leave.

Before Ashton could go, I caught his wrist. He turned to face me. I stared at my red face, my narrowed brows, and my clenched jaw. And I could feel Ashton's anger too. But something lay beneath it. I knew I could access physical senses, but feeling all his emotions came new. Ashton's heart thudded, his eyes stung, and his ears were numb. Ashton was *terrified*.

Knowing what I was doing, Ashton yanked away from me. He reverted to his frustrated posture with a sigh. "Ally, why can't you just trust me!"

"Why do you have to lie for me to trust you?"

Silence overtook the air. I hugged my arms close, thinking everything over.

"I hate being your brother," Ashton muttered.

A gasp escaped both of us.

The words settled in, eerily akin to poison seeping into a wound.

Ashton took a step forward. "Wait, Ally, I didn't mean that-"

"Just go."

Neither of us budged for a bit. I held myself tighter as I couldn't wait until he left. It meant I wouldn't have to stand here thinking everything over. It meant I could go to bed and stop thinking entirely. If only he would just *leave*.

"Good night, Ally." The door closed behind his footsteps.

15

Subconscious Thoughts

Rough winds whipped through my hair, though the cold did not touch me. The dark, starless sky stared down. I soaked in my surroundings as I stood planted at the end of a neighborhood.

Nothing had tipped me off more than the fact that I could see. *This is a dream.*

I cautiously walked down the gravel road, scanning over each home. The house to my left lit up with light, simple blocks of windows bright with a warm orange. I heard distant laughter from the house, despite the harsh fall winds.

The false neighborhood held a familiar air to it. I counted off each house until it clicked. Serendipity Shores. Alison's old home, but not mine.

Like a rodent drawn in with cheese to a mousetrap, my curiosity urged me to investigate. Turning the knob to the warm house, I entered.

Two figures acted as the source of laughter. A young blonde girl sat on the carpet, playing with a short-haired brunette doll. The child's hair coiled into two pom poms on the sides of her head. She didn't bother me a glance, waving the doll back and forth. As I stared at the doll, I found it too detailed, too *real*. The girl turned to me. My steps froze as I took her in fully. Where eyes should be, the fleshy pink of her skin watched me. Spreading far too wide sat her mouth, the only facial feature she still had.

The second figure knelt on the rug, taller than the girl. He seemed my age. His red, curly hair framed his face as he smiled, unfazed by the faceless girl. I listed my head, mouth gaping at the demented scene of the two playing. *He's… Ashton.* The realization made it worse.

"*I have to go…*" the young Ashton said.

"*You can't. You promised.*"

"*I have to go.*"

Their conversation played like a broken record. Ashton would urge to leave, even rising and moving toward the door. The girl would urge him to stay. The scene would glitch back to the beginning.

"What am I doing here?" The two stopped at the sound of my voice. They turned to me, their blank expressions leaving me with nothing to read. I took a step back, waiting on a response. Rising, the girl approached me. I searched her for anything familiar, anything that might clue me into who my mind imagined her to be. My thoughts kept landing on her pigtails.

"Do you miss her?" The girl's smile never disappeared, though her tone grew sad.

"What?"

"You look like her. She knew a lot of things. I doubt I'll ever be able to find someone like her again." Her hands tightened around the doll.

Just a dream. That didn't stop my heart from rising. Against my better judgment, I asked, "Who is she?"

"She's…" Her words fell apart as they left her ever-smiling face. She gripped the doll, choking it. *"I know her name. I cannot say it."* The girl tilted her head up at me. Her smile wavered for a split second, but she smiled, nonetheless. *"And you… I know you too. But it's been so long."*

Water pooled from her hairline. Tears. Despite her smile, she cried. *"I miss her."* Her grip ever tightened on the doll, as if she would suffocate it.

I watched the doll intently, trying to decipher who it depicted.

The girl's young voice snapped me from my vain thoughts. "Tell me your name. Please." Desperate for a sign of real emotions, I scanned over her face. She wouldn't let me on beyond her mask. "I don't want to forget. Not like you forgot me. Like he forgot me." She pointed back to Ashton.

My gaze wandered to the boy. "Will you tell me your name if I tell you mine?"

"They have traded my name. When they think I can't hear, they call me E3."

"Who's *they?*"

The faceless girl yanked at my arm, letting her precious doll fall to the wayside. I pulled back, but her grip proved too tight. "Please! Tell me your name! I can't forget! Not when I'm so close! I can't forget!"

My chest rose rapidly, and I jerked my wrist free in my desperation. I tripped back, landing on a firm, rocky surface. I sat up.

The world around me shifted; the cozy old house was replaced with a dark void before me. The only light emanated from six cylinders. *CAIN's basement.* The girl stood in the middle of the row. Her teeth stretched wider, more tears pouring from her hairline.

Words bounced back and forth from the walls, distorted. It took me a moment to realize they were someone else's words and not that of the girl. A young boy. As the syllables grew more and more distinct, they pounded louder against my ears. My eyes widened as I recognized the sounds.

Forget. Forget. Forget.

The same way I had heard on my first day awake.

The girl crumbled to her knees, screaming in a high-pitched laugh, unmoved from her smile, but distress lined each shout. "No! Please! Not the basement!"

A shadow spread from beneath her, rising into the silhouette of a teen girl. I scooted back on my hands and knees, heart thudding in the back of my head. The silhouette marched toward me.

"She was never supposed to be here!"

Shooting up, I found myself back in my room at CAIN. I gasped for breath as my true senses came back to me. I clutched the blanket draped over my bed. As I readjusted, I shut my eyes.

This is real… This is real. In my consciousness, my mind mulled over every aspect of the dream I could remember.

I rubbed my face with my cold palm. *Did the dream mean anything?* I had only recognized Ashton. Him and the basement. None of this fit with my memories. *That I know of…* Frowning, my mind wandered to the day I had woken up in the hospital. Beyond that, the memories cut off, not a scrap of them left for me to find. Such a strange feeling, to know you're missing a piece of yourself.

The bedroom door opened. "Ally?" I flinched at Vix's voice. "Are you alright? I heard you scream?"

"Yeah," I mumbled tiredly. *Had I screamed in my sleep?* "Yeah, I'm fine. I just had a nightmare."

The flick of the light switch sounded before I felt Vix's warm presence sitting at the foot of my bed. "Want to talk about it?"

My mouth parted with a half-decided answer. *Can I let myself become weak around Vix? He had the potential to fire me or grant me a promotion.* But without an option, I answered, "Alright."

"Tell me how the dream went."

"It was weird… It didn't even feel like mine."

"What do you mean?"

"Well, it was hardly recognizable. Like, if someone else had dreamt it." I realized how stupid I must've sounded. How could I possibly expound upon the horror I had just experienced? "Just a lot of nonsense. Ashton was there, but younger."

"Well, that is strange." Vix ended with a short laugh.

"And a little girl was there too, but I don't know her in real life. She was blonde, and she had this unsettling grin, but she didn't seem very happy. Like you." The last part had left my mouth before I could stop it. I bit my lip, indecisive if I should keep going or wait for his response. I took too long and ended up with the second one.

"Really? How so?" His smile found a way of passing through his voice.

"I meant the smile part, not the unhappy part," I said with a nervous laugh. "Not that I think your smile is unsettling or anything." *Did I just get myself fired?*

"My mother always told me a bright smile is a useful tool to have." His large hand rested on mine. "Something to keep in mind. The rest of this dream?"

"Well, the girl seemed scared of… forgetting something. Certain people. When I didn't tell her my name, she got upset and…" *The basement.* "That was it."

"Well, see? When you talk out a nightmare, it doesn't seem so bad anymore." Vix gave me a pat on the leg. I felt him rise from the bed. "I'm glad I was able to help. Good night, Ally."

"Wait." The shuffling of his feet stopped. My hands fidgeted with the blanket. "You know how dreams usually mean something? You don't think- Well, maybe-
"

Vix sighed warmly. "Look, Ashton told me what happened to you, with your accident and amnesia. I know it must hurt having no clue how much you've missed. But I doubt this dream has anything to do with what happened before. The past can be hard to shake off, even without knowing everything. But you can push through this. You're a strong girl."

"Vix?"

"Yes?"

"Thank you. I didn't know Ashton had told you. Good night." I lay back on the mattress, eyes burning with the need for sleep.

"Of course. If you need anything, I'm always here. Good night, Alison." The switch flicked, and the door closed.

I closed my eyes and drifted back into a dreamless sleep.

Funny. Ashton never told me what happened.

Throwing the front door of his home open, Vix let out a sigh. As he crossed the threshold, his coat hung heavily on his arm. He halfheartedly hung it on the rack before making his way through the skinny hallway from the entrance.

Working for CAIN, Vix's work hours varied from day to day. His watch now motioned 1:00 in the morning, and he was just retiring for the night. Lately, he had been working until later, because he needed to keep an eye on Ally until she was fully adjusted.

A shadow danced on the dim lights of the kitchen against the wall. When Vix recognized the silhouette, his lips spread into a tired smile.

"I'm home, my love," Vix hummed, sliding around the corner.

Red hair pooling over her shoulder, Cherry sipped a cup of tea. Her elbows rested on the counter, eyes closed with sleepiness. "About time." As she rose, she set her steaming cup down. Vix pulled her close by her hips as she reached up to kiss him. "What could possibly be more important than me at that stuffy office of yours?"

"You didn't have to wait for me. You could've gone to bed."

"The bed gets cold without you." Cherry's hands reached up over his shoulders. "What was it this time?"

"Eh, the girl had a nightmare. Nothing too noteworthy. Though she did say one thing you might find funny." Vix split from his wife, moving to the fridge for a glass of milk. "She said someone in her dream wouldn't stop smiling but was still sad. Then she went on to compare the character to me." Watching his milk pour from the carton to the cup, Vix chuckled.

"Well? Are you happy?" His wife smirked at him, a small laugh hiding in her eyes.

"What kind of question is that? Of course, I'm happy. I've got the love of my life, a great job, what more could I ask for?"

Cherry scoffed, lifting her tea mug. "That's a shame. There's a lot more you could ask for." She took a sip as if that would stop him from questioning her.

"Like what?" Vix rolled his eyes at her.

"A bigger house and a better job. Honestly, Anthony, it's one in the morning, and they have you babysitting a teenager. I wouldn't mind being stationed in the First Colony." Cherry pursed her lips.

Shaking his head, Vix laughed at Cherry's sentiments. "Oh, you're so dramatic." He slid over to her, his eyes meeting the emeralds in place of hers. "You know, you are the most beautiful woman I've ever seen. Of course, I only have eyes for you, so there's not a lot of competition, but I think that counts for something."

Cherry let out a condescending laugh. "Well, aren't you quite the charmer? But you're avoiding the problem. She stretched out the word as she readjusted his collar. "You could do so much better."

Vix took her wrist lightly, pushing it away. "Nope, I'm content." Letting out a sigh, he raised an eyebrow at her. "Did you just stay up so you could nag at me?"

"I was bored and couldn't think of anything better

to do.”

Taking his milk, Vix groaned and started toward the bedroom.

“Hey, wait, I was joking!” Cherry laughed, skipping after him. Her steps caught up with his, her tea abandoned in the kitchen. “You know I love you, right, Anthony? I just want you to be the best you can be.” Her lips pursed in a sweet smile, earning one back from Vix.

“Oh, we both know you’d love to be in First Colony, gossiping with all those aristocrat wives.” Vix nudged her, careful not to spill his milk in doing so. He crossed into the bedroom before coming into the bed. Placing his milk on the nightstand, he started taking off his shirt.

Cherry smirked at him from the doorway. “I would adore that. You know me so well.” Cherry stepped around the bed and made her way to her side. She jumped into the covers, the blankets billowing up. “You know, if I didn’t know any better, I’d say part of you enjoys babysitting her.”

“Who? Alison?” Vix scooted next to his wife, sitting up against the bed’s back frame.

“You wanted kids. Well, now you’ve got one. If it wasn’t so sad, I’d find it kind of sweet.” Cherry’s hands tucked beneath her pillow, her eyes shut.

Vix sank to her level, arms stretched under his head. “Darling, it’s too late for your insults.”

“If you say so.” Cherry’s deep-colored lips spread in a dreamy smile.

With a happy breath, Vix joined her in sleep.

16

The Girl in the Mansion

No one paid attention to Lee. And yet, she couldn't escape the constant eyes watching her.

Tightening her grip on her sword, the girl circled her opponent. Her blade twirled with her wrist as she bit her lip within her fencing mask. Lee thrust forward, steel clashing against steel. As she had done repeatedly before, her steps made quick in their practice waltz. She watched the opponent for sneak attacks. Chest already heavy with breath, her lips parted.

"But pardon as you are a gentleman." Due to the duration for which Lee had been reciting the speech, the words slipped off her tongue. With a lunge, she almost landed a hit.

Lee's opponent in turn tried a low swing. She jumped to avoid the touch but immediately regretted it. She would probably be docked for the improper form.

"This presence knows, and you must need have heard." Lee pranced backward, blocking each hit from the other side. "How I am punished with a sore distraction…" After going over it so many times, the words had lost their meaning. Except for this particular portion, that is. No, Lee always slipped up after mentioning "a sore distraction," as if it distracted her itself.

"What- What I have…" Lee paused, allowing the opponent to land their hit.

A woman sitting in the back of the room sighed and lowered her head. "You lost," she said, her glasses framing her face, always holding disappointment, always directed at Lee.

Lee yanked off her helmet, her braid frizzy with sweat. "Line?"

"'What I have done, that your nature, honor, and exception roughly awake, I here proclaim was madness.' Goodness, child, it's not that hard." Patting down her tight skirt, the woman arose from the chair and stepped toward Lee.

"I'm trying, Ms. Kait!" Lee paced back and forth, her posture bored and uncaring. She didn't want to pause to read the distasteful expression on the housekeeper's face. "What's the point of this anyways? When will I ever need to be able to recite Hamlet while also having a swordfight?"

The woman waved Lee's partner off, one of the servants. He left with a nod. "Multitasking is an exceptional skill to have, especially if you're ever to succeed at CAIN." Looking over the clipboard in her hands, Kait readjusted her glasses. "We can be done for the day, I suppose."

Swinging her sword idly, Lee waltzed around the mat. The woman took the sword before Lee could cause any damage and set it on the rack.

"Go change, then you're free to do as you wish until dinner." With a nod, Kait walked off briskly, leaving the young girl alone.

Lee stepped through the mansion. It had been her home for the past month, but as much as they told her that, she didn't accept it. After being adopted, Ms. Kait trained Lee to be the perfect fighter for CAIN. They had spoken of destiny, of how she would fulfill her purpose as one of their greatest assets. They never let her beyond the property gates, and Mr. Titus, the master of the house, rarely ever hung around.

After a quick, warm shower, Lee changed into her favorite pink sweater. She knew most thought the color childish, but Lee wanted to stay a child as long as she could, lest she forgot what it felt like. The soft kiss of her mother. The protective hands of her father. The honey-like laughter of her siblings. All cheaply copied in the yarn and thread that made up her sweater.

Lee sat on the bathroom counter, drawing hearts in the mirror with the fog. Kait would probably reprimand Lee for it later but now wasn't later.

Lee tied her hair into curly pigtails that hung at

her shoulders and stood in the doorway of her bedroom bathroom. Her wide room felt too spacious for the girl who had spent her early childhood sharing a room with other kids. Though she had left a disaster of a bed that morning, the servants had already tidied up the sheets for her to sleep all over again. Cloudy sunlight poured in from the gated window, outlining every corner and dark spot of the room and punctuating the extent of her loneliness.

But that didn't mean Lee could be herself. Someone would *always* be watching her. Waiting for her to slip up and reveal the few cards she had left in her hand.

Humming along to a tuneless melody, Lee walked down the upstairs hall. Her song echoed back to her, her only friend in a lying world. Yellow decorated the walls, along with a few sporadic stray paintings. One portrait framed the image of her and Mr. Titus. Lee avoided this painting because she wasn't fond of looking at her own face. Those rose-tinted cheeks twisted upward in the flawless fake smile. Those eyes were hiding a world of truth behind them. Maybe that truth was what she hated most.

Voices floated from downstairs. Lee peeked around the corner, listening. Mr. Titus walked back and forth before the front door, discussing something over the phone. "So perhaps it would be best to leave her here for the gala…" He nodded along with the conversation. "Yes, we can't be too safe. Dragons are tough to deal with…" Lee slunk further back behind the wall. "See you soon, Vix." The phone clicked. "Lee, my dear, what have I told you about eavesdropping?" His eyes landed on her.

Hesitating to move down the stairs, Lee flinched. She met him at the bottom. "Sorry. Can I ask what that was about?" Perking up, she rocked back and forth on her heels.

"No, you can't. Did you finish classes with Ms. Kait?"

Lee nodded.

Seeing how his tone had affected her, Titus tried again. "I've, uh, brought you a present to keep yourself company." He dug around in his pocket before handing her a square-shaped device.

"What is it?" Lee turned it over in her hands, thumbing what she decided was a lens.

"A Polaroid camera. It's a little old for your time, but it's likely to keep you entertained." Titus took it from her, taking a picture with a snap. An image printed from the bottom, and he shook it out.

The image held her startled expression. Lee smiled at his attempt to make friends. "Thanks." She would rather he didn't attempt at all.

Titus handed the camera to her. "Why don't you go outside and get some nice pictures? I'll see you at dinner." He pat her off, nudging her toward the front door. "Daddy has work to do."

Without another word, Lee went along. Once outside, she sighed. She passed through the front garden embellishing the mansion's front, snapping a few pictures of some lilacs or orchids. She walked all the way the up gravely walkway to the gate, staring off. Lee glanced back at the mansion, her mind mulling over every lie that hid beneath it, the very chains that held her here. Had there been nothing to find, she would've escaped her first day.

As the head of CAIN, Mr. Titus didn't have much time to build a relationship with her, despite his insistence for her to see him like a father. He knew that dealing with Dragons could get messy. Which is probably why he avoided long conversations with her.

Lee always found *Dragon* an interesting term, since dragons in myth could either be taken as dangerous beasts or elegant creatures. Lee didn't know which kind she was. She could hope she was the latter, but her talent had so far proved her to be the first, even if no one else knew what she had done. Dragons, in that sense, seemed a lot like the mansion. It certainly looked beautiful on the outside, but on the inside, a thousand dirty secrets lay in wait.

No one except Lee and her mother knew the girl's talent. Everyone in the mansion just knew that she had one, but they didn't want Lee to know that they knew. To her fortune, lying to Lee proved impossible.

Taking a spot on the edge of one of the flower beds, Lee kicked her feet back and forth. Her gaze drifted back to the gates. Beyond them lay freedom. But freedom remained elusive for her. She had to earn it first.

She had to stay here until she figured out every last one of those dirty secrets and set them free.

Waving her arms, she walked along the flower box, imagining herself a tightrope walker. Below lay death. She could fall and splatter into a million tiny pieces at any point in time.

A squawk from above drew her attention. A crow, standing at the tip of the roof, stared down at her. It screeched again before flying off. She watched it leave, just like everyone else in her life had done.

A group of crows is a murder, her best friend would say.

How poetic, her sister would say.

Do you think it would be hard to catch one? her brother would say.

Of course, none of them were around.

Perhaps they had all been a figment of her imagination, to begin with.

Following along the perimeter of the mansion, Lee took a few more pictures of some wildflowers, the sun, and her hand. She soon found herself at the backdoor leading up to the kitchen. The hustle and bustle of the kitchen staff preparing dinner filled her ears the moment she entered. The savory scent of seasoned chicken floated across her nose. She dodged moving servants, offering to help. They had name tags on their shirts, but she couldn't manage to read any of them with their rushed pace. She decided to just call them all George.

"Lee!" The young girl nearly ran into a frantic Kait. The woman took Lee by the shoulders. "You're in the way. Come on, let's get out of the kitchen and let them work." They moved past the chefs and out into the dining room.

"Can I help with anything? Set the table?" Lee looked up to Titus' assistant.

"No- Just- I don't know- Go read a book or something!" Kait waved her off.

Lee stuck out her tongue in disgust, leaving the room. She got enough books in her classes, no thank you.

Lee stood outside the dining room door, as bored as ever. Snapping her fingers as she went, she tried to think of something to do. Interest in the Polaroid camera had died fast. She could see everything here whenever she wanted, and the pictures she would've wanted were all beyond that gate. One month trapped in a mansion melted her mind.

Taking two fingers, Lee walked them up the stair railing.

Lee had already wasted a month in this mansion, uncovering nothing but a neglecting parent and a bossy housekeeper. She knew one way she could get definite answers, but she had been avoiding the thought as long as she could.

Use your powers sparingly. Only if absolutely necessary, her mother's voice rang in the back of her head.

The last time Lee had used her talent, she hadn't

been able to shut it off on her own. Things did change since then but in the absence of practice, she had no clue if she could turn it off this time.

She forced herself all the way up the stairs. She would go to her room and sit there until dinner. Waiting just like she always did.

The one time she had used her ability, it had saved her. It gave her a chance to hold onto hope and to her family that now hung as a distant memory.

Could she justify using her talent again? Was it *absolutely* necessary? Lee's steps slowed.

Yes.

Pushing her bouncy bangs from her face, Lee focused in. *Come on, talent. I need you.*

Something clicked inside Lee. The feeling she had felt years ago fell over her, and she hated every bit of it. She hated what it reminded her of.

The world opened up to Lee on a whole new plane. Myriad voices flooded her ears, each in an echoed cacophony. She tried to filter through them all. She stepped through the hall, mind distracted.

I can't wait until I'm done with this babysitting nonsense. I have half a mind to quit. Lee rolled her eyes at Kait's thoughts.

As a mind reader, Lee knew she had to be prudent in using her talent. All thoughts were open to her, even thoughts not meant. So many voices in one's head could make someone lose themselves, mistaking thought for a fact. When she used her talent, she had to stay aware at all times. She had been able to loosely communicate through dreams before. She had even tried it once in the last month, immediately regretting the risk she'd taken. Dreams lay in an entirely different field, even harder to discern fiction from reality. But now, letting loose the leash on her talent, even just a little, made her stomach churn.

Lee continued to sift through all the minds in the mansion, searching for any keywords, for anyone who might know how she could get what she wanted.

Lee will have to wait before she can be introduced to CAIN... Lee mentally cheered, reaching Titus' thoughts. She tuned into what he had to think.

Once we're done working with A2, we could probably work her in. And avoiding C1 shouldn't be an issue... The keys I keep in my right pocket... To the secret door, portrait by the stairs...

Lee's eyes widened, and she caught herself before she gasped. She had forgotten how thoughts made their presence felt in the form of haphazard feelings in fragments rather than cogent sentences, but she was able to discern the purpose nonetheless. Glancing around to make sure no one had seen her spontaneous expression change, she quickened her pace to her room.

This time, the thoughts came to Lee as an image, a memory. A train station under construction. She didn't know if that had anything to do with his previous thoughts, but she wouldn't let herself get worked up over that.

Unless… perhaps we can work her into a separate branch. Finding her room door, Lee slipped in, careful to shut the door quietly behind her.

Lee shook her head, chuckling to herself. *Your games don't work on me, Titus,* she thought back. She bounced on the bed, stomach first.

Soon, this will all pay off… I wonder when dinner is, came Titus' thoughts. Lee frowned. This was the part she had been dreading. The ineffectual thoughts and relentless noise, juggling around in her head. She would have to practice drowning it out if she were to stay sane and focus on the task at hand.

"Lee, it's time for dinner!" Kait rapped against the bedroom door.

Lee opened the door and smiled up at Kait. "Can't wait! Will Mr. Titus be joining us?"

"Unfortunately, no. He has a few meetings, so he'll be taking dinner to go." Ms. Kait led Lee down the hall.

"I guess it's just you and me then?"

"Nope." Kait's lips popped with the plosive. "Mr. Titus has reached his hours for me, and since he's not here to arrange an agreement for overtime, I'm leaving." Kait propped her pointed nose upward. "See you tomorrow, Lee." She walked faster than the young girl, probably too excited to be rid of her.

Lee sagged, watching her only company leave. The paintings of Lee stared down at her mockingly. Hugging herself, Lee moved quicker away from them. *I need friends.* She almost mistook her thoughts for someone else's. Her last friends had been stolen from her, and she grew determined to get them back.

Lee just had to play the lonely waiting game.

17

Behind the Portrait

"Good morning." Lee gave a yawn, passing Ms. Kait in the hall. Her pink, collared pajamas hung with static to Lee's body as she went, her blanket clutched close.

"Nothing good about it. It's adequate at best. Come on, get dressed." Kait attempted to turn the girl right back to her room, but talking from downstairs interrupted Lee's attention.

"Has Mr. Titus left yet?"

"No, I believe he's on his way out now."

Lee ducked passed the housekeeper and to the stairs. She ran across to meet Titus, who was putting on his coat and talking with one of the servants.

Titus' stone expression shifted in surprise. He dismissed the servant he had been conversing with. "Lee, what has you so excited?"

"Just happy to get a chance to see you before you go." Lee caught him in a hug before he could resist. She couldn't wait until he left.

He stiffened at the touch before loosening. *Maybe she's more ready than I thought.* Lee had to resist flinching at his thoughts.

They separated. "Lee, before you go to your classes…" Titus straightened, clearing his throat. "I thought I should let you know that I'm going on a business trip tomorrow, and you're coming with me."

Now *that* she didn't know about. "Really? Can't wait!" Anything would be better than another day cooped up in the mansion. If Titus was willing to take Lee somewhere, it meant she had played her part well enough to gain his trust. She was moving on to the next step.

Titus nodded. "Pack your bags later today. I'll be waking you up early tomorrow." He glanced down at his watch. "Shoot, I'm running late. Goodbye, Lee. Perhaps I'll see you later tonight." Mr. Titus turned, dress shoes clipping against the marble.

Lee kept her perfect grin until the door shut behind him. Once in the clear, her lips shifted into a deceptive grin. Her gaze drifted down to her hands, double-checking. The key she had heard in his thoughts lay in her palm. If she moved quick enough, she could find the key's matching door, search for any clues of the whereabouts of C1 or A2, and return the key before he ever noticed. Her chances stretched thin, but she couldn't ignore her first lead since coming here.

Kait trailed down the steps. Lee hid the key in her fist among the blanket.

"Young lady, come back here and change out of those night clothes. We have a class to begin."

Well into the afternoon, Lee's stomach twisted with excitement. After finishing her studies, she would be free to roam the mansion, which meant she would be one step closer to finding the experiments.

Lee sat in Kait's lesson on how to form a proper argument for debate. The girl at least appreciated that Titus had his hired assistant school her, although knowing his true intentions kind of ruined it. She fully intended on using the skills he taught her against him someday.

"Lee."

The girl looked up, meeting an annoyed Kait. Lee had been too distracted in her thoughts, scribbling butterflies on her jeans with a pen, to hear the question the woman had just asked. "Hmm?"

The extra dining room had been decorated as their classroom, with a whiteboard at the end and a lengthy table in the middle. According to Lee, the extra space made it harder to pay attention.

Pacing, Kait shook her head with a sigh. "I asked what the rules are for cross-examination. Stop drawing on your pants. You're ruining them."

With a clink, Lee dropped her pen on the table,

straightening. "Uh… You ask questions, and clarify any misunderstandings, and… something else, right?" Her eyes moved past Kait to the whiteboard, hoping to find some answers. Instead, the answer whispered itself from Kait's mind.

"Expose weaknesses. That one, in my opinion, is the most important," Kait said in that matter-of-fact accent of hers. Nodding along, Lee wrote it down.

As she set the marker down on the whiteboard ledge, Kait gave Lee an exhausted look. "Alright, that's all for now. Go get some lunch or something, then go practice your parries with one of the servants." Nose up in the "I'm better than you" position, her natural resting face, Kait turned and left.

Watching after her, Lee waited with a smile. It was a shorter lesson than most days. More time for her to look for the room.

Lee took the stairs two at a time. She couldn't contain her grin, her brisk steps playing to the rhythm of her eager heart. Thankfully, no one was around to question her excitement.

Lee didn't bother to look up at the judging faces of the portraits. Soon, the fake smiles that awakened guilt within her wouldn't matter. She would be out of the mansion, free to be with her real family, and everything would be okay. *Take that, Titus.*

Swinging her bedroom door wide, Lee spun on her heels. As she dug through her desk drawer, she picked out the key. Lee glanced sideways, double-checking to make sure the hall was clear of servants or Ms. Kait.

With the key in her pocket, a thousand painted eyes glaring down at her, and secrets buried in her chest, Lee trudged on with hope.

Mr. Titus said the door was right... Lee came to stand at the end of the hall, just before it rounded out into the stairs. Her breath hitched. "Here."

The infamous family portrait. So full of everything Lee detested about the place. Titus and Lee, faces molded with lies and deceit; their true colors lay just beneath those eyes. Her stomach churned, eyes meeting her painted image.

Lee pulled herself from the locked stare and tried not to think about it. Digging her fingernails beneath the frame, she tugged at it. It tilted on the nail holding it. A flat handle waited, indented for a hand to pop it open. She pulled it without questioning. The wall slid back, revealing the secret room to be thinner than she thought. It halted at the end of the picture frame, leaving just enough space for a grown man to fit. Lee's petite form could walk through easily.

A metal wall separated Lee from the other side. The door was kept shut by a small lock and knob. Fishing out the key, she inserted it. It clicked in the lock. "You got this, Lee. Just remember who this is for." With a deep inhale, she crossed through the second door.

A thin, dark space welcomed Lee. Something clicked beneath her feet; the wall and door slid back in place when her step came off it. She flinched with a start. Now trapped in a sweaty, claustrophobic, secret closet, a light above her slowly lit up.

Soundproofing foam ensconced the walls. Blue haze illuminated a wide monitor against the longer wall. A control panel sat against it, built into the side of the room, decorated with switches and buttons. Lee leaned over the panel and examined the monitor. The monitor was divided into different screens, all surveying the mansion.

Lee's eyes widened, realizing a camera would've caught her with the key in her room. She hadn't been careful enough. Making a mental note to figure out how to delete that later, she investigated a bit more.

A folder marked *HDE* hung on the wall with a clip. Lee took it down, flipping through the files inside. *A1, A2, C1, E3, M1,* and *P2.* She frowned at the big red stamp over *M1* and *P2. DECEASED.* She had already known about *P2*'s death, but she hadn't heard of *M1*'s.

Sympathy stung deep inside, but Lee did her best to shake it off. She would've loved to help every one of the experiments, but she didn't have time for that. She had to focus on *A2* and *C1.* She knew *A2* would be safe without her, at least for a while, but she had yet to locate *C1.*

Examining *C1*'s file, Lee searched for anything useful. She had read over the *HDE* files before, prior to being adopted by Titus. These files differed from the previous ones. They had notes and scribbles, written in

Titus' own hand. Beneath the printed text, she found a set of commands, inked in pen. *Camera T42.* Unsure, she squinted at it.

Lee looked up from the page, scanning over the panel. She landed on a button labeled *C T42.* It clicked in her head. Setting the file down, she pressed the button. The screen changed to show new sets of live footage. Next to the time, numbers labeled the screens.

The new surveillance pictured a train. Most of the screens held nothing of interest to Lee. Just idle train cars. Agents and guards loaded up a few cars, the train waiting to depart. Her gaze landed on a set of two cameras, focused on the same car.

A thick wall of glass divided the car the long way. On the outer side of the glass, the side with the door, two CAIN agents paced. Blocked off on the other side sat a teenage boy. He had his knees tucked in close, resting on the ground. He shifted a little, his face ridden with a tired frown.

Cupping her mouth, Lee's eyes began to water. Years had passed since she'd seen him, but she could still recognize his face. His cheeks remained fixed on being that tomato shade, his brown hair still insistent on being a spiked matted mess, and his eyes as deep blue as ever.

Lee wanted to scream, squeal, call out to him, *something,* but she refrained. Actually seeing him, even just on a computer screen, made her feel all the more relieved. "Don't worry," she allowed herself to whisper. "We're going to be okay."

Everything is going to be okay.

A wonderful idea sprung into her mind. Lee grinned, a real smile for the first time in years. Composing herself, she focused, reaching out to him in the plains of her mind.

Hello? Hello! Can you hear me!

Lee watched the screen, hoping for any sign he could. *Hello?*

He shifted a little, looking up momentarily.

Clay? Can you hear me?

Clay's face scrunched in confusion, his gaze looking between the guards.

Happy that he could at least pick it up a little, Lee gripped the edge of the panel. *Don't let them know you can hear me.*

Readjusting himself, Clay rested his head on his arms. *Who are you? Where are you? How come I'm the only one who can hear you?*

Lee wiped one of her eyes. Clay had answered back. He could hear her. She desperately collected her thoughts and forced herself to focus. *I'm a telepath, and I'm in your head right now. Don't worry, you're not crazy.*

That's something a crazy person would say.

Trust me. Clay, I'm a friend.

What are you talking about? I've never been outside this room. I don't have any friends.

Lee shook her head. *They just tricked you into thinking that. Do you know where you are?*

Nope. Clay laid his head back against the wall, allowing one leg to stretch out. *Just been sitting here, bored for the past… I don't know how long. No one will talk to me. I don't even know why I'm here. All I've got is my name. Clay… You mind giving me some answers?*

Lee looked around, wondering how much time she had before someone came looking for her. She still had to delete that footage of herself too. She glanced at the time. Titus would be back any minute. *I would love to, believe me, but I'm a little short on time.*

Where are you?

Somewhere far from you, I think. I'm in the First Colony.

I don't know where that is.

I'm in a city called New Old York. It doesn't matter. Clay, I'll find a way to get you out, but you got to hang on a minute.

Don't worry. I'm not going anywhere.

Lee could almost hear him sigh. She wanted to do something more than just give him a few moments of conversation, but even this had seemed impossible days ago. She had to keep herself encouraged, and more importantly, him encouraged. *I'll be back. Just hold out for a little while.* She made herself smile for him, even if he couldn't see it. A thought popped into her head.

Oh, and if you happen to escape before I get to you, look for a man by the name of Ashton.

Flicking a few switches, Lee swapped cameras and dropped her long-distance thoughts.

Once Lee had managed to wipe any footage of herself with the key or talking to herself, she made her way out of the secret room. She readjusted the portrait back in place, refusing to look at it. Clutching the key in her palm, she sighed in relief.

"Mr. Titus, hello!" Making her way down the stairs, Lee saw Ms. Kait help Titus with his coat. Holding her hands out, Lee greeted Kait. "I can get that for you." The woman handed it to her, commenting something about her *finally being a polite young lady.* As Lee hung it on the coat rack, she slipped the key back into the pocket.

"Lee, I hoped you remembered to pack. We've got a trip tomorrow." Titus pat down his shirt then readjusted his dark purple tie.

Snapping her fingers, Lee made finger guns. "Right! Almost forgot. Silly George." With a nod, she turned back to the stairs. "I'll go do that right now!" After making sure she was out of sight, she loosened a little. Everything had gone better than she'd hoped.

She played the role of Titus' daughter flawlessly.

18

Test Run

"All aboard to the Second Colony!" The conductor's voice shouted over the bustle. The train's whistle trumpeted along.

Lugging her single bag ahead of her, Lee stepped up onto the train. Titus pushed her along, hand on her back. He showed her to their room, just the right size for the two of them. After waving Lee to enter, Titus followed with his wheeled suitcase. A man soon came to collect their tickets. Titus gave up the tickets with a curt nod, and the train wheeled them away from the station. The thuds of the train thumped along in a rhythm at first, then they blended.

Lee attempted to distract herself with the window view, anything to avoid talking to Titus. The train ran underground, hidden from remmutants, traversing from the First Colony to the Second. Hands folded in her lap, she lay back in the seat, leaving her mind to wonder what the trip was for. Titus' thoughts searched for small talk, pressing the prompts into her mind.

Titus nudged her playfully. "Excited? Your first trip outside the city." Lee forced herself to try to engage with a nod. *Outside the mansion to be exact.* "I trust you've been learning about the remmutants in your studies?"

Lee nodded. "Yeah. Hopefully, I'll never have to see one up close." She gave a somewhat forced laugh. Would the world be so bad if one swooped down to gobble her up along with all life's stresses?

"Do you have a favorite?"

"Hmm?"

"A favorite remmutant. They're quite magnificent creatures, despite being so deadly. I think the ones from England are interesting."

Lee listed her head. "The squirrels? I don't know, those ones kind of freak me out. I like the crows. They just look so... magical!" She did small jazz hands.

"Yes, I suppose those inky feathers are 'magical' to look at. Too bad they are a mere myth" Titus looked off, a soft smile on his face. *This is going splendidly.*

Lee sunk into her seat, disappointed for letting him think that. She needed him to trust her as much as possible, but she couldn't let herself fall into his tricks. She couldn't forget what he'd done to her. To her family.

Lee turned back to the window, only to be disappointed again by the gray walls. "So, where are we going, Mr. Titus?"

"I thought I'd take my daughter down to Second to see a project CAIN's been working on. After that, you'll be sent home, but I'm staying for a gala at the head branch there. I figured you would want to get out of the mansion." Titus' insistence for her to think of him as her father disgusted her. It was he who was responsible for her father's death, one which didn't even come with a proper funeral. Titus stared out the window as if it were the most piquant view he'd ever seen.

"One of the secret projects? How come you're showing it to me?" Lee asked, letting down her mask just a tad. She fiddled with her sweater sleeves.

"Yes, it is very secret, but I trust you won't divulge it to the entire world. Just stay close to me and you'll be fine." Lee longed to get as far from him as possible. With an inhale, Titus lay back, interlocking his fingers together. "We've got a good day of travel ahead of us."

A few rest stops and two naps later, Titus woke Lee up with a nudge. She sat up yawning, red sweat marks streaked across her face and a little of her hair in her mouth. Taking up her suitcase, she made her way after Titus. As they stepped off the train, she nearly ran into him.

The underground station's dim lights blinded her. The air smelt bad, but Lee couldn't exactly place a scent.

People shuffled about, their thoughts boring into Lee's skull and grinding her mind to powder. She took care to stay close to Titus, to avoid getting lost. Though, it wouldn't be the worst thing.

Lee squeezed past several people. She almost reached out to hold Titus' hand to stay closer, but she refrained. "What time is it?"

"Three in the morning, my dear," Titus said, glancing at his watch.

The flow of people grew smoother as they went through the station. They made their way up the ramp, coming out to the main building of the station. Lee passed through the rotating door, breathing in the cold, fresh air. Squinting, she stared up at the domed sky, making out the curve of the night stars.

"Come along, Lee," Titus said, waving for her to follow. He stood at the curb, waiting. "A taxi should be coming soon, and then in…" He glanced at his wristwatch. "Seven hours, we're off to see the project."

She nodded, rubbing her eyes. "Can't wait."

Thankfully, the taxi wait wasn't long. Instead of staying at a hotel like Lee thought they would, Titus said that he owned a penthouse in Second. He told her he owned a home in each of the Colonies.

Once he showed her where she could set her things, she flopped onto the bed, ready for real sleep.

Titus took his spot on the bed across from her. Slipping off his shoes, he smiled fondly at her.

She's just like Sofia.

Lee sat up at Titus' thought. "Who's that?" she mumbled before she could stop herself.

"What?"

"Nothing." Lee's eyes darted from him. She yanked the blanket over herself, hoping he wouldn't question her further.

Titus sighed. "Look, Lee, I know you don't like me."

Lee's breath hesitated. She watched him with a waiting gaze.

"I don't know why you don't like me, but I hope to be able to fix that." Titus' eyes met hers. "You know, I had a daughter once. Her name was Sofia, and she was a lot like you." His thoughts came bittersweet. "I miss her with all my heart. You miss your real family, too." He gave her a sad smile, trying to connect beyond his usual deceptions. "But they abandoned you."

Lee's heart dropped like a pebble into a still pond. Hearing the words out loud, the thought she had tried so hard not to believe, broke something inside her. All the moving thoughts around her froze.

Lee showed no emotion to Titus.

"Both of us are stuck without a family. But, if I can be a good father, maybe you could try to be a good daughter?" Titus' lips tilted slightly in a smile.

Lee stared at him. His words had come mumbled. Her thoughts grew too loud. They screamed at her, trying to suffocate the girl in doubts and the omnipresent worry that the past month of torture and whatever the future had in store for her, would end up all thrown away, not making a modicum of difference in the world. Closing her eyes, she forced her wavering faith into a polite smile. She could barely manage a nod. "Goodnight, Mr. Titus." She turned on her side, ducking her head under the blanket.

Lee could feel his eyes watching her. When she searched for his thoughts, they came back silent.

"Lee, we've got to go now if we're going to get there by ten." Titus tapped his foot, standing with the penthouse door open.

"Ready!" Lee finished up her hair, tying it in two scrunched pigtails. She skipped out ahead of him. Titus shut the door and the two went down to the street.

The CAIN limousine rolled up to the curb. The manufactured sunlight glinted off the slick black paint of the vehicle. They had an hour and a half drive to the border, cutting Lee's seven hours of sleeping to five and a half.

Lee found this ride far more interesting than the train ride. Out the window was something to look at, for one. The tall towers of the city looked upon them, though they stood short compared to the ones she could see over the mansion wall.

Dreadful quiet settled inside her, the world's thoughts mute to her. She had lost her advantage to her emotions. Her own thoughts no longer had to fight for dominance in her head, but at what cost?

As they went on, the flaws in the sky grew easier to discern. Soon, Lee could see the border, and she realized then that they were driving up to it.

They pulled up to the first wall. One of the CAIN agents managing the border waved. Lee scanned over the area nervously. "What are we doing?"

Titus ignored her, and the car pulled through a gate leaving the second wall. The gate closed behind them.

As she realized what had just transpired, Lee's eyes widened. They had passed the border. They drove outside the city. Where all the terrifying, carnivorous, gargantuan eagles eagerly waited for their next meal. She tugged at her sweater. "Are you sure we're safe out here?"

"Relax," Titus said, laughing lightly. "Our project is so secret we had to hide it out here, away where the rest of society and the government can't find it." His lips spread in a smirk, only deepening her uneasiness.

"Isn't CAIN part of the government?"

"That's just what we want the government to think."

Lee frowned, pulling her arms closer in.

The vehicle tumbled over the bridge across the moat surrounding the Colony. The moat acted as the Colony's source of water, as it couldn't rain with the dome over it. Lee watched as trees flashed past the window. She folded her hands in her lap, her gut tightening in nervousness.

The car rolled to stop. Climbing out the door, Titus helped Lee after him. She came to stand on the unsteady dirt beneath her. When she observed her surroundings, she discovered they had parked just above a wide ditch. Deep in the ditch, a train station was being constructed. A track led in a circle, outlining the ditch. Lee tried to make sense of it, only to turn up further confused. The train took up a quarter of the track, composed of ten cars, give or take, and the front engine.

"What is this?" Lee looked to Titus.

Titus pat the girl on the back, starting down the makeshift dirt path. She nearly tripped, finding it steeper than she expected. "If I told you, I'd have to kill you."

Lee stiffened.

"I'm only joking," he added with a chuckle.

Lee didn't get the joke.

After a good hike, they finally reached the bottom. To keep from breathing in the dust and metalwork, Lee pulled her sweater up over her mouth.

A blond man in a black jacket, marked at the chest with the CAIN logo and a tag that read *O. Casey* came to meet Titus. The men shook hands. "Mr. Titus, good morning!" The man smiled, though Lee thought it looked like his face was new to the expression. "Glad to have you here."

"Casey, glad to be here. Can't wait to see what you've got for us here. Oh, and this is my ward, Lee."

Lee waved. "Hi."

Casey looked her up and down, losing the smile he had reserved for his boss. "Pleasure." He shifted back to Titus. "Sir, if we may have a word, then we can start the tour."

Titus nodded, then motioned for Lee to stay. They walked away from her, whispering to each other.

Rubbing her arms, Lee watched them from afar. No thoughts returned, and Lee frowned at her broken powers. The girl longed for her mother. She would've explained how her talent worked. But now Lee was broken with no means of repair.

Lee's gaze wandered to the train. A train similar to the one she had seen when she'd spoken with Clay. It clicked in her mind. The secret project had been Clay all along.

"So!" Titus clapped his hands together, spinning on his heels to face Lee. Her steps froze before she could sneak off to investigate the train. "Shall we begin?" Nodding to Casey, Titus motioned for her to follow them. "I hope we'll be impressed by what you have to show us."

"I won't waste your time sir." Rushing over, a CAIN agent handed Casey a tablet. He flicked a few buttons on it, scanning over to make sure everything was in order. "Ladies and gentlemen, may I present… Station 42."

The group stepped up onto a shaded platform, adjacent to the track. Casey waved for them to step up into the engine. Two thin doors slid into place after them.

While on the outside had been a slick black, the innards were a blue tinted white. A pair of seats sat placed in front of the control panel, switches and dials decorating it. One blinking red button caught her eye, labeled in an engraved black, *ABORT*. A strange machine behind them. Lee stared at the device to decipher it. Circular shaped, protected with glass, and flooded with strange blue light, the machine only perplexed the blonde girl.

"These dials let you know if everything is stable, and the abort button stops the train entirely in the event something goes wrong." Casey held a rigid posture, his speech probably practiced a thousand times. "We've trained a team of pilots to be able to work all this."

Pilots? What kind of train has pilots?

Moving past them, Casey tapped on the glass of the machine with his knuckle. "And here's our power source. If we've done it right, this is going to revolutionize CAIN forever."

"And the world."

Hesitantly, Lee raised a hand. "What does it do, exactly?" Her lips quirked in an unsure smile.

Casey looked at her bored before his gaze shifted to Titus. "You'll see later. That's all for the engine car." As Casey went past her, he purposely knocked into her. He pressed a button, raising the door for them to exit.

Dirt crunched beneath Lee's boots, eyes glued to the train as they went. As Casey explained it, the other cars would hold passengers or supplies, as with any other train. She still had no clue as to why any of this was so important, but she tried to pay attention in case it came in handy.

"Ready to see what it does?" Casey gripped his tablet tighter as if nervous his boss would be dissatisfied with the tour. Titus nodded, smiling down at Lee. She forced a matching expression. Casey moved them back onto the platform after shouting for the agents to prepare. "Our second test run. Let's see how it goes," Casey said, more to himself than them. Crossing her arms, Lee prepared herself for what might come next.

With the swift movement of his hand, Casey unclasped a radio from his belt. "We're clear out here. Are you ready in there?"

"Just about... ready."

Casey's expression dropped the fake smile, molding it into a sterner look. "We go in 5... 4... 3... 2... 1!"

The thundering of gears shifting and wheels chugging echoed through the pit. The train did a few laps around the track, growing quicker with each turn. Upon gaining a steady pace, the radio clicked again. *"On your mark, sir."*

Casey's eyes followed the train around the loop once more. "Go!"

A sharp *SNAP!* split the air. Lee ducked quickly to block her ears.

When Lee looked up, the train was gone.

Lee straightened, and her wide eyes froze to the last place the train had been. Titus' clapping and the cheers of the other agents broke her from her start.

"Well done, Casey."

Casey smiled with pride.

"What was that!" Lee spun to face Titus, throwing out her arms dramatically. "W-where did it go!"

Lee was met with a condescending smirk from Casey. "Right off the planet." He turned back to the radio. "Hello? Hello?" All that returned was a painful static screech. Straightening himself, he put the radio on his hip. "That is seemingly the only error, sir," Casey said, turning his attention back to Titus. "Once they're gone, we can't make contact with them."

Stroking his chin, Titus considered this. "A few bugs to work out, but nothing too hard for the engineering team, I hope."

"But where is it? How do you just make a whole train disappear? Is it coming back?" Lee stepped forward, almost wanting to touch the air where it had been, to make sure.

"It should come back, any moment now…" Casey squinted at the tablet.

Once the words left his mouth, the train appeared back on the track, still rolling with momentum. Rocky to slow, and it finally screeched to a halt. The pilots stepped off, high-fiving each other.

One comment pressed into Lee's mind. *My sister would love this.*

19

Breakthrough

"Careful… Careful!" Ashton shook my arm.

"Dude, stop! You're going to get us killed!" My heart thumped with each tick on the bomb. I desperately fiddled with the wires.

"Ten seconds, Ally!"

Blowing my hair out of my face, I worked faster. I didn't want to look at the timer, but it sat in the corner of my vision, thus reminding me of my imminent failure.

"Five seconds!"

With shaking hands, I tried remembering what Ashton had taught me, though, it didn't help that he kept bumping me. I mumbled over the steps again. "Red wire… to black… Or, wait, no, that's not right… Black, err, blue maybe?"

"3… 2… 1!" Ashton shoved me out of the chair, and I tumbled to the ground with a start. "Boom! Pshh!

Aaahhhh! There's fire everywhere! Ally, what have you done? You let us all explode!"

I had been practicing diffusing fake bombs all day. Every time I failed, I earned Ashton's dramatic reinterpretation of an explosion.

"Ashton-"

"I can't hear you! My eardrums burst and all the flesh melted from my bones! How could you!" Ashton fell to the floor next to me, throwing his arm over his face. Captain howled along to his owner's lead.

As much as I tried to resist, I smiled a bit. "Ash-"

Rubbing his finger on my mouth, Ashton jumbled my words. "Shhh, we're dead now." He forced us to lay still.

I sat up, shoving his arm off me. "Ashton, this is ridiculous."

"Easy fix. Learn how to defuse a bomb, and then we won't die." Ashton helped me to my feet and brushed me off. "I think that's enough practice for now. We've still got that gala to get ready for." Ruffling my hair, he walked me to the door of the training room. Captain went along, wagging his tail merrily.

"So, on a scale of one to ten, how fancy is this gala?" I listened to the pattern of Ashton's steps and taught mine to match.

Ashton clicked his tongue, swaying as he walked. "I'd say… seven. I guess you don't really have any fancy clothes, huh?"

We reached my room, and Ashton swung my

door open. As he held my hand, I noticed a white box laying on my bed. "Good thing I've got friends who think of stuff like that." He grabbed the box and shoved it into me. "Here, a gift from May."

After inspecting the box, I slipped off the lid. Ashton kept his arm pressed against mine to allow me to see. A crimson gown lay folded in the box. The top portion formed a bow shape, the ruffled straps falling just below the shoulder.

"Tell her I said thanks," I said with a smile.

"She'll be happy to hear you liked it." Ashton rested his hand on my head. "I need to get ready myself, but I'll pick you up later." He nudged me forward, Captain coming along with me. "Till then, Ally-gator."

The door squeaked closed behind me as I stepped across the room to my bed. I pat Captain on the head.

Squeak!

Straightening, I switched to Bolt vision. He sat on my desk, watching Captain and me. The dog huffed at the rat, a low growling itching in his throat.

I calmed the dog with a few strokes. "Bolt is a friend, Captain. Relax."

Taking Bolt, I set him in his usual place on my shoulder. "Gonna need you for my plan tonight, buddy."

The rat twitched his nose in response.

Captain barked behind me. I ignored him and started getting dressed for the party.

Ashton's knocks broke the quiet of the room. "Your royal carriage is here, malady!" he called.

"Come in!"

Ashton entered, finding me finishing up a bun with my hair in the mirror.

"You ready?"

Patting down my dress, I did a double check. "Yup." With Bolt providing me sight, I turned to face Ashton. My brother's face melted into a warm smile. "What?"

"You look nice."

"And you look…" I looked Ashton up and down. A colorfully-patterned button-up hung loosely on his body, sleeves rolled, and bottom tucked into his pants. "Fun."

Ashton's expression quirked, doing a double take on his outfit. "What? What's wrong with it?" He waved the comment off. "Whatever. We've got some time left before we have to go." He walked over toward me before taking Bolt from me. Ashton cupped him in his hands and rubbed the rat. "Why do you have a BL in here?"

"Uh, long story." My sight darkened with the rat in Ashton's hands.

"I think you have time to explain." Ashton plopped himself down on the bed.

"Well, I first caught him in our house, but then I discovered I can see through his eyes *without* touching him. So now I kind of use Bolt when you're not around." My stomach knotted, awaiting how Ashton would react.

"Huh. Vix was spying on us," Ashton mumbled. He lay back on the bed and held the rat up for him to see. "I was wondering why your eyes were darker. Do you know why you've got a connection with *Bolt?*" I could pick up his snicker about the name.

Taking a spot next to Ashton, I flopped back on top of him, crossing our bodies perpendicularly. "No clue." Given how much he kept from me, I would've thought Ashton already knew.

"Fun fact, I use to know the guy that made these things." Ashton poked at the rat. Captain, probably getting jealous, shoved his face into Ashton's free hand. He laughed a bit, petting them both at once. "His name was Blake Landerson."

I shifted, recalling the name from the journal.

"Blake was a pretty cool guy. He used to let me babysit his kids. But he died shortly after figuring out how to make these little cyborg mice." Ashton frowned. "Since rumor has it, he was working for Abel, people around here don't really like him. Or at least, was friends with Abel, the guy not the group. I always thought Blake was nice though." After a sigh, Ashton sat up.

Ashton set Bolt on my face. I jolted upward, grabbing Bolt and wiping my mouth for any loose fur.

"Do you know where his kids are now?" I said.

Ashton turned to me and smiled a little before rubbing his nose. "No clue." He pat me on the knee. "Come on, we've got a party to get to. Leave the BL and Captain. You can just stick by me the whole time."

After a quick drive, we entered the ballroom. Round tables waited for guests, and snack bars lined up against the wall, decorated with plates of little sandwiches and some punch. Guests passed about, initiating different kinds of conversations. Classical music, strung together by musicians on a stage served as the background to the scene. Moonlight glinted through the open ceiling.

"Alrighty, if we should ever split up, which we *won't*." Ashton shot me a warning look. "I'll give you the rundown of people to avoid." We shuffled through the crowd, Ashton pointing out random people quietly to me. "That's Marge, one time she made me cookies and I found cat hair in them. After that, it kind of turned me off to her food. Over there is Casey. He doesn't like me very much and wants my job."

"What's the difference between your job and his?"

"That's a secret." Ashton tapped me on the nose. "Back to the list, that's Jim. One time he gave me a dirty look because I set a remmutant foot on one of the tables at CAIN. Boy, that was a fun story."

"Caleb!" Vix waved at us from a distance. Hanging my arm around Ashton's, we stepped over to meet Vix. He held a glass of wine in one hand, the other in his pocket. "Glad to see you two could make it tonight."

Shooting a finger gun, Ashton smiled. "The party couldn't start until I got here, so I felt obligated."

Vix laughed, though I could tell he didn't find the joke particularly funny. "Come, there's someone I'd like you to meet." Vix showed us to a man standing a few feet away.

A clean suit stretched across the man's intimidating figure. He wore a stiff and well-defined jawline, his crisp hair gelled back. "This is Mr. Titus. Mr. Titus, this is Ashton and-"

"Alison." Titus nodded. I inched closer to my brother, somewhat uncomfortable that he already knew my name. "I've heard so much about the young prodigy." He shook my hand firmly.

Ashton squeezed my arm a bit, eyes fixed on Titus. Leaning down, he whispered to me, "My boss' boss."

"Vix tells me your training is going well." Titus' expression stayed still, making it too hard to read.

"Thank y-"

"I don't think it's the best idea to keep her in CAIN." I resisted the urge to shoot Ashton a dirty look for cutting me off. His gaze darted away from Titus. "Uh, sir," Ashton added quickly. He cleared his throat a bit. His hand rubbed mine. "I just think she's a little young. Maybe in a few years…" His free hand rubbed across his nose.

"Nonsense," Vix said, waving the comment off.

"She's shown herself to be perfectly capable now." Titus didn't flinch at Ashton's proposal. A part of me welled up in pride. "I've got a little girl back home.

I've been trying to convince her to join CAIN. She's got the skill, it's just hard to figure out what's going on in that head of hers."

Ashton's eyes and my sight turned back to Titus at the mention of the girl, somewhat narrowed, but nothing glaring enough to elicit suspicion from the outside. *What are you thinking Ashton?*

"Anyways, we can always discuss it later, in private," Vix offered.

Titus and Ashton locked stares. The latter took a sharp breath, straightening. "Right. O- of course."

Turning the conversation around, Vix clapped his hands, flashing his savior's grin. "Oh, that reminds me. Caleb came up here to talk about a possible promotion, isn't that right?"

Ashton's head bobbed. "Yes, I haven't heard much news about that."

I tapped my foot, growing antsy. I let go of Ashton's arm and focused my sight on getting Bolt to the gala.

Ashton noticed my shift. "Something up?" he asked, sounding more concerned than I expected.

"I'm going to go use the restroom."

"Do you know where it is?"

I nodded before walking off. The three men continued their conversation. I found myself amongst the crowd with Bolt. He crawled up on the ruffles of my dress and onto my shoulder. I maneuvered toward the front door after double-checking that Ashton wasn't watching. As I parted it open, I heard a shout from somewhere in the room.

"Sir, with all respect, no!" Ashton's voice lifted over the crowd.

Glancing back at him, I considered staying to see what had brought the outburst from my brother. But with everyone gone from the CAIN building, I wouldn't get another opportunity like this, especially more so because Ashton was distracted. So, I left.

The CAIN basement chilled my bare arms more than the last time I had been down here.

I passed between the containers, still getting the strange sensation with the last three, but less intense as before. Bolt squeaked, breaking free of my control and starting toward one of the canisters. The hairs on the scruff of his neck pricked upwards as he sniffed the air. I took control again, and taking him in my hand, attempted to calm his nerves.

I stopped at the control panel, taking a closer look. Dragging my hand along the dusty panel top, I moved to the other side. A set of switches designated for each container and marked with their corresponding labels spread across the panel. While I wanted to investigate who the other five experiments were, I had to focus on myself first. *Who was A2?*

My gaze drifted across the basement. I stopped at the spectator's room built into the wall, separated by glass. "Wonder what's in there," I thought aloud.

Crouching, I let Bolt loose. He scampered across the ground, aiming for the containers. Once again, I had to pull him back on focus. Something bothered him about this place. I tried tuning to his other senses in case he heard something I didn't. What was making him so nervous?

Controlling Bolt, I made my way up the wall. I squeezed through after finding a small crack by the corner of the glass created by rubble. The room stretched thin, probably only meant for a handful of people. Monitors lined the panel against the glass, accompanied by a few switches and knobs. I tugged Bolt's round, weighty body up onto the panel. My form waited down below.

The rat's slick nails slid down the slant, knocking me into one of the monitor controls. It flickered on with a static fuzz. Enticed by the glowing light, I paused to watch.

The static confused the image. A woman stood at the panel down below. Her hair twisted in winding, dark braids, light glinting off her glasses.

"Are we almost ready?" The audio screeched awfully. The rat tugged at his ears, but I forced him to stay.

Though gunshots boomed from off camera, the scene seemed uninterrupted.

"Mr. Titus?" The woman stared past the camera, her hands resting on the console.

"You may proceed, Dr. Cleo." I recognized the voice from the man at the gala.

As the doctor messed with the dial, the containers filled with light. Their silhouettes now outlined, the cylinders held children.

The doctor stood at the ready. *"Increasing power now."* Struggling noises came from the containers, along with a few shouts.

"Stop… Stop!" A young boy cried above the others. Squinting, I made his figure out in the C1 container. I was trying hard to make sense of the video. The doctor toggled with several switches. *"No, no, no, NO! Stop! It hurts! I want- I want to forget!"*

The word echoed in the back of my mind.

The woman stiffened. Her hand continued to twist the dial.

"Stop adding power!" Titus called.

The doctor flinched back. Her eyes darted to the rest of the panel as she gasped.

A sharp bolt of electricity burst through the air from the A1 container. It smacked into each container before exploding against the panel.

Blinding light absorbed the camera, and the recording ended.

I breathed heavily and, subconsciously, made Bolt do the same. I didn't know how long I stayed staring at the monitor.

Forget.

Forget.

Forget.

The word hammered in my head. That's what had been stolen from me here. *My memories.* My past. My whole being. Everything I knew before whatever this was. I never wanted the answers so much as now.

Vix had lied to me.

CAIN were the bad guys.

Abel still hid something.

And Ashton… undecided.

Who could I trust now? Could I trust *anyone* at all?

Something buzzed in my pocket. I snapped back to attention, looking over the panel at myself. Scampering down, I moved Bolt back to my shoulder. I dug in my pocket, retrieving my phone. A single text resided on the screen.

Ashton: Hey, where u at?

After taking in my surroundings, I replied:

Went back to my room at CAIN. Wasn't feeling well.

Ashton would probably fall for that. Three dots lined up on the screen. They lasted a moment longer than Ashton usually took to text. Finally,

Ashton: Me neither.

I rubbed my arm, the cold of the room getting to me.

Ashton: Want to meet at the hotel?

Real words proved too hard, so after thinking it over, I sent a thumbs up. I slipped the device back into my pocket, letting out a sigh. As I walked out of the basement, Bolt's gaze lingered on the A2 container.

Knocking on the door, I called, "Ashton?" Captain waited patiently, tail wagging wildly in excitement to greet his owner.

Ashton only took a moment to get to the door. When he saw me, he hugged me a little tighter than usual. I didn't hug back, too stiff and lost in my thoughts. Was this another trick of his to get me to like him?

We split, and Ashton welcomed me in. He shut the door behind him with his foot. "Hey, Ally." He flopped down to sit on the bed. I watched him, sensing something off. We stood staring in silence.

"What's wrong?" we spoke in unison.

We stared a moment longer.

Ashton snorted a laugh. He fell back on the bed, rubbing his face tiredly. "Do you want to go first, or should I?"

"Go ahead," I said quietly. I found myself preferring to stand. Maybe to run just in case something bad were to happen.

"Well…" Ashton's eyes were glued to the ceiling. He huffed through his lips. "After waiting forever before I could go back to Tintview and sleep in my own bed, I finally got that dumb promotion. All the way in the First Colony, away from you, or Kade, or May, or my old home."

"Ashton…" My gut sank, guilt seeping in for thinking so poorly of him all this time. Letting go of my pride, I sat down, not daring to look at my brother. "We could write or something…" Ashton let out a laugh, masking his disdain. "What?"

"It's more than that." My brother's sad chuckle died out. "I wish… I wish I could tell you everything."

"W-what do you mean?"

Ashton raised his hand, rolling it on his wrist. "All the secret stuff about my job. Why it's so frustrating they're sending me away. Why I can't tell you *anything*." His hand fell back over his face. "Look, I didn't mean what I said the other day…" His eyes darted away from me. "About hating being your brother. I just meant…Being the big brother is harder than I thought."

My thoughts kept me silent. Ashton was working for CAIN, the people with the source of my pain in their basement. I couldn't get attached. But I knew I already was.

"Big brothers are supposed to have it all together, be the hero that comes in and makes everything okay at the end of the day, the one who stops all the bad stuff from happening." Ashton clenched his fists, his voice drying up. "At least, that's what I thought. But I'm none of those things."

"Yes, you are." My own voice took me by surprise. I fought so hard against Ashton every single day, but whether he deserved it remained to be seen. He would be moving away, out of Envision City and out of my life. Could I truly handle that?

Ashton chuckled. "Oh, silly George. You have no idea…" Ashton turned his head, his judging gaze drilling into me. "So, what about you? Let me guess: You went around CAIN and dug through stuff because that's *you*. I wouldn't be surprised if you went to the basement, going out of your way to disobey me."

I shuffled uncomfortably. "Maybe…"

"Wait, really! I was joking!" Ashton grinned at me in disbelief. "I can't believe you, Ally," he laughed. "So, what did you find down there?"

Ashton's palpable nonchalance made me even more uncomfortable. I shifted on the bed, setting my hands in a position to get up and run quickly if need be. "You're not mad?"

"Nah. I only told you that because I was paid to. Working at CAIN truly is the worst."

Wait, Ashton's not *on board with CAIN?* My confusion spiraled deeper and deeper.

"Well, it was some sort of lab…" How much was I willing to disclose? Especially with Ashton so dubiously calm? I rotated my body to him. "Are you drunk? Why are you being weird?"

"Nope. Just sad." Ashton didn't bother to look at me.

"The basement was weird." I ended it at that. "It's getting late." Rubbing my eyes, I started my rise from the bed.

Ashton stopped me by grabbing my wrist.

"Wait… Will you stay?" His eyes pleaded with me. "They said I've got to be out of here by tomorrow."

I stared at him, my mouth running dry. Exhaustion kept me from arguing. "… Yeah." I sat back on the bed.

Ashton's lips smiled, but his eyes didn't agree. "Thanks, Ally."

20

Lunch Date

Lunch at one.

Ashton had made the deal with me that morning before I left back to CAIN.

I knew exactly what I would do in the meantime.

With my father's journal hidden in my CAIN-branded jacket, I made my way to the library. I moved briskly through the filing cabinets, Bolt providing my sight. Captain would be moving with Ashton, which meant I would have to get used to using Bolt solely for vision.

Selecting out a large amount of information dedicated to Abel, I collected it up into my arms. I dropped it onto one of the tables with a thud.

I knew CAIN stood against me, and soon Ashton's role wouldn't matter. Now I just needed the final piece of the puzzle: Abel.

I threw the journal alongside the Abel files. I didn't know how it connected yet, but I knew Ashton had wanted me to find it for a reason.

Light glinted off a few CDs. Pinching it in the middle, I moved to one of the computers aligned on the wall closest to the door. I slid the disk in. With the mouse, I pressed play.

What appeared was an ugly image of a man tied to a chair. That man glared at the camera, his eyes adjusting to the light. His dirt-colored hair fell over his face in a mess, bags hanging under his eyes. He glared at the camera, shifting his stubbled jaw.

"Detective Abel Skylor. I assume you know why you're here?" Vix's voice came from behind the camera.

"What do you want?"

Recalling the name, my eyes wandered back to the journal.

"Tell us, how has your little investigation been going?"

Scrunching his face, Abel spat at Vix, who stood off camera.

"Rude," Vix said. *"Do you have a family, detective?"*

"None of your business."

"As one of the moving pieces of the government, I believe it is my business. All I have to do to learn that information would be to check with a few sources, and then I would have everything about them. So, if you want to keep that information more private, turn in your

investigation and tell the rest of the police force it was a dead end. You can move on as if the Hidden Dragon Experiment never happened, and your family can live and die happy lives."

Abel coughed, followed by a scoff and a smirk. "*We both know that's impossible at this point. Would've been nice if you gave those kids the same choice.*" The man stared directly at the camera, sending chills down my spine.

"*A few kids are a price I'm willing to pay for the future. Sometimes you have to make tough decisions.*"

Abel yanked at the rope holding him back in his seat, triggered at Vix's words. "*It wasn't your choice to pay that price! You're a psychopath!*" he tried to kick at Vix, unsuccessful. Instead, he kicked the camera. The image tilted, ending with a shattering sound.

I made a dash for the journal as soon as the recording ended. I flipped through the pages, landing on the next portion of the conversation between Hank Caddel and Abel Skylor.

Red began this time, my father's writing. *Abel, you'll never guess what happened to me in the Interval. While testing an invention of mine, I came across a group of visitors.*

Blue, Abel came back. *What are you talking about? That's impossible. Blake is the only one who can enter the Interval.*

Hank wrote, *He* used *to be, but he's not the only one with the gene anymore. The visitors were children, two of them able to walk the Interval, while the others were tugged along in a red wagon. Not only does that mean my experiment worked, but the Interval is more complicated than I thought. It is a mess of time and space, and there is no predicting where you will land in it.*

Abel. *Hank, you idiot, that's exactly why you have to* stop *using it. You're going to ruin everything! Why won't you listen to me!*

Hank. *I met my granddaughter, Abel.*

Abel. *What did she tell you?*

Hank. *Nothing. She's as stuck up about the rules as you are.*

Abel's blue ended with, *Good kid. Even she gets that you're not supposed to mess with this stuff.*

Thinking things over, I closed the book. The fortune cookie papers sat in my pocket as I ran my fingers through them. I wasn't clear about the meaning of *You're just like your father.* What had he done?

My eyes moved over to the folders, giving rise to an idea.

Thumbing through a folder, I smiled at my findings. Everything they had ever found on the detective was conveniently laid out for me. Including a list of all his past addresses, from where he lived to where he worked. Dated pictures had been taken, each one as an update to the one prior. Pen scrawled along the back of each picture three things: the date on which the picture was taken, the picture's address, and how the place related to Abel Skylor.

A picture of a burnt police department, labeled as his workplace. A quiet suburban home, labeled as his brother's home. Over the years, CAIN had built quite a portfolio on the detective. Picking three images of the same apartment, I laid them out chronologically.

Bolt spun to watch my back. Out the library door, I could see a handful of agents passing through the halls, getting ready to start the work day. Due to time constraints, I hurriedly shuffled the pages back into their proper places. With fewer things to clean up, a quicker escape could be made if need be.

Leaning my palms on the table, I examined the three photos more closely. I noted that Abel's past residency, as it had been labeled, was in Serendipity Shores. The first, taken seven years ago, pictured the curtains encasing the window. Just through the small crack in them, I could make out a cork board, decorated with strings, photos, and sticky notes.

The second photo had dropped all personality compared to the first, empty and ready for someone to move in. Five years ago.

In the third, a whole new collection of things filled the space, and the curtains opened in a homely welcome. Three years ago.

Abel had probably moved after discovering CAIN had their eyes on him. Someone new had moved in since. Maybe the new people had no clue about Abel, but a lead was a lead. Sliding the first two photos back in the folder, I used Bolt to double-check no one was watching. With the third, I folded it up and slipped it into my pocket.

Briskly leaving the library, gears churned in my head with a plan. I would have to let Vix know I was leaving to avoid suspicion.

"Come in," followed my knock on my boss' office door. After moving Bolt to my jacket pocket, I pushed open the door and entered. Since my discovery last night, my view of this room fixed with a whole new light. It was no longer the welcoming space full of potential when I had joined, but rather a mask, a beautiful rose meant to entice people in before revealing its thorns.

Vix sat at his desk, looking over paperwork and marking things here and there. Glancing up, he grinned at me, which seemed to suggest: *Trust me. I'm your friend.* Now knowing the truth, it just sickened my stomach with uncertainty. "Good morning, Alison."

"Morning." Uncomfortably, I sat on the chair.

Still writing several notes on paper, he tried starting a conversation. "You didn't turn in last night. I assume you were with Ashton?"

I nodded.

"He told you about his promotion then? I'm sorry your brother had to go, Alison, but it's for the best. He'll be a great help to the First Colony Branch. And he can always come and visit you."

Again, I nodded, which was nothing more than an

automatic, almost lifeless response. *Ashton.* He had left me to help *CAIN.* After digging for every excuse to make him out to be the bad guy, I didn't want to believe it. Even after it was fairly clear he truly was. He was my brother. I hoped he would never do anything to hurt me, but…

"So, you came to see me? What's up?" Vix finally released the pen, straightening in his chair. I stared up at him, taking in his large stature.

He could easily kill me if he wanted to.

"I was just wondering… Could I borrow some money?" How dumb I must've sounded.

"Sure. What for?" *Well, that was easy.* Now came the part I hadn't prepared for. The lie.

"I need bus money." All good lies were based on truths. "I figured it'd be easier to get around town that way. I need to meet Ashton for lunch later, too." Part of me wondered if I should've dropped that last part.

After digging through a drawer, Vix handed me a small stack of $20's, far more than I needed. "The last hurrah before he goes. Sweet. Here you are, Alison."

I collected it and slid it into my free coat pocket. "Thanks." Rising from my seat, I started toward the door.

Vix cleared his throat. "One more thing."

"Yes?"

"Might I ask where you two are having lunch?"

"Just the diner downtown. Why?" My hands began to fidget.

"No reason. Just curious. You can go now."

With a nod, I continued down my path out the door.

After paying, I picked out my spot on the bus. Shifting in my uncomfortable seat, I waited for the other passengers to board. Bolt curled up tighter in my pocket. I ended up squished against the window by some stranger. Letting out a sigh, I leaned my head in my palm, staring outward at the gray sky. I didn't know whether or not this trip would even lead me to Abel, but I needed to see for myself.

I frowned, still waiting for the bus to move. Pulling out my phone, I checked the time. The bus was supposed to leave at one, which wouldn't be long from now.

I stared at the number, frowning.

I had used lunch with Ashton as an excuse to get money, but I hadn't considered how soon our meeting time would come. I maneuvered Bolt and slid him onto the narrow ledge of the window. The doors still hung open. I could go have lunch with Ashton and try this again later. I had no clue when the next time I'd see him would be.

Putting my phone and Bolt back in my pockets, I shook my head. *Sorry, Ashton. Next time. I need to find Abel.*

The bus started up with an ugly chug and stopped with a harsh screech.

In an awkward file, people stepped off. I took a deep breath while climbing out into the cold. Something buzzed in my pocket. Fishing it out, I found a phone call waiting for me.

The caller ID: *Ashton.* I had no clue how to explain or get away with my plan. So, I didn't.

Pressing decline, I moved toward a map of the town laid out by the bus stop. Spotting the street I needed, I snapped a quick picture and started down the sidewalk, scanning over the surrounding buildings.

Finally, I came up to the run-down building that housed the apartment. Taking the photograph, I double-checked the number. *587. All the way on the fifth floor.*

Before allowing Bolt up, I inched toward the wall of the building. Clinging onto the rough brick, he pulled himself around the building and up along the fire escape.

Without Bolt at my side, I was leaving myself out in the open for any CAIN or Abel agents to attack me, but I tried to stay assured. Neither side knew what I was doing. I would be fine.

Gripped in his teeth, Bolt had a small note I had written for the occupant. *Meet me at the hotel on 6th street in Envision City at 6 pm. Come alone.* Hopefully, it sounded ominous enough to make me sound like a real threat. I likely wouldn't win if someone did ignore the last part and brought a good handful of Abel men. My plan had been structured on a lot of assumptions, but if it worked, it would be worth it.

Finding an open window, Bolt squeezed himself

inside. He broke free of my control, caught off guard by the smells in the kitchen. I allowed him a small corn puff he had found deep under a cabinet. Though gross, I had to remind myself my partner was a *rat*. After, I pulled him from his fixation and back on track.

The home was vacant. A couch posed for a living room divided off with a half wall and a fridge. Down the hall were probably a bed and bath. Lint and dust could be seen against the rays of light pouring in from the window.

Scampering up a stool, Bolt stretched his sacklike body across to the counter. The rat would've preferred to hunt for food in the cupboards, but something on the fridge caught my attention. Two photos, both with a familiar face and slapped on with colorful magnets.

A voice down the hall caused Bolt's ear to twitch, but I ignored it, my gaze fixed on the images on the fridge.

This was definitely not a coincidence.

Click. My eyes darted to the door handle as it began to turn. On reflex, Bolt took off toward the window. He passed into the tight living room when I reminded him of the note. The door creaked open with a cheery voice.

"So then, I told him that that was the worst idea I'd ever heard. You should've been there…"

Dropping the note on the coffee table, the rat bolted up onto the windowsill. *Her* figure filled the doorway, distracted by a phone call pressed to her ear.

"Yeah, so then he laughed so hard milk came out of his nose, and Felix thought he was absolutely bonkers…"

My pocket buzzed again. I jumped with a start, knocking Bolt off course. Shaking myself, I remembered my body waiting all the way on the ground. Nobody above could hear my ringtone. Bolt made it out clumsily, sliding down and landing harshly on the fire escape. He ruffled his fur before scurrying down to meet me.

Mission successful, if I did say so myself.

Once Bolt reunited with me, I moved him to my shoulder so I could check my phone. Another missed call from my brother. I walked away from the building, flicking the device off. *I've got something a little more important than lunch, Ashton.* All I had to do now was get back to the city and wait.

I scanned over the hotel next to me. Just last night, I had been here with Ashton. Now he was off on the road across the nation. I had picked the spot as a meeting place because I knew how to walk there. Now it just filled me with discomfort and memories of my brother. Had I made the right choice to leave him?

I nodded to myself. *Yes. He wasn't going to give me the straight truth, so I must get it myself. That's what he gets.*

I had packed a bag in preparation. It held the

journal, water, and anything else I might need, plus my electric bo staff strapped to my back, which stuck out like a sore thumb.

Scanning over the shuffle of people going in and out of the hotel, I tried to pick out the woman from the apartment.

Why would *May* of all people be living in Abel's old apartment? She worked for CAIN, so I doubted she was oblivious to the fact that it had been the man's old home. If it came down to it, I doubted I could bring myself to fight her.

I tugged my coat tighter around myself. Anxiety tugged at my chest. *Why was she taking so long? Am I just imagining the extensive wait?*

I started down the sidewalk. She had possibly gone to the wrong entrance. My tromping footsteps accompanied another pair. I stopped. The steps still approached, growing louder and louder. I spun on my heels.

Someone grabbed me from behind, and something covered my mouth. I attempted a scream, black pouring in from the corners of my vision. I dug my fingernails into my attacker's arm. Unable to keep focus, my vision flickered on and off. On and off.

Yet still, I attempted to free myself. Another figure approached me, along with hazy audio. My consciousness drained. Something scratchy and tight was thrown over my head.

Blackout.

21

Abel

The bag yanked from my head. Groggily, I came to, mind spinning and vision void.

"Wake up!"

I winced at the loud shouting. I squeezed my eyes shut and reopened them as if that would return my sight. I tried to take in as much as I could without one of my senses. I was sitting, tied to a chair. Kicking a little, I found something in front of me. From somewhere off, I could hear a fan.

Taking a shot in the dark, I attempted to reach out to Bolt. He sat next to me, locked in a small cage on the table (the thing I had felt in front of me). His eyes lit up the room. A bright lamp pointed directly at me, an attempt to blind me. Whoever had kidnapped me didn't know much about me. Bolt spun in the cage, allowing me to see those in front of me.

An older boy and girl, both with curly red hair and similar faces. They couldn't have been older than 20. The girl stood straight up, arms crossed and a black bow tying her hair back. A dirty look rested on her face, so faint that if she were passing someone by on the street, they might think the sun was merely in her eyes. Her brother supported himself on his palms, glaring at me through his shaggy mess of hair.

"Who are you?" the boy barked.

I allowed myself to be looser owing to the impression they gave on account of their age and immaturity. "You kidnapped me, and you don't even know who I am? That's rude."

"We didn't kidnap you." The girl crossed her arms, her voice carrying a softer yet more venomous tone. "We just picked a more secure meeting place."

"If you wanted it to be more secure, then you shouldn't have let a BL in here. CAIN is recording everything as we speak." I had no clue whether my words held truth, but that did seem to be the case.

Leaning into my face, the boy grinned. "Ha! You think! BLs and most other CAIN technology are disabled in this room. Don't think Vix or anyone else is coming to save you for one second."

With the two just as overconfident as I was, it might be easier to escape than I thought. "Is this Abel or not? I want to talk to your boss."

The door flew open. "What's going on here!" May entered, her eyes shifting between each of us in turn. Her gaze finally landed on me. I watched her with a confused gaze. So, she did know about this? *What…*

"Ally? You're the one who left the note?"

"What are you doing with Abel?" I shifted into a glare, remembering I wasn't here to make friends. Just to gain answers.

May sighed, shaking her head. "Felix, Dylan, you can let her go. She's Ashton's baby sister." I wasn't fond of the title.

The other girl rolled her eyes. The siblings untied me. Trying to make sense of what was going on, I rubbed my wrists. "I want an explanation."

"Fair enough." May waved the two out of the room. "Sorry. That was Felicity and Dylan. They're, uh, friends." Pacing, she side glanced at me. "You figured us out quick, huh?"

"Are you with Abel or CAIN? What's really going on here?"

May stopped. Her eyes moved to Bolt, uncomfortable. Rubbing her arms, she turned toward the door. "Walk and talk with me. I'm gonna grab some tea. It'll take a minute to explain everything to you."

Hesitantly, I rose from my seat. I started toward the door before I realized I probably wouldn't be allowed to take Bolt.

May caught onto my waiting. "You can hold my hand if you'd like. Ashton told me about your abilities."

Wonder what else Ashton told you. He doesn't tell me anything. I took May's hand reluctantly, and she led me out of the room.

The door opened into a dusty warehouse. I spotted the large fan I had heard earlier, far above our heads, and bolted to the vents. Felix and Dylan worked on something on the other side of the space, and a few others scattered about, either training or just talking. Retired cars were stacked against the blurry transparent wall outside. The scent of gasoline drifted through the air. A rusty staircase zigzagged up into a watching position.

May led me to a table with a small drink stand, complete with a coffee maker, random flavor packets, and thin stir straws. A toaster also sat at the end, noteworthy due to the sticky note with a scrawled smiley face slapped on it. As she picked out a tea bag, she let go of my hand.

"So," May began. "How should we go about this?"

"Why are you here? What is Abel? Why doesn't CAIN want anyone to know about you guys?"

"I thought Ashton would be the one to break it to you but seems he missed his opportunity. We're on Abel's side. Kade, Ashton, and I." The hot water machine steamed and whirred. "Abel wants to... expose CAIN for what they really are."

"Which is?"

May stirred a straw through her tea. "Years ago, they carried out an experiment on a collection of children, Dragon children, to see if they could somehow harness their powers and use them for… something." She punctuated the sentence with a snort. "I'm not exactly sure what. Vix claims it would be a great way to improve modern medicine. But there's certainly some deeper motive." The stirring stopped. She continued with a sharp breath. "You were one of those kids. That's how I recognized you when we first met."

Hearing it out loud made my hands shake. "That's where Abel Skylor comes in," I said. "He wanted to figure out what happened to the kids, so he formed the organization. Where is he? Can I meet him?"

May took my hand, allowing me to see her shake her head. "Abel was- He was murdered before the group Abel was formed. *I* created Abel." Her voice shook at the mention of the man's death. She held my hand tighter.

"What?"

"Yeah… Abel Skylor was my uncle."

My eyes grew wide. "What? How did you manage to hide it from CAIN for so long?"

"By not doing anything to get myself noticed. I'm kind of in the middle of the social ladder when it comes to CAIN. But Ashton and Kade have a bit more freedom to work themselves up, so that's how we get most of our intel." After taking a loud slurp of her tea, she set it down with a soft *clink*. "There were also five other kids in the experiment, but they-"

An echoing crash interrupted May's sentence. Her head turned, finding the redheads standing over a crashed mess of wood and paper.

"Great job, *Dylan!* You just broke the conspiracy board!"

"Well, *Felix,* you were the one who insisted that it was crooked!"

May turned back to me, her eyes squinted in an awkward smile. "Excuse me, I've got to go deal with that." She shook her head before stranding me in the dark.

I stood there, mulling over everything that had been said so far. Sixteen years of my life, set fire to by CAIN. Ashton missed that time as much as I did.

"Alrighty." May let out a breath as she returned. "I think I've just about got that figured out." The tips of her fingers brushed against mine, both of our hands on the table. She glanced at the dark shadows outside the window. "It's getting late, and I'm sure you're tired after hearing all that."

"Right." I turned to search for the door, only to remember I couldn't control my view as easily from a human perspective. "What city are we in?"

"Envision. But I'm not sure going back to CAIN is the best option. I'd offer you a spot in my apartment, but I'm not sure there's enough room or protection. Um…" May's eyes swept over the warehouse until she landed on a door. "Maybe you could sleep here. We have a cot set up in one of the big closets for when people need to stay the night."

"Why are you so worried about protection? Vix doesn't even know I'm here. It would be less suspicious to go back."

"I'm sure he suspects something. You brought a BL with you and didn't even take any precautions. To be honest, he probably knows I'm with Abel too." May gripped my hand passive-aggressively and took a deep breath. She loosened a little before shaking it off. "Stress isn't good for the baby," she laughed, trying to bring herself back up.

I frowned at my mistake.

May led me to the guest room and sat me down on the cot. "We always keep a two-person patrol, so you can ask them if you need anything. I've got to go back to my apartment and will meet you again in the morning. We can discuss what we should do next then." She combed her fingers through my hair before turning to leave.

"Wait." I held onto her, keeping in touch with vision. "How will I see when you're gone? Is there a way I can keep the rat?"

May's head tilted with a thought. "I think I can move the disabling device in here. It's just a small little box you attach to the wall that works in a small radius. Hang on." Her fingers slipped from mine, and she left.

I sat in the dark until she returned. My thoughts were scattered in all directions.

"Here you are." I felt something warm in my hands as the room lit up. Bolt did a spin, then began a crawl up my arm. May smiled at me, with her hands resting on her stomach.

"Thanks." My voice came out softer than I expected.

"No problem." May drifted toward the door of the room to the left of the bed. Her hand hovered over the light switch. "Good night, Ally."

"Good night." The lights went out.

I stared up at the ceiling after arranging myself into the thin blankets. Bolt curled up close to my neck. With a sigh, I scratched his fur, too scared to turn on my side. I dug through my backpack for water. The familiar crinkle of a fortune cookie wrapper caught my attention.

This one only had one word. *Check.*

What does that mean?

Like a broken record, my mind relayed all the information over to me, again and again. Vix and CAIN had taken so much from so many people. Vix had stolen the lives of not just me, but the five other kids wrapped up in the experiment, Ashton and my history, and May's uncle. Not to mention the safety of everyone who had joined Abel. *How could one man steal so much from so many? Something must be done. He, along with the rest of CAIN, needs to be stopped.*

I couldn't wait until tomorrow to figure out a plan. Who knew how much Vix could take between the night and the morning dawn?

I decided to do something about it.

I was going to kill Vix.

22

Exhaustion

Last night...

As the night of the gala had set in and people flowed out, Vix grew tired. He would've loved for his wife to come and keep him company, but the party rules only allowed CAIN members. After collecting his coat and things, Vix imagined his warm bed, welcoming him to sleep. The tip of his shoe had passed the doorframe when his plans were interrupted.

"Vix!"

Internally groaning, Vix turned with his trademark grin plastered to his face. Titus approached him, not even a hint of a smile. That meant business, which, in turn, meant a longer wait before Vix could melt into his pillows. "Yes, sir?"

Titus pulled himself into his coat, moving past Vix and out the door. "I parked some ways down, so walk with me while I talk to you."

Vix nodded, too tired to protest. *Just keep your head up.*

The starry sky all blurred in Vix's worn-out vision. The coldness nipped at his nose, only increasing his eagerness to leave. What was so important that Titus needed to talk about it *right now?*

"That Caleb is something else, huh?" Titus didn't bother a look at Vix.

"I guess… You brought me out here to discuss Ashton?"

Titus shoved his hands in his pockets, searching for his car. "He and the girl disappeared rather quickly, don't you think?"

"They were probably both tired." Vix could relate.

"Don't be naïve, Vix." Titus' voice grew stern. "It's not that Caleb's patient. He's *reluctant.* He doesn't want her with us." As they reached the car, Titus' steps slowed down. He moved around to the other side of the sidewalk. Setting his hand on the roof, he moved to open the driver seat door. "Hopefully, that nonsense will be over with after tonight. You've got to keep a tighter grip on that girl." He left Vix standing on the sidewalk. After starting up the vehicle, Titus rolled down the windows. "Someday, I'll get tired of cleaning up your messes. Where will that leave you?" Wheels turned, and Titus drove off.

Vix watched after his boss, frowning. He

tightened his fists, shutting his eyes. With a sigh, he gave up. After rubbing his hand over his face, he turned to walk all the way back to his own car.

Just keep your head up.

Titus won't dare *doubt me again.*

Ashton watched Ally disappear into the crowd. This gala was going to be a lot harder for him with her gone. This meant that he would have to talk about the stuff he'd been avoiding.

"Ashton, you've served us a long time." Titus pretended to count thoughtfully. "Going on five years, right?"

Lingering on Ally, Ashton nodded along. "Yeah, something like that…"

"With this promotion, Vix and I were hoping to move you to bigger, better things than our current project."

"About time you moved up to the First Colony, wouldn't you say?" Vix's words drew the young man's attention.

"What?"

"How would you like to work at the capital? It won't be too big of a change from now."

With rising disquietude, Ashton raised an eyebrow. Taking a deep breath, he calmed himself. "And what about Ally?"

Titus rose his head above the crowd, searching

for her. "Well, with A2 gone, I believe we have a bit more freedom to talk. Truth be told, you're moving a little slow with her, part of why we're reassigning you. Another agent can continue her training. Maybe that Casey kid. He seems to know what he's doing."

Eyes wide, Ashton took a step back. "Sir, with all respect, no!" Titus shot him a dirty look, while Vix gestured for Ashton to calm down.

"Caleb, I don't think you know what a great opportunity you're being given by us." Vix side glanced at Titus, clearly trying to appease the man.

Titus looked over Ashton. "She's your sister, right?" Titus scoffed. Ashton frowned, avoiding eye contact. "Cute. But it's time you woke up and remembered what we're trying to do."

"Yes, sir," Ashton said, trying to keep his professional form.

"Excellent. Then tomorrow, you'll pack up and be on your way in the afternoon. It's a long drive, and you'll probably be too cheap to get a train." Titus slipped his hands into his pockets, looking down at Ashton.

"Can I ask what'll happen to her?" When Ashton had first heard of the gala, he couldn't put his finger on it, but he suspected it would go something like this.

"I'm afraid that's confidential information."

Nodding, Ashton fiddled with the cuffs of his sleeves. "Well, then, if that's the end of it, I'll be going now, gentlemen." A title the two did not deserve. As he turned to go, he glanced back. "By the way, that daughter

back home you mentioned? That wouldn't happen to be-
"

"Confidential, Mr. Caleb." Titus glared.

"Right." Ashton made his way out of the gala. "Just like everything else."

"Mr. Caleb." Titus' voice snapped Ashton's steps to a stop. "Your brother gave his life for this company. You better be willing to do the same."

Tonight...

The road lines mixed together in a hazy gray. Ashton went through the motions of driving, his body running down. In an attempt to keep himself awake, he had turned the radio on blast an hour ago, but even that was starting to fail. All routes across the country traveled underground due to the constant remmutant attacks, which meant he didn't even have the stars to keep him company. With nothing else to entertain his thoughts, all he could do was replay the events of last night. When Titus had told Ashton he would have to leave everything he knew and loved if he were to keep his cover.

Captain and the kid's few bags of belongings had been shoved into the passenger side. The dog spun around sometimes, occasionally rubbing up to his owner for petting. Ashton had stopped paying attention to Captain after a while.

Ashton's hands grew sweaty, gripping the wheel too tight. To add to the list of things stressing him out,

Ally hadn't met him for lunch. She hadn't even answered his calls. His first assumption had been that something was wrong. But CAIN was already getting too suspicious. At the dinner, Ashton had caught a pair of CAIN agents watching him. Somehow, they had found out about the lunch plans. So, Ashton got up and left.

For a moment, Ashton's gaze shifted to a slip of folded paper shoved in the middle panel of the car. "Why didn't you come to lunch, Ally?" he let out wistfully. When writing the note, it had filled him with so much dread. The thought of her reading everything, knowing everything he had been too scared to tell her, including what *really* happened seven years ago. And now he knew she would never be able to read it.

Ashton smacked his palm against his cheek, trying to keep the road lines straight.

Shuffling came from the passenger side. Ashton stole a look, catching Captain digging through his things. With one hand on the steering, Ashton tried to shoo the dog out of his bag. "No, boy. No. Come on, I'm trying to drive." He glanced back through the windshield, just to double-check he was still on the right side of the road.

Captain gave up, lying down in the seat. A sigh escaped the tired kid. Ashton flicked on the turn signal, moving to the right lane. He pulled off onto an exit, eyes growing heavy.

"Alright. I'll stop for the night."

With a groan, Ashton tossed his bags on the ground of his hotel room. He expected to pass out the moment his head hit the pillow. Nestling up in the blankets, he shut his eyes but couldn't sleep. Too much shook his mind. He wished he could just shut his thoughts off and deal with those problems tomorrow, but his mind would not allow it. He buried his face in the pillow. Maybe suffocating his thoughts would make them shut up.

If they don't kill her, they'll brainwash her, the kid's mind teased. *By the time you go back, she won't even recognize you.*

A quick, repeated knock came on the door. Ashton forced himself up from the bed. He was too drained to realize he wasn't wearing any pants. Captain added to the din, barking at the possible intruder. Ashton waved off the dog, an unsuccessful attempt to get him to stop.

The door swung open. Ashton's eyes widened at the sight.

"Ally? What are you doing here!" Ashton reached out to hug her, but she took some steps back.

"Ashton." She pushed passed him into the room, her gaze dark. "I know everything."

Ashton frowned, his gut churning with uncertainty. "…You do?"

"Yes. Vix told me." She spun around to face him. Hatred like fire consumed her eyes and being. "He let me in on every lie, trick, and deceitful thing you've ever said to me."

She jabbed him in the chest, knocking him back onto the floor. Ashton shook his head. "Ally, wait, I can explain-"

"You're too late. He even told me what you did. The biggest lie you ever told." She knelt down, her lips nearly against his ear. In a sinister whisper, she said, *"Who you are."*

Ashton shot awake with a jolt. His breath hitched as he attempted to regain himself. He squeezed his eyes shut. *It was only a dream. But it won't always be.* He gripped the sheets.

In a huff of emotions, Ashton threw the blankets off himself and got to his feet. After he turned on the light, Captain shook himself awake. Curious, he stared up at Ashton.

Water rushed from the bathroom tap. Ashton threw it back at his own face, waking himself up the rest of the way. Tugging his pants back on, he called his dog. "Come on, boy. We're leaving."

Swiftly packing up his things, Ashton rushed downstairs to check out of the hotel. He and the dog climbed back into the frost-bitten car. The engine chugged with the key turn. The car pulled out and back on the road, the opposite way they had come from.

Ashton was determined to protect Ally, no matter what. He just hoped she could hold out until then.

23

Freedom

Darkness acted as my accomplice.

I gathered up my jacket and Bolt. Peering around the doorframe, I made out two figures. One's shadows reflected onto the glass roof while the second paced back and forth along the ground. The warehouse sat still, save the footsteps and the air vent. The clock struck 9:00. My plan laid out before me, I was ready.

Scanning over my options, I decided the best way out would be through the vent. Even if I were spotted, it would only be by the watchman on the outside. Bolt's gaze traveled along the vent, following the boxy tube to its place in my room, across the roof, and down, dropping into the ground. I edged the door open with my foot.

Crouching, I stepped toward the vent grate, built into the ground. The lid easily slid off. Raising it, I squeezed myself in. A tight fit, but I knew it'd grow wider by the time I worked my way up. I set the lid over my head and snuck off.

Faint red light filled the space, offered by the camera on the rat's back. I crawled forward before the vent opened up above my head. I came to stand at my full height. Setting my rubber bottom shoes on either side of the vent, I climbed up.

My hand found the ledge of the vent. I hoisted myself up, Bolt giving a short squeak. With a simple finger to my lips, I shushed him. I tread lightly through the maze of the vent on hands and knees. A chill ran through my spine with the cold manufactured air mixed with the autumn night.

After a long crawl, where I solely relied on my memory to tell where I was going, I found an opening to the outside.

The small opening compromised my sight. Leaning down, I allowed Bolt out for surveillance. The watchman remained sitting on the roof, overlooking the junkyard that surrounded the warehouse. I called Bolt back and attempted to open the grate with my bare hands, but it didn't budge. I hadn't accounted for the possibility of screws on the outer vents. With the roll of my eyes, I decided that enough was enough and that I would abandon the secrecy. Abel would be watching for anyone who wanted to break in, not *out*. They might let me go if I ran fast enough and kept my identity a secret.

Turning on my back, I coiled up my knees. My

legs sprung out into a hard kick. A thundering shook through the ventilation system. *They definitely heard that.* Taking a deep breath, I kicked again, and again. Each time it did budge slightly, but not enough.

"Did you hear that?"

"Watch out!"

Heart racing, I gave all that I could muster into a horse kick. It budged, screws ripping from their spots and clanging against the wall of the building. With one last kick, the grate came off. Pumping my fist, I quietly cheered.

Footsteps pounded on the roof of the building. I peered over the side, staring down at the drop below. *Now or never.* Holding my breath, I pushed off.

My insides yanked up as if I would throw up. I aimed for a patch of dirt. Bending my knees, I made an impact. It sent a twang through me, adrenaline pounding in my ear drums. Taking a step, I immediately fell over. Bolt kept himself safely tucked in my pocket. Voices went on in the background. Shaking off the falling sensation, I jumped back to my feet and took off.

Dirt kicked up under my shoes. I dodged past piles of miscellaneous rusty scraps and smokey tires. A gunshot struck near me, dirt exploding upwards. A warning shot, as it was too far for someone to have been aiming for me. I ducked around a trash heap with a skid. The gate lay several yards away. With reckless abandon, I darted for it. I yanked myself up and over, without even checking if it was electrical. My foot slipped from the metal, knocking me to the ground. Air left my body.

I lay there, desperately pleading with myself to get back up. I had no clue whether or not Abel would still chase after me.

Great job, Ally. You made both CAIN and Abel mad at you.

Once oxygen returned to my lungs, my body chuckled. I sat up with a groan, wobbling to my feet like a newborn deer. Stepping backward, I searched for anyone coming after me. The quiet air heightened my senses. Someone was going to come out of nowhere, I just knew it.

When that didn't happen, I allowed myself to relax. Turning on my heels, I ran toward the nearest street and down the sidewalk. I had no clue how to even get to CAIN from here, but a combination of resolve and desperation pumped my veins.

When my body gave out, I could barely see the glowing lights of the Envision. The city felt awake and breathing, even at night. It proved more comforting than the previous silence. I slowed to a walk, huffing. I would need all my energy if I was to go up against Vix. Thankfully, a bus sign caught my eye. A quick ride wouldn't cost too much anyways.

I paid eagerly and took a spot. As I waited, I recounted my plan over to myself. I would grab a weapon from the training room and find Vix in his office. I would have to improvise from there, but soon, the deed would be done, and everything would be over. He could hurt no one else after tonight.

I dug through my backpack, finding the journal to keep me company. It opened with the last entry of the book.

The red, my father, began. *I'm afraid this conversation will have to come to an end. After October 31st, eight years from my time, this journal goes missing. If you have anything left to say, Skylor, do it now.*

Abel picked it up in blue ink. *Hank, you moron! You write a whole book on the rules you've set yourself, and you've broken every single one I can think of. I'm supposed to be dead. You are supposed to be dead. And yet here you are, having conversations with your granddaughter while the rest of the world burns. I can think of several people who need you a thousand times more than she does. Your kids. Your wife. If you don't stop this, you are going to lose everything you've been fighting so hard to keep. You saved my life. I don't know whether to thank you or hate you for it. I know you want me to just tell you everything that's going to happen to you and CAIN. That's the only reason why you would ever allow me to write in one of your precious journals. But here's the thing: I have no clue what happened to you. I have no clue what's going to happen with any of this. Get over it. You're so desperate, we both know what you're thinking. But if you don't get the answers from me, please don't go see for yourself. Reality isn't meant to bend that way.*

But if you do, say hi to May for me. Please. Just

make sure she's alright.

Hank wrote back: *You* could *say hi yourself.*

Abel ended with, *I hope you burn just like I did.*

Whatever argument had taken place between the past and future, the ending hadn't been a happy one. Where did my father and Abel go after this?

As we pulled toward the CAIN building, I requested off.

I found myself staring up at the facility. The guards standing at the front eyed me strangely. Forcing a reserved smile, I moved past them and into the building. Shoving my hands in my pockets, I made my way up the stairs.

As I walked briskly toward the training hall, I passed my room. The place that had once been my home had now turned into a paranoia-inducing sight. It had just been a cage, a way to keep me under Vix's thumb.

Once Vix was dead, I'd be free.

I crossed into the training room. The wall of weapons stood over me, judging my choice. I had no clue how to use half the items. Ashton had only shown me a few things, and though most of my skill belonged to the electric bo staff, it couldn't take a life efficiently. Forcing myself to hurry up and decided, I picked out a knife, decorated with a simple red leather handle. I stared into my own reflection, taking in what I was about to do. I nodded to myself. Bolt stared up at me curiously.

I pat the pocket the rat lay in. "Stay close, buddy."

Each step to Vix's office took an eternity and yet seemed too quick. A thousand panic signals went off in my head, but I pushed them away. Now was not the time to be indecisive.

Before I could question whether or not I should, my hands moved to knock on the office doors.

"Come in," came Vix.

Taking a deep breath, I entered.

The devil in the skin of man glanced up at me, smiling tiredly. Seemed he had run out of grins to fool me with. "Evening, Alison."

I nodded, dagger behind my back. Breaking the eerie quiet, Vix gave a yawn. In turn, I yawned too, shaking off my sleepiness. *Stay focused. He's not your friend. Just think of all he's done to you.*

When I still said nothing, Vix looked up from his work. He narrowed his eyes at me before his gaze passed to my hand behind my back. "What's up?"

My throat caught dry. My hands shook. *Speak! Say something!* Do *something!* With eyes shut and my blood full of emergency, I plunged the dagger forward.

My heart stopped.

When I dare open my eyes, Vix rose to his feet, tightening his grip on my wrist. He clicked his tongue, stepping from around his desk. I stumbled back, unable to break free of him. I knocked into the chair opposite his. It fell over with a screech and thud. Bolt tucked deeper into the pocket, impairing my sight.

"I'm disappointed in you," Vix said, his smile

dropping. He twisted my hand back, forcing me to drop the knife. With my free hand, I attempted to pry him off. "You lied to me and your own brother. You never went to lunch with him. My spies tell me you left the poor kid waiting there, heartbroken." The last word came like spit, hitting my cheek.

Vix's fist caught my stomach in a punch. I doubled over with a harsh cough. "Why? I assume you were stuck on your own little investigation about the basement, and you finally decided you wanted to know more about Abel."

I threw my fist forward, desperate to land a punch anywhere. Vix caught my knuckles, twisting them to match the other hand. The hand that had once held the blade started to go numb. Clenching my teeth, I yanked back like a desperate mouse.

"So, you hunt down Abel, thinking you have everything under control. And you're *smart* enough to bring a BL with you so we can see everything. They explain the truth behind every little lie he told you, and now your ego grows unabated because you were *right*. I was the bad guy all along, at least in your eyes."

Vix yanked me forward before jabbing his knee upward into my stomach again. Tears tugged at my eyes. "So you decided you'd be the noble one, the one who *kills* me." Letting go of my wrists, he swept my legs from under me. My back hit the ground, adding to the pain in my chest. "Well. Doesn't sound too noble to me."

Vix rolled me over with his foot. In a move

dictated by abject desperation, I dug my elbows into the ground and crawled away at a snail's pace. He dug his heel into my hip, earning a scream from me. Bending over, he whispered, "But do you know what I'm most disappointed in?" His foot came up, returning a kick to the back of my head. A ringing thundered through my brain, my teeth. My connection with Bolt snapped off.

Darkness circled me like a shark, with no one to rescue me from it.

"You weren't brave enough to do it. I thought I raised you better."

Again, Vix turned me over, just for the fun of kicking me in the gut several more times. I cried, eager to lose my consciousness already. I felt something wet in the back of my throat as I coughed it up. Blood.

"I'm not as cruel as you, Alison." I could feel his breath up against my face. "I'm not going to kill you. You're too precious to me. All I wanted was a better future for this city. For the world. And if that means beating some sense into you, so be it. I hope we can still be friends after this."

I wanted to scream at him but couldn't. Every breath was a struggle.

Grabbing me by the neck, Vix lifted me up. With his vision, I could see my own dirty and broken face. I wanted someone to save me. I wanted somewhere to go if I did live. But there was no one.

I had pushed everyone away.

"You are a very special girl, Alison."

The door threw open. Vix's gaze darted toward it, letting me see who it was. My body trembled.

"Ah, good. You're here." Vix smiled.

"Mr. Vix, have you seen" Ashton's jaw dropped, body switching to a defensive position. His hand went to his hip, only discovering a lack of gun.

Vix tossed me to the side. My hair fell over my face as I winced. My pockets felt empty. Bolt had left me at some point.

"Ashton. I would've thought you'd be across the country by now." Vix's tone shifted back to his welcoming one.

"Vix-"

"I suggest you run along, Mr. Caleb. Wouldn't want Kade or May to end up hurt, would you?"

My breathing hitched, waiting for my brother's response. *Please. Please.*

Footsteps followed the silence, and the door slammed.

"Well." Vix's voice. Fear dug into my heart. "Looks like he chose his friends over you." I squeezed my eyes shut, refusing to believe it. Hot tears singed my cheeks. More steps, then a mechanical click. "Send a handful of agents up here. I have some cleaning up to do." Another click echoed the first.

Vix tossed something in front of my face. In my desperateness, I got a flickering connection of Bolt. He watched me from afar.

Broken as I was, the object in front of me was a

fortune cookie.

The paper read, *Checkmate.*

I felt something stiff against my skull. "Good night, miss Alison." He kicked the back of my head, and I blacked out.

24

Stumbling Through the Dark

A coughing fit erupted in my chest. Something next to me shifted in an alarm. My breath shook, pains in my body springing up and reminding me of my fight with Vix.

I shook at the memory of how miserably I had failed.

The logical thing to do would be to breathe, take in my surroundings, find answers, and devise a new strategy. Drum up a new plan that would fall flat on its face along with me like every other time I had come up with a dumb plan. Seek for answers that were just out of reach and should've never been mine in the first place. Find the layout of my new surroundings that would probably be ripped away from me the second I was alone and replaced with terrifying darkness. Breathe in a breath that would be my last.

I could see, telling me that a living being was placed next to me. My vision proved stiff, stuck facing forward. I sat in a car, a gun positioned uniformly in the man's hands next to me. A CAIN escort.

I drew in a sharp, stiffened breath like the scared, illogical animal I was. My heart drummed with anxiety and fear. Picking up as much as I could with just peripheral vision, gears churned in my mind. The car ride suffocated me, soreness building in my chest. My limited sight aggravated my claustrophobia, much like a broken dream, boxed in and fragmented. The car paused at a red stoplight, a small handful of vehicles filling the lanes. The wait lasted an eternity, my beating heart acting as the timer. A blue-tinted night filled the void of the sky, hypnotic and tiring.

My mind bounced back and forth, teeter-tottering on a choice. Shutting my eyes tight, I chose. I pushed myself into the darkness. I pulled, taking hold of the door handle. Cold air burst in through the open door. The man's hand tried to grab my shirt, but I had jumped from the car before he had the chance. Shouts arose from behind. My heart trumpeted, echoing back and forth in the walls of my mind. I pushed myself, harder and harder.

My feet slapped against concrete. Whether or not I would run into something was at the flip of a coin. My toe stubbed against the sidewalk slab. I stumbled along it, following an invisible path. My whole chest hurt, but I couldn't afford a second's hesitation. With no clue of the destination, I ran. I ran as far as my weak body could take me. I ran for my life.

In a desperate attempt to lose those chasing me, I darted to the side. I ran into bystanders, giving me short glimpses of where I was headed. I had no time to apologize. My cheeks were wet with tears.

I dropped off the sidewalk and into the road. Honks sent shivers through my spine. Thrown off by the sounds and lights and a million signals flooding my nervous system, my pattern turned zigzag across the road.

And then, my legs finally gave out.

My eyes burned, begging for rest. My voice caught in my thought, not daring to alert CAIN where I hid in the open. My foot caught along the ledge to the other side of the street. I smacked down on my chest, hyperventilating. My ribs screamed in agony. With scraped hands, I pushed myself up to my knees.

Forcing myself up, I reached out for a wall. My fingers found the soothing brick surface of a building. Unable to hold my own weight, I leaned up against it. I lay my head back in agony. As much as I needed to rest, I couldn't stay in one place for long. CAIN kept spies everywhere. Despite my instincts, I didn't dare attempt to find Bolt. Even he would rat me out, no matter how much I needed him.

No one could save me now.

Ashton had abandoned me.

I had betrayed Abel.

Vix wanted to use me.

I could trust no one.

Wincing with pain, I edged along the wall, off to pause and think. My whole self yearned for sleep. I shook my head. I couldn't, as warm as the thought sounded. My fingers shook, scraping against the wall, frozen and numbed. Where to now, I had no idea. The overwhelming, infinite, and grotesque void of darkness did no good to give me any succor. My plan to end everything tonight had fallen to pieces before it had started, and it was all my fault.

I couldn't even trust myself.

25

Emergency Number

Ashton forced a shaky grin at the guards at the CAIN entrance. He darted down the sidewalk, and after ensuring he was out of sight, sped up to a run. His car waited around the corner, hidden in night's shadows. Throwing open the door, he quickly took hold of the wheel and started it up. Captain sat up at the suddenness of it all.

Ashton drove down the midnight street, occasionally stealing a glance at the rearview mirror. With one hand, he quickly dialed a number. The ID read *Mother,* a codename come up with years before. "Come on, pick up. Pick up!"

"This is May. Leave a message!"

Before starting the next call, Ashton glanced up at the street. He rolled on through a red light. Two black cars behind him glistened in his mirror. Ashton took a turn at the next opportunity.

Selecting *Marksman,* Ashton held the device up to his ear. *"You've reached Kade. You could leave a voicemail, but I probably won't listen to it. Bye."*

Eager to go faster, Ashton hunched down over the steering wheel. The cars following him grew slowly closer. "Dang it," he muttered, pressing harder on the gas.

Ashton's phone shook in his hand, startling him. He nearly dropped the device in his eagerness to answer. "Kade! Listen-"

"Ashton, it's one in the morning. I thought you were on your way to First. What are you-"

"CAIN knows we're with Abel. They're coming for you and May. Ally's in trouble- I messed up. Kade, I- I can't." Gathering his composure, Ashton took a deep breath. The revving of vehicles behind him caught his attention. "Kade, you've got to run."

"What happened to Ally?" Shuffling came from the other end. Kade's tone became sterner.

"Vix got her. I came back to fix everything, but when I got here, it was too late and I just… froze. I don't know what he plans to do with her, but I can get an idea. I was supposed to protect her. I was supposed to-" A loud snap drew his attention away from the phone. His head darted back to see gunfire from his pursuers. "Shoot."

"What?"

"Just getting shot at by CAIN."

"Where are you?"

"Envision City. Listen, get rid of your phone after this conversation, and go. You'll have to live off the lam or something."

"Alright... Have you heard anything from May?"

A chorus of honks interrupted Ashton's frantic driving. After almost hitting a pedestrian car, he tried to focus more on the road. Captain stumbled in his seat with the shifting gravity. Ashton glared at the CAIN vans. "Come on, you guys don't have a siren or something to warn bystanders?" Pinching the phone up against his ear with his shoulder, Ashton let out a tired sigh. "No, she wouldn't pick up. I tried calling her before you."

Two more black cars poked out from around the corner in a goading fashion. Their headlights met with Ashton's. He dug into the brakes, shifting the car to reverse. His hands glided across the steering wheel, maneuvering back at high speed. He winced at a few trash cans he had hit. He turned a corner, CAIN only coming from one direction now. When he had enough distance between them, he spun the car back around and into forward drive.

The glass shattered at Ashton's side as a bullet hit the mirror. Ashton ducked, stretching his arm over to sit Captain down too.

"I hope she's alright. Keep your head up-"

"Can't at the moment or else I'll get shot."

"We'll get Ally as quick as we can. Ashton... When this is all over, are you going to tell her?"

Ashton's grip tightened on the wheel. Once he realized he was in the wrong lane, he swerved. CAIN headlights flashed in his eyes. He spun the wheel around and turned down another direction. They drove up the highway arching over town. With less direction to go, Ashton knew it would be easier to corner him. Subconsciously, he sped up. "No. Yes. I have no clue. This is a question for a less chaotic time, Kade!" His fingers grew tenser by the second.

"Ashton, just..." His friend stopped.

A bullet flew past Ashton's head. His eyes widened, spotting more CAIN coming up the other side. "Kade? What's up?" *I need you, buddy.*

The phone gave muffled static. *"There was a knock at the door."*

"Don't answer it." Patting his lap, Ashton motioned for the dog to get on the driver's side. Though an uncomfortable fit, Captain did as told. Ashton pushed against the gas like a lead brick. The engine revved, charging headfirst at the oncoming CAIN vehicles.

A gun clicked on the other side of the phone. *"We'll catch up again soon, ok?"*

Ashton unlatched the door and kicked it open. "That's a deal."

With the car running on inertia, Ashton jumped from the seat along with his dog. He did a barrel roll, managing to land on his feet. Dirt and road oils mixed with a few scrapes stained his skin. Captain's bark let Ashton know he made it safe. Ashton watched as his car collided with the oncoming CAIN traffic. Ashton began running, Captain tagging close behind. The cluster of cars exploded behind him, a shattering boom following.

Heart trumpeting in triumph, Ashton took off in the opposite direction. Ashes fell from the sky, accompanied by burning pieces of paper. His eyes widened as he realized what the paper was.

"No, no, no…" Ashton's shoes skidded to a stop, contemplating whether to reach out and grab a piece. He had completely forgotten about the old photographs he had left in his bags. One of the few things he still had as an omen to his past. Back before everything crashed. A piece landed at his feet, fizzing away. The smiling face of a seven-year-old Ally and a fifteen-year-old Ashton.

Ashton's moment halted as a new wave of cars drove up from the other side. The CAIN vans blocked off his path, guns aimed at him. Ashton raised his hands and took a few hesitant steps back. Captain began to bark ferociously at the opponents. Ashton stopped at the concrete wall that kept the drivers from falling off the highway.

"Stand down, Caleb!" Bright lights blinded him, and without a weapon, he had limited ways to defend himself.

Ashton sighed, waiting as a pair of agents came out to cuff him. A smirk crossed his face as they took his first hand. He let out a sharp whistle. On command, Captain pounced his master's offender. While the one was occupied, Ashton took out the second with a quick punch and kick. Immediately, gunfire started up again in chorus.

"Come on, boy." Ashton waved for the dog, darting past the cars and down the highway as quickly as he could. All he had to do was get off the highway, and he would be able to lose them easily.

Ashton turned his mind to Ally, trying to sustain his focus. He had to protect her no matter what. If he couldn't do that, he had no right to call himself her brother.

Keep going. For Ally.

26

Escort

My feelings settled in my chest. My ribs ached. The icy air numbed most of the outward pains. I tried to remember what hope felt like. Ashton's warm and worn hands were all that I could picture. Concrete slipped beneath my feet, throwing off my already unsteady balance. My fingers shook along with the shaky breath in my chest. Everything felt awful.

I tasted all the pain I had forced myself through. Salty remnants of blood lingered in my mouth. A cough stung in the back of my throat, unable to come out. My tongue begged for water, something to flush away the disgruntled feeling in my gut. *If only I had gone to lunch with Ashton.* I would have more than guilt filling my stomach now.

I sniffled my tears away. Oils and dirt stung my nostrils. Ashton's smell had been engraved in my memory now. I would give anything to just smell that cedar-sweat scent again. All I could smell now was the betrayal of the city I had once been so proud to protect.

Too many sounds banged against my eardrums, emerging as accusations for my missteps. The whirring of a car zoomed past me. Thunder from outside the dome accompanied the drumming of my heart. Every time the lightning hit, my thoughts would be broken with a start. Footsteps picked up in the distance. Paranoia bounced around in my ears. I could almost hear what Ashton would say. *Things will get better.* At least, that's what the version of himself he had allowed me to meet would say. But I had heard too many lies in my life to believe those words.

In the end, I had been thrown out and abandoned in the dark. I had no one to blame but myself.

"Ally!"

My movements stiffened. CAIN. They'd found me. Things would *not* get better. I would be their lab rat for the rest of my life. I would never taste freedom again.

"Ally!" The voice sounded familiar, like… *No. I'm delusional. He left. He's not coming back to save me, not now or ever.*

"Oh, Ally!" His strong arms gripped my form, almost knocking me over. My voice was caught in my throat. For the first time in my life, I didn't mind this stifling feeling. Ashton's eyes squeezed shut. He fell to his knees, still hugging me close. My arms hung in the air, unsure of what to do. I soaked in the warmth, too taken back to move.

I broke down crying.

Ashton opened his eyes, looking up at me. Rubbing his thumb along my cheek, he pushed my hair from my face. "Hey, hey, don't cry. I'm right here. I've got you."

Without a word, I threw myself around his neck. My brother held me close, his hand moving up and down my back in a warming motion. I never wanted to let go. I didn't want him to leave me again. Never again. Together, we sat on the dirty street, too terrified to pull out from each other's grasp.

My face pressed against his neck, and my breath left cold and shaky. "Ashton…" I finally said.

"…Yeah?"

"I'm scared."

Ashton hesitated. He stared out at the street, vision watery. Taking a deep breath, he said, "Me too."

I choked on a laugh. After one final squeeze, I loosened from my brother. He took my hands in his and helped me to my feet. Captain brushed against my leg, tilting his weight on me. Ashton cupped my face in his palms, his chest rising and falling uneasily.

Just being here with my brother alleviated my pain. I wanted to see him, not just my own dumbfounded expression, but being able to see at all was enough. It meant I wasn't alone.

"What made you come back?" My voice came broken and tired.

"I didn't want to lose you. Not again." Ashton's hands slid down to my arms, finding rest in my palms. "I need to tell you... *everything.*"

"I already know."

Ashton's breath hitched, gaze narrowing. "You do?"

I nodded. "Yeah, May told me about how you were working with Abel the whole time and about the Hidden Dragon Experiment."

"And?"

I frowned up at him. "And? That's it. Why? Is there something else?"

Ashton's eyes darted away, thinking it over. With a huff, he shook his head. His hand came up to rub his nose. "Nope. Everything's fine."

I wiped away a few stray tears tickling my cheek. "What are we going to do now?"

Ashton's gaze swept over the street, then up to the sky. "Well, for one, let's get out of the open." Taking hold of my hand, he pulled me along down the sidewalk. Captain trailed along, tail wagging happily. Ashton found us a spot blocked from sight by the highway above.

Refusing to let go of my hand, Ashton whipped out his phone with his free hand. He dug through the contact lists, stopping at one labeled *Marksman.* His thumb hovered over the call button. Frowning, he sighed. "Dang it, I told him to throw away his phone, didn't I?" He clicked the phone off and tapped his foot. "Hang on, Ally-gator. We need to get out of the city and find May and Kade. Then we'll work out a plan there. I'm going to figure everything out."

The phone vibrated in Ashton's hand, lighting up with a new call. The ID read *Vix "murder is science too."* I shot Ashton a look. He smirked a little. "What? I've got nicknames for everyone I don't like on my phone. Casey is 'the child trafficker.'" His smirk disappeared as he hesitantly answered the phone. "Wonder what Vix wants." He pressed the speaker button for me to hear.

"Ashton." Vix's voice came cool and collected, smooth as molasses. My ribs stung with remembrance. Ashton gripped my hand tighter.

"Anthony," Ashton said, purposefully lowering his voice in a mocking tone.

"You have something that belongs to me. And I have something you'd probably like back. I'll let Kade and May walk away with a clean slate if you turn yourself and A2 in." I exchanged a look with Ashton. Any form of politeness had fallen from Vix's voice, referring to me merely as an experiment. *"Meet me at Station 42, and they can go scot-free."*

With a roll of his eyes, Ashton hung up. "Yeah, we both know that's unrealistic." He let the device drop with a crack. He crushed it with his foot before kicking it into the road to be run over. "Hand me your phone too. We can't give them a chance to track us." I obeyed, and he repeated the process. His fingers locked with mine, and he started a new walk.

"Where are we going?" I stumbled after his brisk steps.

"Well, I can't just let Kade and May die. We have to go to Station 42. If I don't come, they'll have no other reason to keep them safe." Though Ashton did his best not to show it, I could tell he was very worried. He scanned over the street signs, trying to find his way around the city. He turned us down the sidewalk.

"What's Station 42?"

Ashton clicked his tongue thoughtfully. "I'm not entirely sure, but from what I've picked up, it's where one of the other... experiments, for lack of a better word, is being held. It's some dumb train out in the middle of the woods."

I lit up at the mention of another Dragon like me. I hadn't paused much to wonder where the other experimented kids were. I had no idea one was so close. *What were they like? What powers did they have that CAIN had kept such a tight grip on them?*

"Have you ever met this other kid?" I ventured.

Somewhat startled by the question, Ashton glanced back at me. "Yeah. I have." He turned his head before crossing the street.

"Really? What are they like?"

"Well," Ashton said. "He's a lot like you. Hopefully, we can find a way to save him, and you two can meet." My brother took me around a corner. His face split into a saddened smile. "But we'll have to focus on that another time. My main goal is keeping you safe..."

As he went on, he seemed to be growing distracted.

"Ashton? What's up?"

"I- I think you should stay here while I go."

The statement quickened my heart. "But-"

"I can't give Vix another chance to hurt you. I'll find somewhere safe for you to stay, and then I'll go after my friends by myself."

"No, Ashton." I gripped his hand with both my hands. "Ashton, I can't- I need you. Please. Please don't leave me again." *Don't leave me in the dark.*

Ashton stopped. He turned to me, frowning. "Ally, I messed up before. Vix got to you, and I can't- I couldn't live with myself if that happened again."

"So, you're going to abandon me all over again?" Tears tugged at my eyes, but I was too stubborn to cry now.

Ashton stared at me. His gaze shifted up and down. "Ally…" His hand wavered in mine. He shook his head determinedly. "No. No, I won't. I'm not going to leave you again." He pulled me closer, wrapping me up in another hug.

A limousine came down the road, the streetlights glinting off the shiny pitch-colored hood. Ashton broke from the hug, eyeing the car with suspicion. I stood just behind him, taking up a defensive position.

The car pulled up to the curb, the window sliding down. A man in a suit stared at us, his face molded in a stoic expression. "Caleb. Mr. Vix would like to speak to you." After pressing a button, the doors shifted to unlock.

My brother and I exchanged a look. I stared up at him, pleading for him not to leave me. Ashton turned back to the driver, glaring. "Fine. But for the record, I know this is a trap." He popped the backseat door open and waved for me to enter. Captain jumped in behind me, earning a look of disgust from the driver. Ashton sandwiched the dog in. With Captain pressed up against me, my vision switched to black and white.

The drive fell uncomfortably silent. Ashton intertwined his fingers, fidgeting with his thumbs. I sat stiffly, watching the already gray world with a gray view. We crossed over a few highways before landing near the border. The twenty-minute drive ended with us passing through the CAIN gate. We passed the dome wall, making me uneasy. The sky cried tears, and though they had been blocked in the dome, they now dropped in freeform. I scanned over the sky, wary of any remmutants. Sensing the tone of the car, Captain nestled his head into my lap, almost frowning. I pat his head, trying to reassure myself. *Ashton isn't going to leave me. We'll get through this.*

Shadowy trees blotted out the night sky, blockading us from the giant eagles. The car pulled up to a crater dug into the ground. Mechanical sounds whirred below, along with commanding shouts. Down the dirt road we went. Train tracks circled the pit. The train stood at the end of the crater, the direction we were heading. *Station 42.* Vix stood on a platform along with a handful of agents.

Anxiety crowded in my chest. My visions went back to that moment everything had fallen apart. When I had drawn up the dagger and taken a stab at fate. The memory of the knife handle stuck in my hand. I rubbed over my wrists, trying to stop the shaking. *I'm fine.* I gave Ashton a reassuring smile, hoping for one in return. He fulfilled my hopes.

The car parked, but the man told us not to exit ourselves. Rather, he climbed out and help us both from the vehicle. Ashton kept giving the agent dirty looks.

"Well, well. If it isn't the Caddels! So glad to see you made it." Vix outstretched his arms, stepping toward us, his face smothered in the lying grin.

Ashton scrunched his nose at him. "Where are they?" His hand found mine, lighting up my world. Captain sat attentively at his master's side.

Casey stood afar, gaze shifting from the dog to the man. Hatred burned in his eyes, but he remained quiet.

With a chuckle, Vix said, "In a moment, Caleb. Patience." He turned to me, waving his hands toward me. "You know, Alison, your family really was quite something."

Ashton stepped forward, growing annoyed. He stepped in front of me, still holding me close. "Get on with it, Vix."

"Yes, I agree with him for once." Casey stepped forward, scrolling through a tablet in his hand. "The next train car is ready, and I don't like wasting time."

Vix's grin wavered at the comment, but he went along. "Alright then. Come along, kids." He turned on his heels, though his head was still facing back in case we pulled something. We followed, keeping our guard up.

"You see, Caddels, I would have originally preferred to meet at a nearby CAIN training camp. I intended to take miss Alison there before she escaped. But Casey was keen to show off his model train." Vix gave a teasing look to the aforementioned agent. "Titus liked the idea, so welcome to Station 42!" Vix waved toward the train cars.

The train was pumped with machinery. As we made our way closer to the engine in the front, the din rose in a crescendo. Captain brushed against my leg, giving me more freedom of my gaze. Unfortunately, with Ashton still holding my hand, the conflicting views caused my head to ache. Rather not splitting with my brother, I merely shut one eye, focusing on the dog's sight.

Casey cut in without looking up from the control tablet. "Titus was only so fond of the idea because Vix has failed so miserably with every other case he's had. So now it's my turn."

Vix shot the younger man a look. "Casey. I hope you know I have the power to request your next mission be under Dr. Cleo. She might need help after losing A1."

The mention of the woman prompted Casey to look up. He paused, taking in Vix's words. "Let's continue the tour, shall we?"

The tops of the cars domed over tinted windows allowing a foggy view in. Vix went on and on about the brilliance of the train, and how revolutionary it would be for CAIN. I couldn't care less. I was only concerned about rescuing Kade and May and getting out as soon as possible. The cars were labeled with numbers, printed on in boxy form and each starting with the digits *4-2*.

As we passed a car labeled *421,* a strange sensation came over me. I tried to peer in through the window, but the tinted black prevented me from finding out what lay inside.

My steps faltered; Ashton's hand slipped from mine, and Captain walked on past me.

And I could still *see.*

Not just see, but through my own eyes. My heart stuttered.

"Ally? Something wrong?" Ashton glanced back at me once he realized my touch missing from his.

"I just… no. Nope." I reached out for my brother's hand again, not wanting to draw Vix or Casey's attention. I continued walking. My vision shifted back to the mix of Ashton and Captain's.

"And now, we come to the end of the tour," Vix said, folding his hands.

"Kade and May," Ashton demanded, narrowing his eyes at his old boss.

"First the trade." Casey snapped his fingers, summoning a group of agents who then surrounded us.

Ashton took a defensive position. One agent grabbed me from behind. I lost touch with Ashton, but I could still see from my attacker's view.

"Hey! Let her go!"

Whipping around, I kicked the agent in the knee, forcing him down. My elbow dug into his gut. Just as he fell back, a new agent took his place. His arms wrapped around my torso, suspending me in the air. My legs flung wildly, but the escape attempt proved futile.

Ashton came toward me, only to be jabbed in the gut by the butt of a gun. He doubled over before an agent jumped him, pinning him into the mud. Ashton gave a sharp whistle, signaling Captain into attack mode. With spirit in his growl, Captain dug his teeth into the arm holding me back. I dropped down to my feet, sending sharpness through my body.

"Ally! Go!"

I ducked underneath the next agent's arm, going as quickly as I could. Without touch, my sight had left me. I face-planted after tripping over some track and the hitch between two cars. Determined not to get caught, I shoved myself back up. My shins hurt from the fall, but I did not pause. My chest burned with energy. Eyes squeezed shut, I felt the wind rush through my hair, mixed with rain and mud.

I smacked into a larger form. My stomach tightened as I realized another agent blocked my path. He scooped me over his shoulder before I could process. Balling up my hands, I punched his shoulder in a desperate attempt to free myself. He seemed unfazed as he took me away.

I dropped hard on my back, the air knocked from my lungs. Though I couldn't shout, I quickly sat up and tried to move forward. I ran into a smoothed wall. Knocked back, I rubbed my nose and shook off the pain. I ran my hands against the wall in front of me, trying to feel out my surroundings.

"Let me out of here!" No answer came. "Ashton!" I called. Still nothing but the mumbling outside the walls. One of the train cars turned out to be my prison. I paced the space, unsure of how to escape. As I came toward the right side of the area, my vision lit up again from my own eyes. I paused to stare at my hands. "What in the world…"

Unsure whether I was really seeing, I blinked several times. I shook away the strange feeling. I needed to get out of here. That was my focus.

I scanned over the room that trapped me. The train car split in half by a glass barrier, me on the smaller side of it. The tinted windows came easier to see through on the inside. I hoisted myself up to peek through one. My arms strained to hold me.

I spotted Ashton just outside, still pinned down. Captain growled at his owner's captors. Casey knelt to Ashton's level, evincing a fiercer bark from the dog. "You have no idea how long I've been waiting to see you like this. Defeated. Weak. Scared." His voice filtered into the train car poorly, but I managed to make it out.

"Guess you're gonna have to keep waiting." Ashton whistled again and Captain launched at Casey. Ashton pushed himself up from the ground, knocking the agents back. My brother started down the row of the train, Vix calling after him. Once Captain had kept Casey down long enough, he went after Ashton.

"Yes!" I cheered, running out of breath while using my upper body strength. I allowed myself to drop.

Turning my head all around, I searched for a way out. I stepped across to the left side of the car, only to have my sight stolen from me. Curious, I walked back to where I once stood. It came back. Some sort of invisible barrier seemed to be the difference between dark and light. As I crossed all the way to the seeing side, I stared at the wall suspiciously. I pressed my palm against it, thinking it over. *Whatever's in the next car over must be doing it.*

"Hello?" I ventured. The walls probably did no good to make myself heard. "Hello!" I tried again; hopefully, it would be loud enough to be picked up past the two walls of the cars, the space between them, and the pounding rain.

"Hello?" The response took me back. I had possibly put the sounds of outside into a word in my head, but I tried to stay optimistic.

"Is someone there?" I waited patiently for a response. All I got in return was whipping rain against the outside. I sighed, accepting defeat. I didn't have time for conversation anyways. I needed to escape first. The mysteries surrounding my powers could be dealt with some other time.

Peering through the glass, I spotted a keypad on the wall, I assumed the way to let me out. I couldn't get to it through the glass; even if I could, I wouldn't be able to see it on that side of the car. A hatch sat above my head, just beyond the glass. I turned back to the window to the outside. Just to check, I banged my elbow against it as hard as I could. It refused to break, only sending a shiver up my funny bone.

As I rubbed it, I weighed the possible options. A few BLs sat hunched in the corner, keeping an eye on me. Knowing they wouldn't care, I stuck my tongue out at them. Light glinted against the metal plating on the black-furred one.

BL32.

I gaped, taking a few steps back. The little traitor had already been repurposed to keep an eye on me again. The BLs on patrol were plucked out of a hat, but the chance that Bolt would be the one on patrol stunned me. Nodding my head back and forth, I weighed my options. I thought about using him to my advantage (just like he used me), but then I would run the risk of getting caught all over again. I glanced at the keypad. With the roll of my eyes, I decided I needed the rodent. Once I had escaped, I would leave him behind as one of CAIN's dumb puppets.

With a deep breath, I took control of the rat's body. My vision swapped from my own to a view from the upper corner of the wall. I directed him up toward the hatch and popped open the lid. I had to admit, the Blake Landerson guy who had engineered these little guys had done a nice job.

Casey stood below, flipping through the tablet. "Dang it." His hand brushed through his blond hair nervously. "I can't wait until that idiot is gone for good." He selected a button to lock all the car doors. To do so, he had to type in a quick password. I could hear the doors of the car click in place. With a frustrated composure, he looked up from the device and began with his orders. "Hunt down agent Caleb! Kill on sight!"

"No, don't do that." Vix shook his head, confusing the agents. Casey side glanced at Vix, hatred in his gaze. "Bring him here, and then we'll decide what to do with him."

"Yes sir." The agents marched off with a nod.

Casey mumbled something under his breath and walked down the back of the train.

Bolt crawled back into the car. I worked him down to the keypad. I tried the password I had seen Casey display. The light above the keypad turned green and the glass wall slid apart.

I swapped off the rat. Fighting my instincts to collect him and give him a job well done pat, I made my way out the hatch.

Stomach pressed against the roof, I climbed. The night acted as a shield. Vix and Casey found themselves too busy discussing matters with other agents to notice me. I carefully crossed over to the next car. I allowed myself up to a hunched walk. Spreading my legs, I managed to touch the ground on the other side. I made my feet light over the roof. The rain nearly made me slip, ending in a squeak. I covered my mouth, to make sure no one noticed me. I quickened my pace, knots winding in my gut. I crossed the halfway point of the train, giving me a good amount of ground to cover before I found Ashton.

I attempted a jump to the next car. I caught myself, though somewhat unsteady. As I treaded briskly across the metal, my vision cut off. *Something in that last car...* I stepped back and bent down to catch the number of the car. From my angle, too much light reflected off it to see. Shaking my head, I forced myself on. I had to find my brother.

Lowering to a crawl, I felt for the edge of the train car. I stretched out my foot and found the next ledge in the dark. My sneaker slipped back on the wet surface. I frowned, having no clue how to gauge the distance. I steadied myself up and took the leap of faith.

The car thudded beneath my feet. I stumbled some but caught myself.

"What was that?"

"Over there!"

"Stop!"

I picked up to a run, startled by the agents. I guessed the length of the cars, counting my steps. *7... 6... 5... 4... 3... 2... Jump!* I repeated the cycle, growing clumsier with each car. As luck would have it, rain tumbled against the train, making me miscount. I hit against the next car, slipping. With all the strength I could muster, I yanked myself back up. I wobbled to my feet and pressed on.

"Shoot her down!"

"No, don't!" Vix and Casey flew into an argument below.

A gunshot rang from somewhere. I could feel it vibrate through the car beneath me. A yelp escaped me. My feet tangled in another attempted jump. My shoes slipped from under me, knocking me back. As I fell, I screamed on reflex, giving away my position.

Something yanked the front of my shirt, pulling me into the next car. His hand pressed against my forehead.

My face brightened. "Ashton!"

Ashton shushed me. "They're gonna be here any minute." His voice cracked with a hushed panic. "We've got to find Kade and May and get the heck out of here." He spun me around to the other side, letting his hand linger on mine. Captain waited at his master's side.

The stretched car split with a wall and another door. Based on the wall structure, it didn't seem to lead outdoors. Ashton's attention turned to this car's key panel. Strewn apart, loose wires dangled about.

"How'd you get your door open?"

"I just rewired it. The only problem is I can't get it closed now." It snapped at Ashton, smoking. He backed off, frowning. "Shoot." Coming back up to his lengthy height, he turned to me. "Come on. We've got to go." He dragged me behind him, taking several steps.

A figure blocked the door. Casey had a gun aimed directly at Ashton's chest. "You're not going anywhere."

27

Running

Ashton shoved me behind him. Captain barked with spite. "Casey. Hi."

"No one's going to miss you when you're dead." Casey stepped forward, backing Ashton and me farther into the car. "And then, after I kill you, I'm going to kill her." Waving the gun, Casey gestured to me. "I'll tell Vix it was an accident, and I'll never have to worry about this stupid family again."

"Well." Ashton kept his eyes locked on Casey so as to not miss any opportunities. "It's good to have goals, I guess. I miss the days when the worst you did to me was give me dirty looks."

Casey gripped the weapon more firmly. "Don't taunt the guy with the gun."

"Exactly." Ashton uppercut Casey, whipping around and knocking the gun from his hand. Ducking down, Ashton caught the weapon before it hit the ground. His legs sprung up to set him at his full height again. Extending his arm, Ashton clicked the bullet into place.

Casey jumped back, hands raised defensively. Ashton stared him down, edging his attacker outside the train car. Once Casey stood at the step before passing the door, Ashton stopped moving. In a swift action, he swapped his aim to the door lock. A bullet shot forth, sparking the key panel and slamming the door shut.

My brother flashed a smirk at me. "We'll save that fight for some other time." He blew at the top of the barrel coolly before sliding it into his holster. "By the way, don't do that. You're going to shoot yourself in the face," he added quickly, referring to the blowing thing.

"What now? Casey's waiting for us outside." I followed after my brother to the door on the opposite end.

"That's not the only way out." Ashton flipped a security card between his fingers, probably collected from Casey's person. He slid it in between the door and the wall. The latch unpressed itself, allowing the door to unlock. He threw it open, revealing another room.

"Why didn't you just use the card on the keypad?"

"Because I didn't think about that." Ashton pressed on through the door.

Tied upside down to the wall was Kade, his face lighting up at the sight of his friend. "Am I glad to see you guys!" He moved the best he could while strung up by all four limbs. Thick ropes held his hands while iron locks bound his ankles.

"How long have you been upside down?" I didn't think anyone could last long in that position.

"It's some weird mechanism. If you try to move, it spins you around so you can't escape."

Ashton looked over his tied-up friend, frowning. "It takes a key lock. This card isn't going to do it."

"I've got a lock pick in my boot." Kade wiggled his foot. "That's what I was trying to reach when I flipped."

With a nod, Ashton reached up to remove Kade's shoe. Ashton found the pick underneath the soft part of the shoe, hidden in the sole. Eyebrow raised, Ashton questioned whether the hiding spot was necessary. Taking the pick, he handed it to me. I scrunched my nose at how sweaty it was. "Here. You unlock his feet while I figure out how to handle the ropes."

"Spin me around first, so I don't have to worry about holding my feet up," Kade said.

"Okay." Placing my hand against the wall, I slid the platform around like a record. Kade turned face up, shaking from gravity pulling his blood back and forth. I shoved the pick into the locks, unsure of how the tool worked. The task proved more difficult with Ashton's view elsewhere. After wiggling it around aimlessly, I finally managed to get it.

"I don't have anything to cut the ropes with…" Ashton fiddled with a rope around Kade's left hand.

"Pocket knife in the other shoe."

Ashton rolled his eyes, kneeling to get Kade's other boot. "Why didn't you just keep it in your *pocket.* Hence the name *pocketknife.*"

"They took the one in my pocket." I finished up the final lock while Ashton cut the ropes apart. Kade dropped to his feet, rubbing his wrists. "So ha."

"Fine." Ashton succeeded to point to his friend.

Kade held out his hand for the tools back. He stuffed them back into his boots and slid them on. "What's security like out there?"

Ashton paced to the door before realizing there was no window. "Uh, on a scale of one to ten, I'd say a six and a half."

"Not a lot but still tough to get through. Got it."

"You don't think that's a lot?" I frowned.

"When you've been in the CAIN and Abel game as long as us, you start to realize how tough CAIN can actually be." Ashton looked off in disdain. I squeezed his hand tighter.

If I couldn't get through this moment, how was I supposed to survive at all?

"Do you know how many are watching the door?" Instinctively, Kade went for a gun at his side only to remember CAIN had it. Ashton handed Kade the one he had gotten from Casey.

"I don't think many. Casey found us, but he didn't want to sound the alarm. He and Vix are fighting." Ashton chuckled a little.

"If Casey doesn't watch it, he's going to get sent to his room." Kade checked the number of bullets in the gun. Once he was done, he reloaded the magazine and gripped it with both hands. "Exit strategy? Where do you want to meet if we get separated?"

Ashton's eyes wandered, thinking it over.

An alarm rang through the car, the lights going haywire. My hands shot to my ears, separating me from Ashton and his sight. Captain howled along.

"We've got to go," Kade said, impatiently. The door behind me flew open, allowing a wave of chilled air in.

I felt Ashton's hand grip mine before my world lit up again. Kade stood outside the door, watching our back. Hand in hand, Ashton pulled me outside, his free hand bunched in a fist. Staring down the long line of the train, I found the prisoner car the only one emitting sound and lights. *Looks like Casey decided he was better off reporting us to Vix.* Agents headed in our direction from all ways but one, the wall of the crater. I doubted we would be able to climb it easily.

We were surrounded.

Ashton and Kade exchanged a wary look. The tocsin alarm split my eardrums. Part of me hoped that it could be heard from the city, that way CAIN would be exposed. The crater added to the din, bouncing back and forth in echoes. The alarm suddenly stopped. In the distance, I could see Vix exiting the head of the train, his face contorted in a scowl. I figured he had been the one to shut the sound off. The air fell eerily quiet now in comparison.

Casey made his way to the surrounding group but was still a good way off. "You're free to attack when ready, men," he shouted from afar.

The agents closed in tighter. Ashton took several defensive steps back, Kade facing the opposite way. "Not if we attack first! Kade, shoot them!"

"We have limited bullets, Ash. No."

An agent ran at Kade. He ducked, allowing the man to roll over him. Spinning around, Kade landed a punch to his face. Another attacker was already on his way.

Ashton tried to fend off a group with his elbow, but it was difficult with me holding back one of his hands. To his credit, he refused to let go. Five agents surrounded us. Ashton's guard proved ineffective. Ashton gripped my hands with both of his. "Get ready. Just kick your legs wildly."

Before I could protest, my brother swung me up and around at the group. I did as told, holding my breath. The five were knocked back or out. Either way, they couldn't get at us anymore.

When Ashton put me down, my head spun. I shook it off, waiting for the new wave of agents. With Kade combined, we had taken out about of quarter of the original agents. Kade worked on the other side of the fight with Captain, knocking out two with a quick punch.

A gunshot landed a few inches from my feet. Dirt

blasted up, stinging my eyes. I rubbed them in pain. I could still see through Ashton, but the burn persevered.

"Ally!" Ashton cried out in alarm, probably still worried about the gunshot.

"I'm fine," I groaned.

An agent jumped Ashton from the side, impelling him to let go off my hand. My hands shot up over my head in defense. I could hear Ashton struggling with the agent near me. My heart thundered, no clue whether he was winning.

Only darkness painted my path. I could be attacked from any direction. Casey wanted to kill me. Vix wanted to brainwash me. Nowhere was safe.

A strong grip from behind sent a jolt across my spine. I struggled, the agent refusing to let go. With no other choice, I dug my teeth into his arm. I dropped, landing on my stomach. With a disregard for my surroundings, I bolted. I crashed into people, quick to collect myself and keep going. As long as I stayed moving, I wouldn't be an easy target.

I couldn't trust anything in the darkness. Rain mixed up my sense of smell and my sense of touch. In my eagerness for escape, I had gotten too turned around. *I need to find Ashton again. We were almost home free. Why did I have to mess that up? I mess everything up.*

The grunt of an agent in my path drew me back to reality. A quick knock to the head made the darkness light up with blurred spots. I fell back, my elbows scraped against mud. I rotated my jaw, trying to readjust myself. I pushed myself up, steadying on my weak legs. A hand gripped firmly around my wrist, raising me in the air. I scratched to pry off my attacker's fist. The bruises I had gotten from Vix grew sorer by the second. My memories filled in the blanks of my vision, flashing me images of my own terrified face when I confronted Vix. I shut my eyes in an attempt to shoo the vision, but it remained at the forefront.

The sound of an impact reached my ears. My wrist was released. My stomach flipped at sudden falling. Arms caught me wedding style. Color filled my sight.

Ashton smiled down at me. "Hey, Ally-gator."

A screech rained down from above. A massive form swooped up an agent. Another remmutant made contact with the ground, shaking the earth. Screams erupted from the agents. Kade ducked away from one that dropped a little too close to him. Ashton held me closer. Another eagle pinned down a man, clawing at his body. Its beak dropped like a weight, shredding the man into bloody bits. Ashton's eyes widened in horror. Remmutants still circled the air. One came down in an attempt for food, but only shredded one of the train cars.

My brother's hand flew over my eyes. "You don't need to see this." Once he realized blocking my eyes wasn't doing the trick, he threw me over his shoulder. My skin left contact with him, thereby blinding me. He guarded himself by keeping his head down. I bumped up and down as he ran, his steps dodging, avoiding agents and horrific eagle monsters.

"You idiot! Why would you use sound alarms? Now we have remmutants to deal with!" Vix's voice carried through the air, panic lining it.

"Shut up! I'm dealing with it!"

"We've got to get out of the open." Ashton's voice came heavy and quiet. I didn't want to see men being ripped apart, but I would've preferred he put me down and give me his hand so I could have some sense of where we were going.

More gunfire launched from somewhere. My brother finally sat me down. The thing I sat on shook as Ashton climbed up next to me. As he helped me up, my sight resumed. We stood in an open train car, spacious for cargo. Several boxes lined against the back, along with a few loose weapons and tools.

"We should be safe in here." Ashton peered around the opening, back pressed against the wall.

Ashton sprinted across the car to the other opening. I stood close behind him, awaiting his call. "It looks clear… if we go this way, we can run up out of the ditch and get away into the woods."

"Not so fast, Mr. Caleb." Vix's statement ended with a cough. Ashton whipped around and saw his former boss climbing up into the car, Vix's shirt stained with crimson blood. He held his wound tightly, a gash from the birds in his shoulder. I couldn't help but focus on it, my mind returning to the remmutants and the horrors they had committed. Vix's welcoming grin had vanished, nowhere to be found.

Ashton's hand moved over my chest defensively. My sight swapped back to darkness.

"Hand over A2. No more deals."

"I can't do that."

"Fine." A gun clicked. "Let's see how you survive getting shot in the face this time."

"Ashton!" My voice cracked with desperation. I tried to shove my brother over and out of the way.

Screech!

Boom!

Thud!

Shhhhh!

The train car thudded violently, knocking me forward.

"Ally!" Ashton's familiar hands yanked me away from what I heard to be the crates sliding around the car. Rumbling vibrated beneath my feet.

The train had begun moving.

28

The Interval

My knees buckled under me at the sudden movement. Ashton stared down the train, showing me a remmutant that had ripped the roof from the front car. The train curved around the corner and gathered speed. The wheels rotated with an unnatural whir. Ashton stabled himself back into the car.

Vix dodged past a sliding crate. His gun rose unsteadily. "You're running out of time, kids. Get over here, Alison."

"Heck no!" I jerked back, clenching my fist.

"That's my girl," Ashton said.

The train car swung with the curve of the track, and the crates yanked around with it. One moved directly for us. Ashton shoved me over, his hand touching the tips of my fingers just long enough for me to see him get pinned against the wall. He let out a groan. Given the pace at which the train moved, I found it hard to get back to my feet.

"How cute." I could imagine Vix's stupid grin. "Ashton wants to protect his little sister. He's not as righteous as you think, you know?"

Ashton's voice grew strained. "Vix-"

"He's told you quite a few lies, hasn't he?" Vix's hard shoes approached me, slowed by the wobbling car.

I pushed myself up, hair tumbling over my face. I shook my head to ignore Vix's mind games and shifted to a defensive position. The whirring of the track increased.

"You think Abel was his only secret? That was just the lie he was fine with you knowing. But when Caleb wants a secret kept, he finds a way to keep it. Isn't that right, Caleb?"

"Vix, don't you dare!" Ashton grew harsher. I could hear him struggling to get the box off himself.

"Ever considered how you ended up in the Hidden Dragon Experiment in the first place? The six kids weren't chosen in a random manner. At least, not you…" I could feel his breath on my face now.

"Ally, don't listen to him!"

I frowned, wishing for a minute to think. Uncertain breath caused my chest to rise and decline. Those questions had crossed my mind, but I hadn't had the chance to learn the answers.

"Just so you know, Alison, I have never lied to you. I think we both know you can't say the same for your brother." The quickening pace of the outside wind and wheels overshadowed his soft voice, but I could hear it crystal clear.

"Ally! Don't-"

"Everyone just shut up!" I shut my watering eyes, growing fed up with both their pleas. "Vix. With the fortune cookie, you said I was like my father. Tell me. What does that mean?"

The air stood quiet.

Vix broke it with a chuckle. "Your father was just like you. He gave up everything for something so trivial, so vacuous. He was always after the next thing while ignoring what was right in front of his face. And his family paid for it."

"Don't you dare talk about Hank that way!" Ashton snapped. "Ally, your father loved you more than anything-"

"Telling more lies, Caleb?" Vix spat venom.

I swung my hand, making contact with Vix's deceiving face. I could see past myself, albeit for a split second. A snap broke the air, white flashing on the outside, and then… the whirring stopped.

The train chugged on, sounding like a regular train but echoey. I heard a grunt, thump, and a shuffle. Ashton's hand found mine, lighting up my view. His gaze fixed on a stumbling Vix.

"Let's go." I started to the car door, Ashton stumbling behind me. I didn't want to stay any longer and listen to Vix's sickening words. Losing my touch, I yanked the door handle with both hands. It slid open.

Though I expected cold rain, nothing came. Ashton gave me sight again, and we rushed out. Together, we balanced on the median. When Ashton attempted to jump to the next car, the scene around us forced him to stop. We stood in astonishment.

Twisted and disorganized land lay before us. A rolling sea of desert, snow, forest, and winding static. Islands of floating chunks of space and land hung in the sky. Faint voices of male and female, young and old, played as background. The world constantly rearranged itself, taking new broken shapes and forms. The air constantly morphed from claustrophobic heat to stunning cold and every weather in between. The land stood odorless, tasteless, and formless. A clock fixed in the sky where the moon should've been.

"Thought it would be easy, huh?" Vix appeared at the other side of the car hitch. He laughed hysterically, hair was strewn from its professional state. "Welcome to the Interval. The world between worlds. If you jump now, you could land yourself in any given time or space." He straightened, leaning on the door. "You're stuck here until I say so."

The train is… a time machine.

Ashton's gaze fixated on the corruption below us. The track constantly appeared to catch the train and disappeared as quickly as the wheels came off it.

Ashton's mouth gaped. "*It's C1…*" he muttered.

"What?"

"We need to get to the front of the train and figure out how to get back to earth." Sticking out his tongue, Ashton turned to Vix. Once my brother was done taunting, he hoisted himself up onto the roof of the next car. He could do that easily due to his height. He yanked me up by the arm. Vix called after us, but we didn't stop. The hollowed cars echoed beneath us.

I spotted the ripped-up front car in the distance. "Are you sure it'll still work?"

"We can hope."

A chunk of dirt appeared before us in a strange glitch. Ashton ducked quickly, yanking me down with him. Just as soon as it had come, it vanished.

"Is Vix chasing us?"

"I don't think so." Ashton panted between sentences. "His shoulder looked pretty bad. I don't think he has the strength to climb up here. He's probably following through the cars."

A puddle formed before Ashton's steps, causing him to slip. The puddle revealed itself to be an ocean, dunking his whole form in.

"Ashton!" My sight turned watery as I yanked him back up. Shirt soaked, he plopped down on the steel roof.

Ashton caught his breath in the form of coughs. He stared down at his hand, which was already drying. Soon, no physical reminder of the ocean remained, his clothes completely dry. He grimaced. "I don't like this backward place."

"You mentioned something about C1. Is that the cause of this chaos? Is that the other experiment?"

Ashton shook out his hair in reflex, though no water remained to get rid of. "Yeah, but… We have to hurry. Vix has the upper hand on us because he doesn't have to jump between the cars."

We had taken but a step when a thundering creak came from all directions, a strange side effect of the Interval. A massive, sideways skyscraper formed itself in front of the train. In response, the track spun around, crashing through one of the building's windows. Ashton dropped to his knees, shielding me from falling glass. Like a snake, the train dug through, winding in strange curves. It had made its way past the skyscraper, dipping down hard. My stomach dropped with the train. My hair flew up, frosty air smacking against my face. One more quick jerk and the roller coaster was over.

I wobbled to my feet, my stomach hurling itself into the back of my throat. I shoved the bile back down, taking my next step. We moved on toward the front of the train, only a couple of cars away.

Ashton jumped down, leaving me in the dark for a moment. I sat on the edge and slid off into his arms.

My brother pumped a fist in the air. "Yes! Made it here before Vix!" Extending his arm, he pushed the engine door open, which was somehow still intact after the damage the remmutant had caused.

I frowned, stepping in after him. "Speaking of Vix…" My thoughts trailed off to what he had said.

Ashton shot me a confused glance. "Ally?"

"Stop right there!" Vix slid the car door open, fire in his eyes.

Ashton moved swiftly, slamming the engine door shut with his foot. He searched for something to block it but turned up empty. "Aw, darn," he said. He pulled me over to the control board, squinting it over. Clicking his tongue, he tried to decipher the buttons. "Alright. I've got it. Ally, I'm going to have to leave you for a second. But there's something you need to do for me."

"What? But- But Ashton, I can't see without you. I need you." I hadn't expected my voice to sound so desperate. I tightened my fingers through his.

"Don't worry, we'll be fine." Taking me by the shoulders, Ashton moved me in front of the console. He moved my hands over each switch and button. "Here, this button controls what time we land, and here's the place. Swap them to the correct coordinates and time before pressing this button to send us back home. I'll distract Vix while also getting rid of the power source. It's in one of the cars. I'll unlatch it once you tell me we've almost arrived, that way CAIN can't use the train anymore. Got it?" He made to leave, but I wouldn't let him go.

"No, I don't- I *can't* be alone again… You said you wouldn't leave me. Ashton, please."

Ashton stared at me, forcing me to look at my own stupidly desperate face. My cheeks turned red against my pale skin, frustrated.

"Ally…" Ashton hesitated. Pulling me by the arm, he yanked me into one final hug. His hand combed through my hair, his eyes shut. "I'll always be there for you. I'll come back. Just… trust me. Please."

My hands shook, wrapped around his torso. Could I? After every obvious lie that he uttered to me. After every time he left me in the dark. After every time he had avoided me. After every time he had shown me how much he truly loved me. After every time he sought me out when I shoved away. After every time he had pulled me into the light.

"Alright," I breathed. "I trust you."

We separated, and Ashton showed me the buttons one more time, explaining the coordinates and time. A keypad worked for assigning numbers to the various functions, which made it easier for me to count.

"When it's ready, call me. Sound works differently here, so I might be able to hear you. See ya later, Ally-gator." Ashton ruffled my hair one last time before heading off.

The fight between him and Vix echoed behind me. It came from all directions and, at the same time, nowhere at all.

I focused on the task at hand. I rubbed my finger over each button on the keypad, determining which was which number. I pressed them, recalling the numbers my brother had given me. The darkness meant I was constantly second-guessing my decisions. With a deep breath, I reminded myself of my confidence. I just had to trust and take a leap of faith. Ashton would come back. We'd get out of this nowhere space, the Interval. We'd get home and…

And what? Ashton had moved out of his house, and even if we could go back, CAIN would easily find us there. I couldn't fathom a way of escaping this mess that lay before me. CAIN would always be after me. I would only learn information that would make things more complicated. I could only lose what little I had. *Things could only get worse from here.* I couldn't go around it.

No. There must be a future. I wasn't carried this far to be dropped. If I gave up now, nothing would get better. Never ever. I didn't know every little detail of what lay ahead, but maybe I didn't need to. Maybe I could trust that when it came to it, I would be able to handle it. Ashton would be at my side, and maybe that was enough. I couldn't go around, but I could go through.

I continued typing numbers. *Only a few digits left to go.* Sounds bounced off into my ears, each made up of fragments of the universe. My pinkie pressed against the final number. Hand hovering over the pad to avoid losing it in the dark, I took it in. Mustering my biggest shout, I called for my brother.

"Ashton! It's ready!"

Nearly forgetting, I smacked the enter button. The train whirred louder, picking up speed. I ducked down, nearly tripping. A loud *clunk!* reached my ear, repeating itself over and over. The sound of the train's power source dropping off into the constant shifting deep. The train shook unsteadily without it. The echoes thundered too loudly for me to pick out any other noises. Until one morphed into a footstep.

"Way to go, Ally!"

My eyes opened, scanning over the train engine. Ashton smiled at me, but it immediately fell at a new sound.

"Yes. Way to go, Alison." Vix's voice bled furious sarcasm. Ashton and I backed up into the console. Vix approached, hands formed as claws, ready to tear us apart. "You were my last chance, Alison. My last *real* chance to make an impact on this blind world. Then Casey and Ashton had to rip that from me. I should've known this would've happened. We were antithetical from the moment we met."

Ashton shot me a look, telling me he had no clue what the word meant. We climbed up onto the nose of the train. Ashton's hand stretched across my body, his grip on mine. He stared at the upside-down numbers on the console, still flipping through to find the correct destination.

"We're a few digits off still," I said.

"Well, we'll either end up in the forest or in the ocean a few days back or forward." He now turned his attention back to Vix, then to the messy sea below. "We could also end up falling from the sky and dying." Taking another step back, Ashton narrowed his eyes at our enemy. "Guess those odds are going to have to do."

I had some thoughts on the prospect. "Ashton, wait!"

My brother jumped off the train, taking me with him.

29

Freesias

I smacked against hard, dirt ground and continued on rolling. Unable to make sense of anything, completely shrouded in dark, I let out a scream. As I tumbled down, my chest filled with panic. The earth, littered with rocks and knots, knocked into every bone in my body. I hunched myself into a ball, unable to stop myself. My ankle twisted underneath my body, sending a sharp pang up to my brain. The hill grew steeper. Forced from my ball, my head slammed against something. All sense was knocked from me.

My eyes fluttered open as I slowly regained consciousness. I bobbed up and down, being carried. My sight worked its way into focus. Forest lay before us, surrounding all sides. My sight glanced over his shoulder, smiling at my worn face.

"Good morning, Ally-gator," came Ashton's soothing voice.

"What-" My voice fell groggy and hadn't quite woken up yet. "Where are we?" I said in a jumbled mess. My arms sagged over his shoulders and around his neck.

"Not in the ocean." Ashton carefully stepped over a tree root.

I readjusted myself on his back, moving my hair away. "What happened?" The bright sun rose over the trees, blinding my morning eyes.

Ashton shrugged. "Well, we fell down a hill. And now we're lost in the woods." He trudged on, his steps weighty and tiredly swaying.

With a frown, I pat his shoulder. "You can set me down now."

"Right." Ashton knelt somewhat clumsily and let his hands drop from under my legs. I set my foot on the ground and lifted my whole weight onto it. A jolt sprung up my leg, impelling me to pull back up. I winced, falling to a sit. I pulled my foot up, rubbing my cold hands over it.

"What's wrong?"

"I think I sprained my ankle." I bit down on my lip, trying to ignore the pain.

"Here. I can still carry you." Ashton set his hand on the ripped hole at the knee of my jeans. He held out his other hand to me. I stared at my own dirty face. At Ashton's skinned palms, likely scraped from the fall. We were trapped in the overgrown forest. My eyes glazed over with water.

Ashton flinched, somewhat panicked. "What's wrong? Did I do something?"

I let my head drop. "This… This isn't how I wanted this to go."

"What?"

"All of this. We wouldn't have even ended up on that stupid train if I had just gone to lunch like you had asked."

Ashton's breath filled the silence. He gave up, moving to sit next to me. "What *did* you want, then?"

"I don't know." I crossed my arms over my knees. A single tear ran down my cheek. "I just… I wanted the truth. I wanted answers. I wanted to know *why.*"

With a sigh, Ashton moved to sit next to me. "Well, then, I guess we both messed up… I haven't been completely honest with you, Ally."

A small laugh escaped me. "Really?"

Ashton rolled his eyes at my sarcasm. "Yes, *really.* I'm sorry, Ally." He rocked his feet, outstretched in front of him on the grass.

"Can you tell me now?" I stared up at him, my hair falling over my shoulder. "Please. I think… I *hope* I'm ready. I can take it."

Ashton smiled with a tinge of sadness, looking down. "I have no doubt you're ready… *I'm* the one who's not ready. Once you know what happened, you're going to look at me differently, and I don't want you to. But I will tell you. When I finally get over myself, I'll tell you." His mouth spread into a smirk as he ruffled my hair. "I love you, Ally. You are my very best friend. Never doubt that." He stood up, dusting off his pants. Holding one hand out to me, he said, "Come on. We've got to keep moving."

I nodded as he helped me onto his back again.

We continued to navigate the forest, trying to make sense of the brush and mangled path. The wet dirt from the rain stuck to the bottom of Ashton's shoes. He took in the wonders of the woods, soaking up the sun pouring in through the leafy canopy.

"I guess if I'm ever going to tell you what happened with the Hidden Dragon Experiment, I should work my way up, huh?" Ashton sighed, contemplating. I hunched closer to him, curious about what he would tell me. "How's about a story?"

"Okay. It's a true story, right?"

"Right. So…" Ashton ducked under a tree branch. "There was once this brilliant scientist, who went by the name Blake Landerson."

"That was the guy who designed the BLs, right?"

"Yep. He had a wife and three amazing children. Even some pretty cool neighbors. One family lived across the street, the Skylors." Ashton smirked at me, waiting for a reaction.

"So, he *was* in league with Abel."

"This was before the formation of the Abel

organization, but he was friends with Abel the person." The trees grew clearer as we went. "Blake worked at CAIN because the company was mostly about giving Dragons a brighter future back then. But he couldn't help but worry something bad was coming, and things were taking a new turn for the worst."

"How come?"

Ashton smiled as if he was about to drop the most mind-blowing piece of information ever. "Blake was a Dragon."

"And?"

Ashton climbed over a rock and slid to the other side. "He had the ability to do a lot of time-related things. For example, he could go through time and space, mostly. But he could also see the future, I think. That's what Abel told me anyways. But I thought there was some catch to seeing the future…"

I leaned in closer. I wondered if this Blake guy somehow related to how strange Ashton had acted in the Interval. "You knew Abel? What was he like?"

Ashton nodded. "He was… complicated. As much as I hate to admit it, he didn't like Blake that much. In his words-" He lowered his voice in a mocking tone. "-'he's an idiotic moron that doesn't know how to take good advice when it slaps him in the face.'"

My hair fell over his shoulder as I lifted my head. "I thought you said they were friends?"

"Oh, they were. Anyways, back to Blake and CAIN." Ashton shook his head. "My knowledge of the events after this point might not be entirely accurate. I was your age back then, so Abel didn't tell me much."

"Sounds like someone else I know," came my singsong voice.

Ashton laughed dryly, shooting me a glare. "Very funny. Now, Blake had impressed Vix, so he got a promotion. His first real project."

"The BLs."

"Exactly." Ashton nodded along, maneuvering around a twisted tree root. "That night, Blake went to Abel for help, but Abel felt odd about it. He was a detective at the local police station, and he had been investigating some shady CAIN stuff prior. Blake didn't entirely disregard Abel's warning. He instead designed the BLs as a spy for himself, not for CAIN."

I nodded along, considering as my brother spoke.

"But, not wanting to seem too suspicious, he talked about the BLs as if they were for the use of CAIN. And then, the night came. The Hidden Dragon Experiment."

I leaned in, triggered by the mention of the experiment. Ashton came to stand over a short, steep cliff. It slid into a wide patch of white flowers, fresh with morning dew. Angling his feet, Ashton skidded down into the patch, careful not to drop me or step on any of the flowers.

"Vix requested that Blake help with the experiment, though I'm not sure he knew what all he was getting into." Ashton tiptoed around the blossoms. "With him and his wife out for the night, they asked me to babysit for them…" His voice drifted off. Whatever memory he was reliving caused his breath to go shaky. His gaze shifted to the ground, sweeping over the flowers.

"Freesias."

"What?"

"Oh, it's the name of the flower." Ashton grew distracted from the previous conversation, maybe on purpose. He breathed deeply, taking in their scent. "May loves these things." A gasp escaped him. "*May!* That's it!"

"What about her?" I quirked my smile, curious. Ashton moved quicker, not quite avoiding the flowers, but sparing most of them. He made it past the patch, examining each tree he passed. "Ashton, what are you doing?"

"Remember that story I told you about that time Kade shot me in the face?"

"Yeah. What about it?"

"We told you that all we found when we were sent out here was a squirrel. That was a lie. First off, I can't believe you even bought that-"

"I didn't."

"-And secondly, we found something much more important than that. And, if we're in the forest I think we're in…"

Ashton squinted at a tree. The wood had been marked out, the shape of a circle with two circles inside, on top of each other, one slightly offset. *Just some misshapen knots.* Ashton moved from one tree to another, which had an almost identical carving. *Or maybe not...*

"What is it?"

Ashton pointed at the top circle and allowed his finger along the outer circle. "A head, arms, and another head." His hand stopped at the bottom circle. "It's a hug. Our code for Mother. May's been this way, and she wanted us to know it." He readjusted my legs over his hips, beaming hopefully.

"I know somewhere safe we can go."

30

Experiment C1

Clay found it hard to sleep through the screaming going on outside. Muffled voices and the usual hush of machinery were nothing new for him. Over time, he had learned to block it out. But this sounded different. He wondered what could be going on being the walls of his prison, although he didn't care enough to check out the small window. He sighed, nestling back into a spot to sleep.

The shouts were silenced after the train had been activated. The thud of the train rolling down the track knocked Clay from sleep once again. A sharp sting snapped through the boy like an electrical shock. This happened every time they reached the Interval, as those on the outside called it.

An argument shot back and forth several trains down. Clay longed to be in the argument. Even an argument would be better than the loneliness he was fraught with every day. His thoughts wandered to the girl in his head a while ago. That had been nice, but he couldn't shake the feeling that it had all been a figment of his imagination. A desperate attempt to give himself some purpose other than sitting in a box.

When several minutes had passed since Clay heard from the fighting people, bangs smacked repeatedly above him. Just moments before the car door burst open, his attention shot up to the ceiling. An angry, graying man with a strong build ran through, not pausing a glance at Clay. In a moment, he was gone, already off on his hunt to the front of the train.

Clay stared after him, confused. What he wouldn't give to stretch his legs, to go somewhere other than the three yards of space allowed to him. He put off the thought, reminding himself that his duty belonged to the box. To forever be trapped in this shipping container had been determined as his fate, and he did not know why. He'd just woken up in the box one day and accepted it as his life.

More voices came, twisted by the Interval. In a moment, the train car dropped along with the boy's stomach.

Clay stiffened his hands against the wall, forced to his knees. His feet lifted from the floor with the new gravity. Tightening his chest, he prepared himself for the worst. The car made contact, thudding hard. It rolled, tumbling its young cargo around.

Fortunately, there was nothing else in the car, meaning nothing posed a threat of crushing Clay.

Clay did, however, smack his head against the wall, knocking himself out.

Something poked at Clay's face. "Oh my gosh, are you okay?"

Clay squinted, trying to take in his surroundings. A girl stood over him, her figure upside down from his view. He groaned, readjusting himself.

"Are you hurt? Do you have a concussion? How many fingers am I holding up?" The girl continued to press, Clay too distracted to answer.

The boy sat crossed-legged in the dirt, staring at the green around him. Snow-coated trees towered over the two, stars peeking through and winking down at him. Crickets hummed a unique tune carried on the wind. Clay breathed it all in, enjoying a new world of peaceful silence.

"Hello? Can you speak?" The girl waved at hand at him. Her frosty hair framed her heart-shaped face and fell just beneath her neckline.

"I…" Clay's voice caught in his throat, his gaze stuck on her odd-looking brown eyes.

"Where... Where did you come from?" She looked past him at the scraps left from the train car. The walls twisted and stabbed at various angles. Clay would've questioned how he had survived the crash if he wasn't so captivated by the new world beyond the box.

Clay wobbled to his feet.

"Wait, where are you going?" The girl rushed to his side, helping him up.

"I don't know. Somewhere." His words slurred as a headache increased.

"Hang on, you're hurt. Do you need a place to stay?"

Shaking his head, Clay tried to push her away. He had no clue where he would go, but he wanted to get as far from the boxcar as possible. He needed to gain distance, lest the people who had trapped him come looking. "No, no, I-" Finding the pain far too excruciating to bear, his whole bodyweight fell to her.

The girl nearly toppled. "Let me help you. I'm Pidge."

Clay straightened and sighed with defeat. "Fine. Name's Clay."

SIGHT SEERS

BOOK

TWO

COMING 2023

SIGHT SEERS

Acknowledgments

Over the course of my writing journey, so many people have been supportive of my dream.

First things first, heartfelt gratitude to my family. You guys are my very best friends in the whole wide world, and I'm so thankful to God for putting you in my life. I don't think I could be the woman I am today without your influence and love. All the times my mom yelled at me for not writing when I said I would. All the drives with my dad, talking through plot holes or just weird ideas. All the times my sister told everyone she met about the book years before it was even close to being published. And all the late-night talks with my brother, laughing while it was way past our bedtime. I thank you for each and every moment.

Thank you to my friends. Though I've lost a whole bunch along the way, even the ones I'm not on good terms with today, I want to thank you for being supportive when you were and for being a huge encouragement. The fact of the matter is that you were inspirations for characters, plotlines, or even just tropes hand fisted in here to make you smile. Writing can be a lonely career, but I don't think I could've made it this far without a buddy pushing me on. Thank you.

Thank you to my community. To all the random internet strangers struggling along with writing just like me. To you, I challenge you to pick up that story you've been working on for years but haven't touched in weeks and finish it. Your support helped me here, with one book under my belt and more to come, and I hope I can return the same support to you. Thank you.

Thank you to my beta readers. You guys are a writer's greatest tool. Without you guys, this book could never reach the quality is now. When you've been locked in your room for hours typing out whatever idea pops into your head, you tend to lose focus of what actually makes sense. For getting this story back on track, thank you.

Thank you to my readers. You who are holding this book in your hands right now. You have made all my dreams come true. The idea that you have taken time out of your life to read my little ramblings of the fictional people living in my head is absolutely insane to me. I hope you see yourself in the heroes of this story, in the themes of these pages, and that you have been made better for it. I hope these words were not a waste of your time but something you enjoyed and can appreciate. Thank you.

Sincerely, P.S. Singleton.

About the Author

 P.S. Singleton is a fiction writer from Arizona. She has dabbled in writing all sorts of genres, from fanfiction to comedy to sci-fi spy thriller. Sight Seers is her first published work, but she plans to write many more in the future. She was homeschooled through the Classical Conversations program and has lived in four different states over the course of her life. She is seventeen and in college going for a degree in Digital Media Arts. Someday, she hopes to work in television, specifically writing for cartoons. When she's not writing, she's either drawing or binge-watching kid's shows. You can follow her on Instagram at @ps.the.writer to keep up with writing updates, bonus content, and more!

SIGHT SEERS

P.S. SINGLETON